Deny Me

KAREN COLE

Quercus

First published in Great Britain in 2020 by Quercus
This paperback edition published in 2020 by

Quercus Editions Ltd
Carmelite House
50 Victoria Embankment
London EC4Y 0DZ

An Hachette UK company

A CIP catalogue record for this book is available
from the British Library

PB ISBN 978 1 52940 866 9
EB ISBN 978 1 52940 381 7

10 9 8 7 6 5 4 3 2 1

Typeset by CC Book Production
Printed and bound in Great Britain by Clays Ltd, Elcograf S.p.A.

MIX
Paper from
responsible sources
FSC® C104740
FSC
www.fsc.org

Papers used by Quercus are from well-managed forests and other responsible sources.

To Jim

Prologue

She was still breathing – a revolting wheezing and hissing that made him feel sick and angry. He stood over her, his arms hanging limply by his sides, waiting for her to stop.

Once it was all over and she lay still, he crouched beside her, watching the blood trickle at the corner of her mouth. He lifted her head, feeling the curve of her skull beneath her hair. He used to like to twine her hair in his fingers, breathing in the scent of her shampoo as she held him close and feeling the laughter shake in her belly when he said something funny. He used to love making her laugh. She hadn't laughed all that often, even before. But when she had, when he'd succeeded in making her laugh, it was like winning the lottery or like finding something very rare and precious – something that was all the more valuable because it was so rare.

But in the past few months she hadn't laughed at all. She'd just watched him carefully with big, disappointed grey eyes.

Thinking about that made him feel sad and angry again. He'd loved her once, he supposed. But she'd ruined everything. She didn't want him anymore. She'd betrayed him and he wasn't the type to forgive.

He let go of her head, gently setting it down on the concrete. There was something about her eyes – her blank accusing stare. It gave him the creeps. Looking into her dilated pupils, he was reminded of something he'd read recently – about how forensic scientists back in the early 1900s used to think that a murderer's image would be imprinted on the retina of his victim. It was a stupid idea really, but in the early days of photography, they believed that the eye worked like a camera – that whatever a dead person last saw would be retained inside like a negative. He knew it was nonsense. The human eye didn't record images.

Even so, he leaned forward and closed her lids so she couldn't look at him anymore. Now she was dead, his anger was slowly evaporating, leaving a residue of sadness and fear. He was afraid of what he'd done and afraid of what would happen to him when people found out. What was he going to tell them? He wasn't sure that even he could explain this one away. On the plus side, no one had seen it happen. No one could prove it wasn't an accident. Yes, that was his story and he was sticking to it. An accident – just a terrible accident.

Feeling calmer, he sat back on his haunches and stared up at the wide blue sky. He watched as a bird of prey wheeled above him and a single white cloud drifted past. But then, sitting there, he caught *something, a movement or a shadow, out of the corner of his eye and he turned.*

With the glare of the sun on the window it was hard to tell what was reflection and what was not. But, just at that moment, he could have sworn he saw someone – someone standing there, watching him.

Chapter One

'He killed her.'

We're talking about my parents' neighbour, whose wife died a few months ago. But when Mum makes this shocking assertion the conversation stops abruptly, and Dad and I both turn and stare at her. For a moment I think she must be joking; that it's just her mischievous sense of humour. But she seems deadly serious. Her fork is trembling in her hand, bits of potato and gravy dropping onto her kaftan. Her bright red lipstick is smudged, her hair sticking out at wild angles and there's a look of what I can only describe as horror in her eyes.

Dad sighs, picks at the potato bits and wipes the gravy off his mouth with a napkin. 'He didn't kill her, love,' he says patiently, patting her hand. 'It was just an accident, a terrible accident.'

Mum bats his hand away crossly. 'It wasn't an accident,' she insists. 'I saw him, clear as day, through the window.'

She's getting more and more agitated, waving her knife and fork around. I know from Dad that her dementia occasionally makes her aggressive in between bouts of inappropriate friskiness, but I haven't seen this side of her before. *I've been away too long*, I think sadly. I've been so wrapped up in my own life and my own problems. My mother has changed. She's not the same vibrant, funny woman who used to dance on the tables in restaurants, who had us all in stitches with her impression of the head teacher at my school.

'She gets confused sometimes these days,' Dad whispers loudly to me. 'It's the Alzheimer's.'

'I'm not confused,' Mum retorts. 'I know exactly what I saw, and I'm not deaf, by the way.'

'You've been watching too much *Midsomer Murders*, that's all, Jean.' Dad says. 'You're thinking of that episode we saw the other day, the one where the gardener hit his wife over the head with a spade, remember?'

'How did she die, exactly?' I ask, a faint anxiety churning in my gut. Ridiculous, I know, but Mum's distress seems to be infectious.

Dad shakes his head. 'It was horrible. A real tragedy. She fell from the top-floor window. They added a third floor only last year. The racket the builders made was insufferable, wasn't it, Jean?'

5

'What? Oh yes,' Mum nods vaguely.

'It went on for months.' Dad presses his lips together disapprovingly. Something about his tone suggests that he feels her death might have been a fitting punishment for all the noise they had to endure. 'Kate was so young too – only thirty-two. The same age as you, Jessie.' He looks at me with a worried frown, as if it had something to do with her age; as if I too might be about to launch myself out of an upstairs window.

No doubt he's thinking about his conversation with Matteo last night. How much did Matteo tell him? I wonder. How much was Matteo's particular brand of bullshit and how much was true? Under the table I dig my nails into my thighs. The room is hot and stuffy, and I wish I could open the door, but the draft bothers Mum so we keep it closed. I'm starting to feel that sense of panic I sometimes get when I'm shut in.

'Apparently, she hit her head at just the wrong angle,' Dad continues. 'It's such a shame. She's got a young daughter too.' He shakes his head gravely. 'That poor child. That poor man. It doesn't bear thinking about.'

I imagine a handsome couple with a cute little girl. In my head the little girl is about seven – the same age as Anna Maria. I close my eyes, trying to block out an image of big, frightened brown eyes and tear-stained cheeks. Why did I have to go and think about Anna Maria now? I don't want to

6

think about her, or about the English Academy and Madrid. That's all behind me now. An unfortunate chapter in my life best forgotten.

'How long have they lived here?' I ask, trying to focus. I run my finger along a groove in the pine table, where someone, either me or Howie, dug into the soft wood with a knife.

Dad frowns. 'About three years now,' he says. 'They moved in shortly after you went to Spain. Ajay's a vet at the practice in the village. He's very good apparently. He's been great with your brother's dog.'

I wonder if Howie's still got the same dog, an irascible pug called Bella, who never stops yapping and who tried to bite my ankles last time I visited. I'm about to ask, but Mum is breathing strangely, clutching her chest, and her face has turned puce.

'Are you OK, Mum?' I ask anxiously. 'Dad, is she OK?'

'She'll be fine,' he says, carrying on eating. He has a look of studied calm on his face – an expression that suggests he's seen all this before. Like it's a regular occurrence.

'He wants me dead,' Mum hisses dramatically in my ear. 'Because I know too much.'

'Nonsense,' says Dad sharply. 'Ajay Chandry is a very nice man. He didn't murder his wife and he certainly doesn't want to kill you. Jessie, can you pass me the salt, please?'

I pick at my food, not really tasting it. I want to make a joke or talk about something happy to lighten the mood and comfort Mum, but I've no idea what to say, and I know all too well that when someone is in a delusional state like this, there's not a lot you can say.

We eat in silence for a while. There's nothing but the sound of our chewing and the steady monotonous ticking of the clock on the wall. Dad gulps down his beer, staring broodingly at the label and picking at the edges with his thumbnail. He's put on weight since I last saw him and his belly is straining over his trousers. Next to him Mum looks delicate and ethereal, like an aged Titania. She's looking at her fork, twisting it in her hand as if she's never seen one in her life before, and there's an emptiness in her eyes that scares me. It's way too warm and stuffy in here and the silence is oppressive. I've always hated long silences. They just allow space for dark thoughts to fester.

'Well, it's nice to be back,' I say brightly at last, just for something to say.

'It's lovely to have you, darling,' says Mum, smiling at me fondly and cupping my face in her thin, blue-veined hands. Her moods these days are as changeable as a child's. And, just like that, she's happy again, as if our earlier conversation has been wiped clean from her mind. 'Isn't it lovely to have Jessica home again, Brian?'

'Mmm.' Dad nods and clears his throat. 'I was just wondering what your plans were, Jess? How long are you going to stay in England?'

And I realise with a sinking heart that he hasn't fully understood the situation. He doesn't know that I'm never going back – that there's nothing to return to.

'I'm not going back to Spain,' I say firmly. I think about the flat I shared with Matteo in Madrid – the expensive wooden floors, Matteo's wardrobe full of designer shirts and jackets. I think about Dr Lopez with his kind, grave face and I shudder.

'But Matteo gave me the impression . . .' Dad starts.

'Matteo is full of shit . . . Sorry about my language, Mum, but he is. He can't accept that I've left him. I'm never going back.' I stare at Dad defiantly, waiting for the backlash. My parents were so upset when Howie divorced his wife that they refused to speak to him for more than a month. And even though Matteo and I weren't married, they were pleased that I'd finally settled down with someone. I know from the less than subtle comments they'd made recently that they really hoped we'd eventually tie the knot, which was strange, considering they'd never actually married themselves.

But the reaction to my news is surprisingly muted. Mum looks confused and Dad just frowns.

'What are you going to do for money?' he asks.

'I've got some savings. That'll tide me over for a bit until I get a job.' I want to reassure him I'm not going to be an extra burden – that I can look after myself.

'But are you sure you're well enough to work?' Dad asks. 'Maybe you should rest and recuperate for a while. Matteo said—'

'What's wrong?' Mum interrupts, looking alarmed. 'Are you ill, Jessica?'

'No, I'm fine, Mum. I don't need to rest.' I pat her hand. I'm thinking about the days after I was fired from the English Academy. Those days were the worst – being trapped in the house all alone with my thoughts and the awful gnawing boredom and loneliness.

'I think work will be good for me.'

'But what will you do?' Dad asks. 'There can't be much call for EFL teachers in the village.'

'Maybe not,' I agree. 'I was thinking of having a break from teaching. I might do some photography.' I took a few photos at Matteo's friend's wedding, before everything went pear-shaped, and they turned out well. Photography was part of my degree at college before I dropped out to move to Spain with Matteo. It feels like a logical choice.

But Dad doesn't seem reassured. 'How much money can you make as a photographer?' he asks doubtfully. 'It doesn't seem like a very steady job.'

'Nonsense.' Mum shuts him up with a spark of her old fire. 'Not everything's about money, Brian. I think it's a marvellous idea, Jessica. You're so talented. You should take up painting again too. Your painting was always fabulous.'

I haven't done any painting for ages, I think sadly, and I try to remember exactly when and why I gave up. It must have been shortly after I arrived in Spain. Matteo never liked me painting. He didn't like the smell of turpentine and even when I bought odourless paint thinner, he still objected. Sometimes it was easier just to give in to him.

Thinking about Matteo, my chest feels tight and the room seems unbearably warm and humid. I thought that I would escape the heat when I returned from Madrid. But I've come back in the middle of a heatwave, and I feel hotter than I ever felt in Spain. At least in Spain we had air conditioning. Mum and Dad haven't got any fans, and no one ever opens a window in this house.

'Do you want afters?' I ask, standing up abruptly. I feel dizzy and am sure I'm about to faint. I need to get out of this room.

'I'll just have a cup of coffee, please,' says Mum. 'You couldn't fetch my shawl from the bedroom while you're up, could you, darling? I'm feeling a bit shivery.'

How she can be cold when the temperature must be at least thirty degrees, I've no idea, but I escape willingly upstairs, glad for an excuse to get away from them both. I love them but being back home hasn't brought the relief I thought it would. Dad can't help treating me like a child and I can already feel myself slipping back into old ways, old patterns of behaviour. *The sooner I move out, the better*, I think, as I push open the door to my parents' room.

It's like a time capsule – practically unchanged since we first moved here, when I was three years old. There's the same wallpaper, the same aubergine-coloured curtains, even, if I'm not mistaken, the same aubergine duvet cover. I can't find Mum's shawl, so I open the wardrobe and pick out a warm fleece. I'm about to take it downstairs when I get distracted by the photos on the bedside table. There's a picture of Mum looking super glamorous with big eighties hair, me propped up in her lap. And there's a school photo of Howie, chubby cheeked, about twelve years old, grinning cheekily at the camera.

As I turn towards the door, I feel a sudden wave of claustrophobia – like I haven't suffered in ages. I stagger to the window and open it, leaning out, gulping in the humid air. Everything in the close is completely still. Nothing is stirring. There isn't even a hint of a breeze in the trees. It's as if the world is holding its breath, waiting for something.

There's a clear view of the house opposite and the silver Toyota parked outside. I look at the window at the top of the house, but the sun is low, reflecting off the glass, and it's impossible to see in. I think about Mum's strange outburst, musing on how little we really know about the people who live all around us. Unlike the other houses in the close, which have small, neatly clipped lawns, the house opposite has a concrete front garden with a stone statue of an owl at the centre. I imagine Kate Chandry tumbling to the ground, smashing her head against the concrete, and I shudder.

Chapter Two

It's dark and I'm crushed into a ball, hardly able to breathe or move. I know I need to stay calm or I'll use up all the oxygen, but panic is welling up inside me, banishing all logical thought. My chest feels like it's about to explode and my whole body is shaking. Where the hell am I?

Then I realise that I'm trapped inside my own head. I can see the shape of my face, my nose and mouth and eyes, but from the inside as if it's hollow, like the inside of a jelly mould.

'Let me out!' I shout. But the sound snags in my throat and no one hears me.

Outside my head someone is coughing loudly, and I don't know why, but I sense that Mum is in danger. I'm aware that I'm dreaming, that I need to escape from this nightmare and get out of my head to help her, but I can't. I'm trapped inside.

'Let me out!' I scream, desperate now. And summoning a huge effort of will, I tear open my face, bursting out of the dream.

I wake up with tears rolling down my cheeks. The duvet is twisted in my arms and I'm sweating buckets. Prising my eyes open, I stare up at the white ceiling, at a band of light shining through the heavy curtains. *It's OK*, I tell myself as my breathing returns to normal. *It was just a stupid nightmare.* I often have dreams that involve being trapped in enclosed spaces, but this one is new. *It doesn't mean anything*, I tell myself. I'm at home now. Matteo is more than a thousand miles away. The past few months are behind me. But the dream lingers with me and there's a feeling of dread in the pit of my stomach that won't go away as I heave myself out of bed, pulling on a pair of jeans and a T-shirt.

I can hear clattering in the kitchen downstairs, punctuated by the sound of Dad's rasping cough. Looking in the mirror, I force my lips into a smile – it's more of a grimace really. I've read somewhere that just the physical act of smiling is supposed to release endorphins that make you happy, but it doesn't seem to be working today. I still feel and look like shit. I look completely washed out. Three years' living in Spain hasn't given me a tan, just more freckles and a prematurely lined face. My red hair is frizzy, my eyes are pale and bloodshot and my lashes without make-up are pale, like ghostly spider legs. I brush my hair and scrape some mascara on my lashes. Then I root in my handbag for my medication. I pull out a packet of pills and swallow down two with the glass of water by my bed.

Depression with psychosis was what Doctor Lopez called it. I close my eyes, trying to block out an image of him in his clinic, his handsome, grave face, long fingers tapping on his desk. Matteo sitting next to me holding my hand, pretending to be all loving and concerned.

Anyway, I'm all better now. I haven't had a delusion or a hallucination for at least a month and I'm even starting to feel a little happier, more optimistic. It was because I was so stressed and tired with work and Matteo. All I needed was to get away from the situation I was in. Today is a new day. The start of a new life. Matteo is history and I can focus on the future. I'll have breakfast and then start setting up my new photography website. After that, maybe I'll go into town and visit the estate agent's to see if I can find a new flat. I need to buy myself a new car too. Maybe I'll even get a cat or a dog.

First, though, I need to talk to Dad, find out exactly what Matteo told him and give him my version of events. But when I get downstairs, Dad is on the phone trying to call someone, a worried frown on his face.

'No answer,' he says, flinging it down on the table. 'I wish she'd leave her bloody phone on.'

'What is it, Dad?'

'Ah, Jessica,' he says. 'I'm afraid we've got a bit of a problem. It's your mother. She's wandered off.'

'Maybe she's just popped out to the shops,' I suggest, putting two slices of bread in the toaster. I'm not overly concerned. Mum is an adult after all.

'You don't understand,' says Dad. 'She doesn't go out on her own anymore, not since she got ill. She forgets where she is and gets confused and distressed.'

I'm sure he's making a mountain out of a molehill. Mum seems fine to me. Apart from the confusion over the neighbour yesterday, she's been her old self, more or less. When I spoke to Dad on the phone in Spain, he'd given me the impression that her illness was far more progressed than it is, and I'd been half afraid to come home, afraid she wouldn't recognise me, scared that we'd already lost her. I was so relieved to find her essentially the same. A little confused sometimes, a little forgetful, but still the same Mum that I love and find exasperating in equal measure.

'Are you sure she's not somewhere in the house?' I suggest. 'Or in the garden?' I peer out of the window at the lawn and the flower beds. The small summer house and the neat vegetable patch – Dad's pride and joy.

Dad sighs. 'No, I looked everywhere. When I woke up this morning she wasn't in bed. I went downstairs and couldn't find her. It's not the first time this has happened. Last time they phoned me from Budgens. She was there insisting on buying three bottles of whisky in her nightdress even though she didn't have any money on her.'

'She doesn't even drink.' I can't help laughing at the image.

And Dad smiles wanly. 'Yes, I know,' he says. But there are dark circles of worry around his eyes and I realise how tough all this must be on him.

'I'm just going to have to go and look for her,' he says. He fetches his trainers and sits at the table, tying the laces. 'Do you want to come and help, Jess?'

'Of course.' I turn off the toaster. Breakfast can wait.

Outside the sky is grey and a very light, thin drizzle is misting the air. The close is quiet, the mock-Tudor red-brick houses with their neat lawns and sleek cars forming a tight circle of respectability. *Nothing to see here*, they seem to say. *Nothing shocking or awful ever happens here. We just mind our own business.* Not for the first time, I wonder if the facade is truly representative of its inhabitants. And, as if in answer, the front door of the house opposite bursts open and a man emerges, toting a little girl and a briefcase in one hand and rummaging in his pocket with the other.

This must be Ajay Chandry, I think, with a slight thrill of curiosity. This is the neighbour Mum was talking about yesterday over dinner. I must admit, he doesn't look much like my idea of a wife-killer. He looks like a normal, hassled, middle-aged British-Asian man with greying hair in a slightly crumpled white shirt. He waves at Dad and Dad hurries across the close. I follow him over, curious, to inspect the Bluebeard for the first time.

'Ajay, hello!' Dad blurts.

Ajay looks politely surprised to be accosted so early in the morning. 'Good morning, Brian,' he says.

'Sorry to bother you but you haven't seen Jean at all, have you?' asks Dad breathlessly. 'She's wandered off and she hasn't got her phone with her.'

The car beeps as Ajay finds his keys and unlocks it. 'Oh no, not again.' He looks around vaguely as if Mum might be somewhere in the close. 'No, I'm sorry, I haven't seen her. But I'm driving towards Aylesbury. I'll keep an eye out on the road for you and let you know if I spot her.'

He catches my eye and smiles quizzically, and I redden because I was staring at him, trying to imagine him pushing his wife out of a window. On closer inspection he's quite good-looking, especially his eyes, which are an extraordinary grey-green, large and luminous in the sunlight. He looks kind and capable – the sort of person you would trust with your beloved family pet.

'This is my daughter, Jessica,' Dad explains. 'She's staying with us for a while until she finds a place of her own. She just got back from Spain.'

'Oh?' Ajay says politely.

'Yes. She's been living in Madrid but she's back now. She's looking for a job.'

'What do you do?' he asks.

'I'm going to set up my own photography studio,' I say with more conviction than I feel.

Ajay smiles – a normal, nice smile.

'You're a photographer?' he says to me. 'That's a coincidence. I'm looking for a photographer for Izzy's birthday party. This is Izzy, by the way,' he says, patting the little girl in his arms. 'Say hi, Izzy.' Izzy squirms and tries to get out of his grasp, reaching for the car.

'She isn't a morning person,' Ajay says apologetically. 'You're not free on Saturday afternoon, are you?'

'Er . . . um, sure,' I mutter, slightly taken aback. *Shit*, I think. Apart from the photos I took at Matteo's friend's wedding, I've never taken a professional photograph in my life. I'm not even sure where I packed my camera, but I can't really afford to pass up on the opportunity to get paid work.

'Good. I'll see you on Saturday then, three o'clock?'

'OK,' I say. He hasn't even asked how much I charge. But then, judging by his sleek car and the renovations that have been done to the house, maybe money is no object to him.

Izzy wriggles violently in his arms, impatient to get going, and covers his mouth with her hand.

'Well, I'd better get going,' he laughs, removing her hand. 'I think that's a hint that Izzy wants to get to summer school. She's got some important playdough animals to make, haven't you, Iz? Well, it was nice to meet you, Jessica. I'll keep an eye out for Jean.'

'Thank you,' says Dad. 'That's very kind of you.'

We stand and watch Ajay strap his daughter into her car seat before they drive off.

'Which way should we go?' I ask as Ajay's car turns out of the close.

Dad looks around. 'We should probably check out Budgens first.'

We climb into Dad's Honda and crawl along the main road towards the village centre, stopping every now and then to peer down side streets.

'Are you OK Jessica?' he asks as we reach the centre of the village. He clears his throat, which is what Dad always does when he's embarrassed. 'Because Matteo said you had a spot of bother before you left.'

If by 'a spot of bother' he means a full-on nervous break-down, then he's right, but the last thing I want to do is get involved with psychiatrists again. I nearly ended up being sectioned the last time. And I don't want to worry Dad either. He has a lot on his plate right now.

'Yeah, well, Matteo can't accept that someone in their right mind would leave him, so he's decided I must be crazy,' I say lightly. Dad smiles uncertainly and glances over at me. 'You're sure you're OK?'

'Absolutely,' I say brightly.

'I'd be happier if you went to see someone,' he says, frowning. 'There's a good therapist in the village. I could make an appointment for you, if you like.'

'I'll think about it, Dad,' I promise. 'But let's just concentrate on finding Mum for now, shall we?'

We park outside Budgens but there's no sign of Mum inside, and the cashiers don't remember seeing her, though they offer to show us the CCTV footage to make sure. We decline and walk down the high street until we reach the clock tower at the end of the road. There's a small roundabout and one road leads into the village and the other out towards Halton airbase. To the right there's a footpath that leads to the play park, Hampden Pond and the church. I used to walk up there with Mum when I was little. We used to go and feed the ducks.

'I might have a look this way,' I say on impulse.

'That's not such a bad idea,' Dad says. 'She might have gone to church. She's found religion in her old age and she's always hanging around, bothering the vicar. I'll go and search down by the canal. Call me if you find her.'

I head up the path by the side of the stream. There hasn't been much rain lately and the water is low and smooth like a thin glaze over the riverbed. It trickles under the bridge where Mum and I once played Pooh sticks. The First World War memorial orchard is new. But the play park is still there, though they've taken away the swing and put down astroturf. I remember coming here with my school friends, Alice and Holly, when we were teenagers. Alice, as the oldest, would buy the cider from the off-licence and we would all sit on the swings: me, Holly and Alice, the three musketeers, talking and laughing, staring up at the black sky and the stars.

I walk on alone, passing an early dog walker, a middle-aged man with one Great Dane and one terrier, but otherwise the path is empty. The water level is low in Hampden Pond too, the muddy banks exposed, spattered with bird droppings and feathers. When I open the gate the ducks and coots and swans waddle up to me, thinking I'm going to feed them.

I don't spot her at first, because she's hidden behind a tree. But then I catch a movement and a flash of white out of the corner of my eye, and I realise she's sitting there on the bench – a lonely figure in her nightdress and slippers, staring pensively at the water. I'm relieved to find her safe and sound, but also appalled that she is out here in nothing but her nightie. Her illness must be more advanced than I realised.

She smiles slyly at me as I approach. 'Oh, there you are, Evie. I was looking for you. You're going to be in so much trouble.' She wags a finger at me, and my heart sinks because she doesn't seem to have a clue who I am.

'Mum, it's me, Jessica, your daughter,' I say.

'What are you talking about? Of course it's you, Jessica. I know that,' she says crossly. 'I haven't completely lost my marbles yet.'

I sigh with relief. 'What are you doing here, Mum? We've been looking all over for you. Dad's beside himself with worry.'

She looks around, alarmed, as if she's suddenly noticed where she is. She smooths down her nightdress which is covered in leaves and grass. God only knows what she's been doing.

'I don't really remember why I came here,' she admits and for a moment, there's such a look of alarm and bewilderment in her eyes that I want to hug her. Instead, I take her hand in mine and stroke the blue veins and the liver-spotted skin.

'Never mind, Mum. We've found you anyway. That's the main thing.'

'Yes,' she says, catching my hand and raising it to her lips. 'It's so lovely to have you back with us, Jessica. I missed you.'

Her eyes well up. Maybe it's a side effect of the Alzheimer's, or maybe it's the drugs she's on. Whatever it is, Mum has become much more sentimental lately than she used to be. Perhaps it's just the knowledge of the fragility of her life and of our relationship. Like me, maybe she's terrified that she will one day forget who I am.

'I missed you too, Mum,' I say softly, blinking back my own tears.

'I never liked that young man, what was his name?'

'Matteo?'

'Yes, Matteo. Far too full of himself for my liking.'

'No, I know. You told me at the time, Mum. I should've listened.'

She laughs and we sit there hand in hand for a while, staring at the mud, the murky-green water and the ducks squabbling. Then I take my phone out of my pocket and ring Dad.

'Any luck yet?' he says, sounding breathless and agitated.

'Yes, I've found her. She was by the lake.'

'Oh, thank God for that. I'll drive round and pick you up by the church.'

'No, don't bother.' I'm suddenly overwhelmed by a feeling that I want to spend as much time as possible with my mother, before it's too late. 'We'll walk back. Don't worry about picking us up.' I turn to my mother. 'Is that OK with you, Mum? Do you fancy a walk? We could go back along the canal.'

She smiles brightly and politely like the Queen at a garden party. 'Why not? It's such a lovely day.'

So, I hang up, then wrap my jacket around her shoulders and we walk hand in hand as if I am a child again, only now the roles are reversed and it's Mum that needs looking after, not me. We make our way back to the main road. Mum walks briskly, her back straight, and I don't have to modify my pace at all. Her brain may be going, but physically she's remarkably fit.

'Who's Evie?' I ask as we cross over the roundabout and turn onto the canal path that runs along the back of the houses.

'Evie?'

'Yes, you called me Evie just now.'

She looks confused for a moment. Then she says, 'Oh yes. Evie was a school pal of mine when I was at the convent. We were great friends, Evie and I.'

'You've never told me about her before.'

I know so little about Mum's childhood, I realise, and now it might be too late. How can I know now that she's telling me the truth? How can I differentiate the truth from her fantasies?

'Haven't I?' She tilts her head to one side like a bird and smiles. 'I'm sure I have. You probably weren't listening.'

It's probably true, I think guiltily. Mum told me a lot of stories when I was a teenager, but I was too wrapped up in my own life to take much notice. Now I wish I'd listened more, asked more questions while I still could.

26

'Well, why don't you tell me about her now?' I say. 'I'd like to know.' I slip my arm through hers and feel how thin she has become. Her arm feels like a dry twig, easy to snap.

'Evie? Well, where do I start?' she says, her eyes misting over again. 'She was my best friend in the world.'

'Are you still in touch?'

'What? Oh no. I don't know where she is now. We were naughty little girls. But the nuns were so strict. They used to tell us not to shine our shoes so that no one could see the reflection of our knickers. I mean, what kind of perverted mind thinks of something that?'

'That does sound a bit extreme.' I wonder if it's the truth or something she's seen in a movie.

'Of course, convent girls are the worst. All that repression, it has to come out somehow.' She laughs and pats her hair. 'As soon as I left, I went completely wild. I was determined to go on the stage. I joined a theatre troop and we did a tour of the country. That's when I met your father.'

The next thing I know she's happily recounting a story about when she and Dad first met. How he towed her home after her car broke down.

'Oh, you should have seen him, Jessica,' she says dreamily. 'It was love at first sight for both of us. He had magnificent sideburns, a moustache and these piercing blue eyes. He looked like Tom Selleck and Clint Eastwood rolled into one. Of course, my parents were furious. They couldn't accept that their daughter was going out with a lowly mechanic – the son of an estate worker. And when we moved in together . . . well, then they really hit the roof.'

I've heard it all before. How Mum and Dad were two star-crossed lovers, as Mum likes to describe them. How Mum's family were so snobby they refused to accept Dad and how Mum broke off all contact with them. I think now that it's a shame that I didn't get to know my grandparents before they died, even if they were as awful as Mum says.

'There was one night he climbed up the trellis,' she continues lost in her thoughts, 'and he snuck in through my bedroom window. He had to hide under the bed when my Mother came in.'

'Really?' I laugh. 'How come I haven't heard this story before?'

'Haven't you? I'm sure I told you. I've told Howie for sure.'

We walk on. Mum seems lost in her memories, her eyes cast downwards.

'By the way, I've got a job,' I say. 'Taking photos for Isobel's birthday party.'

'Isobel? Who's Isobel?' she asks.

'You know. Ajay Chandry's daughter. Your neighbour.'

'Oh.' She's stops and looks vaguely at the dark water.

A family of swans glides up to us. The signets are big and grey. Their eyes are belligerent.

Suddenly Mum grips my arm, surprisingly tightly.

'I should have gone to the police at the time,' she hisses. 'He said it was an accident, but I know that it wasn't. He pushed her. I saw him through the window . . .'

There's so much conviction in her voice that, for a second, I'm sucked into her fear.

'What exactly did you see, Mum?' I ask, repressing a mounting feeling of apprehension.

Mum glances at me sideways. 'Just be careful, Jessie. He's a liar and he's dangerous.'

Then she loosens her grip on my arm and walks surprisingly fast. A swan blocks our path and Mum shoos him out of the way. The swan hisses at us but reluctantly slides into the water and glides away.

'That swan is a big bully,' she says. 'Never did like swans, nasty vicious things.'

Chapter Three

Claire Matteson welcomes me into her office with a limp handshake and a sad smile.

'Hi. Jessica, isn't it? I'm Claire,' she says. She's got a spaniel face with drooping dark hair and dark, moist eyes. Everything about her is moist and limp, like a piñata left out in the rain. It's as if she's soaked up all the misery of her patients, as if she needs therapy herself. I can't really blame her. I guess it would make anyone depressed, listening to other people's problems all day.

'Hello, nice to meet you.' I grip her hand firmly and smile brightly to show that I'm fine, and that I don't really need her help. But she just smiles faintly and gives me a sad, searching look. She's on to me. She can tell that my cheery bravado is just an act.

I survey the room. It's not large. There are just a couple

of chairs and a small, round table with a box of tissues on it and a long, dark green couch.

'Am I supposed to lie on that?' I ask.

'Whatever you feel comfortable with,' she shrugs.

I perch gingerly on one of the chairs and there's a short silence as Claire gazes at me compassionately. The window is open and as the wind stirs outside, I can hear the tinkle of a wind chime and I shiver. I know wind chimes are supposed to make you feel relaxed, but they've always had the opposite effect on me.

'Where do we start?' I ask.

'Why don't you tell me about yourself,' she says gently. 'Tell me why you've come here.' Her voice is as soft as cotton wool. Some people might find it soothing, I suppose. To me, it's just slightly annoying.

'What do you want me to say?' I cross my arms defensively. I really don't want to be here in this small, stuffy room with her. I had enough of doctors and psychiatrists in Madrid. I've only come to keep Dad off my back. If I go along with counselling, I reason, then hopefully he won't probe too deeply into what happened in Spain.

'Whatever you like.' Claire lifts her shoulders. 'This is a totally non-judgemental space.'

'I don't know what to tell you.'

'Why don't you start by talking about your family?'

31

So that's the kind of therapist she is. Problems in later life must be caused by your family, your childhood.

'Your mum and dad fuck you up or something like that?' I say, trying to remember the Philip Larkin poem I learned at school.

'What?' Claire looks startled.

'That's what they say, isn't it?'

'Oh, I see.' She chews a nail thoughtfully. 'And do you think that's true for you?'

'No, not really. My dad was quite strict, and my mother had a bit of an unpredictable temper, but they did their best. I always felt loved – that's the main thing, isn't it?'

When I think of my childhood, I think of camping holidays in Cornwall: Mum and Dad bickering about how to put the tent up. Sitting on a wall by the sea eating fish and chips – me screaming and Howie laughing raucously when a seagull swooped down to steal a chip. It was a pretty normal upbringing, as far as I know.

Claire nods but doesn't speak. She's waiting for me to say more, reveal all my secrets. But I can beat her at her own game. I zip my lips firmly and wait for her move.

Eventually, after what seems like the longest silence, she caves. 'Your father said you've been living in Spain. What was that like?' she asks.

I hesitate, wondering how much to tell her and how much she already knows. What exactly has Dad told her?

'For the most part it was great,' I say. 'It was just in the last six months I had a bit of . . . trouble.'

Claire leans forward, all attentive now. 'What kind of trouble?'

I bite my lip. 'I got very stressed. I was hardly sleeping and eventually the stress led to depression. But I'm all better now. It was just . . . I was in a bad relationship and there was the pressure of work. Getting fired from my job probably didn't help.' I give a short, ironic laugh.

Claire doesn't smile. 'I see,' she says slowly. 'Why did you lose your job?'

I close my eyes, trying to block out Anna Maria's tear-stained face. 'It was all a misunderstanding,' I say.

'Oh?' Claire tilts her head to one side, inviting confidence.

But there's no way I'm ready to talk about Anna Maria, and I definitely don't want to share the truth with Claire. If she knows everything that happened, she'll have me labelled as crazy.

'It's not important,' I say, lips pressed firmly together.

She waits for a while, until she finally realises I'm not going to open up, and then she tries another tack.

'What about your boyfriend in Spain? You said you were in a bad relationship,' she says.

'Matteo?' I hug my knees to my chest. 'Well, it started out good. He was very romantic, very passionate. But over time he changed.'

'Changed how?'

'I don't know.' I shift around in my chair. 'He had a cruel sense of humour.'

Claire sits straight, alert. 'In what way, cruel?'

'I don't mean in a physical way but . . .' I hesitate for a moment. It's still painful to talk about. 'For example, when he found out that I suffer from claustrophobia, he locked me in the bathroom. He said it was just a joke, but to me it wasn't funny. It was very embarrassing.'

It was at a friend's party and when he finally let me out, I was having a full-blown panic attack, lying curled around the base of the toilet in a gibbering heap. And everyone was standing around staring at me.

'It doesn't sound funny,' Claire agrees, shaking her head sympathetically. She looks down at her hands in her lap. 'Anything else?' she asks.

'He got very angry sometimes.'

'About what kinds of things?'

I wince as I picture him standing red-faced in our bedroom amongst a pile of woodchips and sawdust.

'What the fuck?!' he was shouting. 'What the fuck are you doing?'

I don't remember it all very clearly. But I do remember looking up and having a moment of lucidity, seeing myself in the mirror. Seeing myself as he saw me – as a mad woman crouching on the floor, clutching a pair of scissors in my hands. All around me there were deep gouges in our expensive wooden flooring. And there was that sound, a sound that cut through me – the plaintive crying of a young child.

'Can't you hear it?' I'd pleaded with Matteo, pressing my ear to the floor. 'There's a child trapped under the floorboards.'

'No, I fucking can't. You crazy fucking bitch. You're not right in the head, you know that?' he shouted, tapping his head to emphasise his point. Then he paced the room, fuming in Spanish about how much replacing the floor was going to cost him. When he'd finally finished ranting and raving, he crouched beside me and spoke quietly. But his voice was still loaded with anger.

'And what exactly do you think a child would be doing under the floorboards, Jessica?'

I know now that I didn't really hear a child – that it was a hallucination, part of the psychosis I was experiencing. But I'm better now, hallucination and delusion free, and I have been for a while. There's no point in bothering Claire with the details.

'We would argue over anything and everything,' I tell her. 'He was very precious about his things. I once accidentally damaged the floor in the bedroom and he completely flipped.'

I go on to list all the times when Matteo was unreasonably angry over 'little things' and Claire seems to lap it all

35

up. If I can convince her that my problems were all caused by Matteo and the situation I was in, she might decide I don't need therapy after all.

No such luck, unfortunately. I suppose she needs to make her money somehow because, when the session finally wraps up, Claire takes out her notebook and books me in for another appointment, insisting that, 'We have a lot to work on.'

And I walk back home along the canal, breathing the damp air, trying to shake off the oppressive atmosphere of her office and all the painful memories that have been stirred up.

Chapter Four

'Where are we? What's going on now?' Mum asks plaintively, gazing out of the window as we pull up outside my brother's large, new, Georgian-style house.

'We're at Howie's,' Dad informs her crisply. 'He moved, remember?' I don't really like the tone he uses with her, but I suppose it must get tiresome, constantly having to repeat everything.

It's the day after my therapy session, and my brother's wife, Vicky, has decided that it's a good idea to invite us all round for dinner – to welcome me back home. It's a sweet thought, but I'm not exactly thrilled about it. I'm never sure what to say to Vicky and they both make me feel like a loser – Vicky with her perfect gym-toned body and hectic social life, and Howie with his mountain climbing and thriving law firm. Howie is the success story of our family – the one

37

who took Mum's energy and charm, and Dad's common sense and ran with it. Me? I never got past the starting post. I just seem to lurch from one disaster to the next.

Still, I've dosed myself up with medication and I should be able to handle a family dinner. Family is family, I suppose, and there's no avoiding them.

We park at the front on the gravel driveway and I climb out of the car, looking up at the house. *It must have cost a small fortune*, I think. And I can't help feeling we're like the poor relatives in a Jane Austen novel as we climb the steps to the large, imposing front door.

'It's Jessie!' Howie exclaims, opening the door and enfolding me in a bear hug. 'How are you, little sis?' Even though he's forty-four, more than ten years older than me, he looks very fit and youthful for his age. I suppose there must be pressure to stay looking good when you've got a young, attractive wife like Vicky.

'It's lovely to see you, Jessica,' says Vicky, hovering behind him clutching a growling Bella in her arms. She puts her down and Bella snarls and snaps at us, her whole little body quivering.

'Just ignore her,' Vicky says apologetically, tucking sleek blonde hair behind her ears and kissing me lightly on the cheek. 'Her bark is worse than her bite.' She smiles awkwardly at Mum and Dad. Even though Vicky's been married to Howie for at least six years, she never seems totally at ease with my parents. It's not that surprising, I suppose. They've never gone out of their way to make her feel welcome. They loved Howie's first wife, Louise, and although they never said anything explicitly, they made it fairly obvious that they blamed Vicky for the break-up of their marriage.

Howie and Vicky show us through to their state-of-the-art kitchen-diner and Vicky checks the lasagne in the oven while Dad helps himself to a beer from the fridge and Mum drifts off to the French windows, staring out at the garden with glassy eyes.

'So, I expect you want a tour of the house?' Howie says to me and I smile and nod wanly. The last thing I really want is to have to admire all their expensive fixtures and fittings – to have to hear how difficult it is to choose between Italian marble and slate or how it's impossible to find good plumbers to install a jacuzzi bath and a walk-in shower.

'Where are the kids?' I ask as we look in the freakishly neat playroom. I know Lara and Luke, Howie's children from his first marriage, are staying with them for the summer and you can't usually miss Howie and Vicky's five-year-old, Brandon, if he's within half a mile. He's a force of nature – a ball of noisy, belligerent energy.

'Brandon's asleep, thank God,' says Howie. 'We have a policy of not waking him if he's asleep, because nobody gets any rest when he's awake. And I think Luke is in his room – it's hard to know where people are in this house, it's so big. Sometimes I don't see Vicky for days.' He laughs heartily and opens the door to what he calls the blue room. It doesn't seem to serve any purpose that I can tell apart from to display expensive works of art, ornaments and pictures of Howie at the top of K2. 'And Lara's still at work,' he adds. 'She should be back for lunch.'

'At work?' I say, surprised. The last time I saw Lara she was a pimply fourteen-year-old with braces, and it's hard to imagine her grown-up enough to have a job.

'Yeah. She's been doing work experience at the clinic in Wendover. She decided recently that she wants to become a vet.'

'In Wendover? So, she must know Ajay Chandry then?'

Howie leads me up the stairs and we pause on the landing. 'Yeah, that's right, do you know him?'

'I just met him the other day.'

Howie shrugs. 'I don't really know the guy. But he's been quite good with Lara, encouraging her and helping her with choosing courses and so on.' He opens another door to a massive master bedroom. 'His wife died recently, I believe, an accident of some kind.'

I examine the view from Howie's room – the sloping lawn down to a fringe of pine trees.

'Yes, Mum said something weird about that the other

40

day. She said she saw him through the window – that she saw him kill her.'

Howie stops and stares at me. 'Really?' Then he laughs. 'Well, you know Mum's not exactly been herself lately. She gets muddled and invents stuff. The other day she told me quite seriously she was a spy in the Cold War. Now I don't know everything about what Mum did in the fifties, but I'm pretty sure she wasn't old enough to be a spy.'

I can't help laughing too. Howie is right, of course. She saw something, something that made her scared, but I'm not saying she really saw Ajay murder his wife. That's clearly ridiculous.

'And this is Luke's room.' Howie knocks on a door with a sign on it that says *Enter at your own risk*. He opens it without waiting for an answer.

Luke doesn't seem bothered. He's sitting on his bed watching YouTube on his phone.

'Hi, Aunt Jess,' he says breezily, taking off his headphones and standing up, striding over to shake my hand firmly as if we're in a business meeting. He's shot up since I last saw him and I'm struck by how much he looks like a younger, slightly skinnier version of Howie, the same floppy blond hair, the same slightly clumsy good manners.

'Wow, look at you,' I say, realising I sound like every aunt ever. 'You're all grown-up.'

41

'I'm taller than my dad now,' he grins. 'Look.' He stands on his tiptoes next to Howie.

'Like hell you are,' says Howie, pushing him playfully as they jostle together, trying to get the upper hand.

'Who's taller, Jess?' Luke asks me but I'm saved from answering because at that moment Vicky calls upstairs to say that dinner's ready.

The family meal is about as relaxing as I expected. Vicky keeps fussing and Brandon refuses to eat anything, deciding halfway through the meal to crawl under the table while Dad attempts to tell a story about his childhood – about how he and his friend got lost one time on the Langley estate where his father worked.

I'm interested in his anecdote. Dad never usually says much about the past and I'm intrigued by the image of him as a boy running wild and getting up to mischief. But he's interrupted by Brandon, who decides he's not getting enough attention and starts barking like a dog and pinching our ankles. Vicky apologises and tries ineffectually to coax him out from under the table. And Dad breaks off, lips pursed. He doesn't say anything, but I can see that he's fuming. He believes in old-school discipline and I'm sure he thinks that Brandon would benefit from a good smack.

To make matters worse, Howie decides, with his usual tact, to quiz me about Matteo.

'So why did you leave him, Jess? What was wrong with him?' he asks bluntly. 'I quite liked the guy.'

Shortly before my breakdown, Howie had come out on a business trip to Madrid, and he and Matteo had bonded over fitness and fine wines. Matteo was at his charming best, showing Howie the sights and being extra sweet and thoughtful towards me.

'Yeah? Well, you didn't know him,' I say.

'What didn't we know?' asks Dad, giving me a sharp glance.

They're all looking at me now – even Mum, her mouth hanging slightly open, a worried frown creasing her forehead. I feel the heat rising in my neck, beads of sweat breaking out on my forehead. I feel as if they can read my thoughts; as if they know the real reason that I left Madrid.

It's a relief when Lara storms in, flinging her bag down on a chair, distracting them.

It's obvious she's in a foul mood, but she manages a brief, curt 'hello' to me and Mum and Dad, before announcing she doesn't want anything to eat and heading out of the room.

'Come back here, young lady. You've got to eat something,' Vicky says. 'Besides, Jessica is here, and you haven't seen her in three years.'

Lara stops in the doorway and rolls her eyes. 'But I'm not hungry.'

'You didn't eat any breakfast either. You have to have something,' insists Vicky.

'I don't see what it's got to do with you, you don't—'

'Oh, just sit down,' Howie snaps impatiently.

Lara glares at him and he glowers back until she gives in, sighs and flounces to the stove, dishing herself out a miniscule helping of lasagne. Then she sits at her place, slamming her plate down on the table.

'Oh Jesus, what's this?' she says, chewing with an expression of distaste on her face.

I can't help staring at her. She's changed so much in the three years since I last saw her. She's lost a lot of puppy fat, and despite the sour expression on her face, she looks beautiful in an edgy, waifish kind of way with her pink-tipped, black hair and her huge kohl-rimmed green eyes.

'I thought you liked lasagne,' Vicky says.

'Yeah, the way my mother makes it, not this' – she waves her fork around trying to think of a suitable word – 'shit.'

A tense silence settles over the table. Vicky seems like she might burst into tears. Dad appears embarrassed and Howie looks annoyed. No one tells Lara that she's out of order for speaking to her stepmother like that. No one ever says anything in this family. So much is repressed and left unsaid. In a way, Lara is a breath of fresh air. At least she speaks her mind. Though I must admit, I'm starting

44

to feel sorry for Vicky – which is something I thought I'd never say.

'Well, I think it's delicious, Vicky,' I lie. 'I was going to ask you for the recipe later.'

When it's time for us to leave we drive home in silence. Dad stares broodingly at the road ahead and Mum drops off, her head nodding against her chest. I feel emotionally drained and very tired. I think I must have taken too much medication, because I fall asleep too, and when I wake up, my face is pressed against the window, dribble running down my chin. I open my eyes and see that we're already back at home, parked in the driveway. Dad is opening the garage door and Mum is snoring away in the passenger seat.

Chapter Five

Pink and yellow balloons are tied to the gatepost, bobbing in the breeze, and loud shrieks of children's laughter billow out of the open windows.

I like the contrast of the colourful balloons against the dark grey sky, so I take some snaps with the camera I found packed away at the bottom of my suitcase. Then, taking a deep breath, I ring the doorbell, fingering the packet of beta blockers in my pocket that I've brought with me in case of emergency. I've already taken one, but it hasn't kicked in yet and I feel nervous and jittery. I'm not sure whether that's because I've bitten off more than I can chew, and I'm worried that Ajay will discover that I'm not really a professional photographer, or because there's a part of me that can't help thinking about what my mother said.

Be careful, Jessie. He's a liar and he's dangerous.

46

'You made it,' says Ajay, opening the door and greeting me with a warm, natural smile. He seems genuinely pleased to see me and my reservations about him evaporate. It's ludicrous to even consider Mum's delusions. I mean, we're talking about a woman who put on one slipper and one trainer this morning and then proceeded to accuse my father of stealing her silver watch. Dad was almost certainly right – she must have seen something on TV and got the whole thing muddled in her head.

'Where do you want me to start?' I ask.

'There's no rush,' he smiles. 'The adults are all in the kitchen. Come and have a drink first and meet everybody.' He places his hand lightly on my arm and steers me into the kitchen where a few mums and one dad are sipping white wine, and an elderly man wearing a turban, presumably Ajay's dad, is sitting in a corner looking awkward. I smile and nod as Ajay introduces them and they nod back warily.

Searching for something to say, I look around at the gleaming kitchen. It's barely recognisable from when I used to come and play here after school with Holly.

'Wow, this is nice,' I say. 'You've knocked the wall through to the dining room.'

'You've been here before?' Ajay asks, pouring me a glass of wine.

'Yeah, a long time ago.' I take a cautious sip and smile nervously. 'This house used to belong to my school friend,

47

Holly. But I would never have recognised it now.' I shake my head, looking around at the expensive, tasteful decor, and wonder who chose it, whether it was Ajay or his wife, Kate.

Ajay smiles and nods, uninterested or unsure how to respond.

I place my drink on the counter as Izzy comes rushing in, clutching a present someone's given her. Her face is glowing with excitement and she's wearing a beautiful shimmering grey dress with silver fairy wings – the effect slightly spoiled by the pink cardigan which is bunched over the top. I take a couple of photos as she rips the paper off, pulling out a fluffy pink unicorn, and she glances up at me with surprise.

'Don't mind me,' I say, feeling like the paparazzi. 'Just pretend I'm not here.'

She shrugs and dashes outside onto the lawn. Through the French windows I can see the children and an elderly lady in a sari watching them.

'Is there anything in particular you want me to photograph?' I ask Ajay.

'Um, well . . .' He looks around vaguely.

'She has to get a shot of the cake, Ajay,' says a woman with a sharp face framed by a mop of curly brown hair. 'I spent hours making that.' She lifts a cover off, and reveals a fantastic creation, a huge pink castle with turrets and a chocolate drawbridge.

'It's beautiful,' I say truthfully.

'Thank you,' she says, looking gratified. 'I'm Miriam, by the way.'

'I'm Jess.' I shake her proffered hand. My flattery seems to have broken the ice and I feel mildly encouraged. *I can do this*, I think. *I can appear normal and professional. I can make new friends and a new life for myself here.*

'I wanted to do what I could for Ajay,' Miriam explains. 'He didn't want to have a party, but I told him that we would all help and that he has to keep things as normal as possible for Isobel.' She lowers her voice to a whisper. 'Poor little mite, losing her mother like that.'

'Yes, it's tragic,' I agree. 'Were you and Kate close?'

'Very.' Miriam nods emphatically. 'My daughter, Adriana, is in the same class as Izzy. Did you know her at all?'

'No, I didn't, I'm afraid.'

'Oh, she was amazing. She was so funny and vivacious and, of course, she was a fantastic mother. She just adored Izzy.' Her eyes fill with tears. 'Sorry,' she sniffs. 'It's just still so fresh, you know?'

'No need to apologise,' I say, feeling my own eyes well up in sympathy. 'It must have come as a real shock.'

I want to talk more to Miriam and hear more about Kate, but another woman rushes up with some party-bag related emergency and whisks her away. So I wander out into the garden, reflecting on the fact that Ajay didn't have to prepare any of this party himself. There seems to be an army of mothers falling over themselves to help him to organise everything. I'd like to believe that they're all motivated by nothing but kindness, and I'm sure that's part of it, but I can't help wondering if they would have been so eager to help if he wasn't so good-looking. There's nothing so attractive as a handsome, solvent widower, I suppose.

There are a lot of kids out in the garden, scampering about. I wonder vaguely if I need permission from their parents to take pictures. Though it's hard to get any of them to stay still long enough to photograph. I take a few random action shots, hoping some of them will be decent, and then I persuade Izzy to sit on the swing. She agrees readily enough and sits obligingly, gazing pensively at the grey sky while I snap away.

'How old are you, Isobel?' I ask, pausing to check the photos I've already taken.

'I'm five today,' she says, holding up five fingers.

'Wow, what a big girl you are.' I feel a wave of intense pity for this sweet little girl who's just lost her mother. Right now, she seems happy and excited, but underneath I sense her grief and confusion.

She nods. 'Mmm. I can read too. My teacher gave me three stickers yesterday.'

'Three? Really? Wow, that's brilliant.' I press the button on the camera. She's not a difficult subject to photograph, totally unselfconscious and beautiful with huge brown eyes, and in that dress, she looks like a woodland fairy. Only the cardigan ruins the effect.

'Can you just take off your cardigan so I can get a good picture of your dress?' I ask. 'It's so pretty.'

She stares at me dubiously. 'Daddy told me to keep it on. He said it's cold today.'

'It'll be all right, just for a minute while I take a couple of shots.'

'OK.' She shrugs it off her shoulders and flings it carelessly onto the grass.

'My mummy died. Did you know?' she says out of the blue. And my finger freezes on the shutter button. How the hell do I respond to that? Her expression hasn't changed, and her tone is matter-of-fact. But what's going on inside her little head?

'Oh yes?' I say cautiously.

'Yes, she did. She went up to heaven with all the angels.' She kicks her feet and frowns. 'Do you believe in angels?'

'Sure,' I say. 'I remember one that used to come to me when I was about your age.' It's not a total lie. For a while, when I was about six, I used to have a recurring dream that a woman came and stood at the end of my bed. I could never see her clearly, but I knew that she was there, that she wished me well and she wanted to protect me.

'I don't,' says Izzy. 'They're just in stories.'

51

I stare at her open-mouthed. 'Who told you that?' I ask.

But she doesn't answer. She just stands up and picks up her cardigan. As she does, I notice for the first time that the top of her arm is covered in dark grey and purple bruises.

'What happened to your arm, Izzy?' I ask, feeling a twinge of unease.

She looks down at her arm. 'I don't remember,' she says. Then she pulls her cardigan back on and runs off to bounce on the trampoline with some of the other children.

It's nothing, I tell myself as I watch her clamber on and throw herself around, laughing like a loon. Children bang into things and hurt themselves all the time. *Remember what happened in Madrid. You don't want to go down that route again.*

'I hope it doesn't rain. I don't like the look of the sky.' The elderly Indian lady interrupts my thoughts. She's holding a tray of strange-looking sweets.

'Please take one,' she says.

'Yes, hopefully it'll stay dry,' I mutter, picking up a sort of syrupy dough ball.

'Mmm, these are delicious.'

'I made them myself.'

The children scream and scatter as Ajay announces a treasure hunt in the garden.

'They have so much energy, don't they?' she sighs,

placing the tray down on the table next to me and adjusting her sari. 'It makes me tired just watching them.'

'Yes,' I agree.

'Especially my granddaughter. She's a real live wire.'

'You must be Izzy's grandmother?' I venture.

'For my sins,' she smiles proudly. 'I'm Gita, by the way.'

'I'm Jessica. My parents live in the house opposite.'

'Oh?' She gives me a short assessing stare.

'Izzy seems to be coping well,' I say. 'With losing her mother, I mean.'

Her mouth forms a tight line. 'Children are resilient,' she says.

Are they? I wonder. They appear to be on the surface but then again, trauma when you're very young can have a deep, long-lasting effect.

'And anyway, maybe she's better off without her,' Gita says crisply.

I gawp at her, not quite able to believe those words have come from her mouth.

'You're shocked, I can tell,' she says. 'But really, my daughter-in-law was not a good woman.' She frowns and then looks at me. 'I'm sorry, I should be more tactful. Were you a good friend?'

I smile and shake my head. 'It's OK. I didn't know her. I don't really know Ajay either. I'm just here to take photographs.'

53

'Oh?' she nods.

There's a moment of silence as I think about what Gita just said.

'I hope you don't mind me asking, but in what way was she not a good woman?' I ask tentatively.

Gita frowns. 'Well, I don't like to speak ill of the dead . . . She was a woman with a lot of problems, let's leave it at that. Excuse me.' Before I can press her for a real answer she glides off, carrying the tray back into the house.

I spend the rest of the afternoon taking photos until, at six o'clock, Miriam announces that the cake is about to be cut, and we all troop in and stand crammed together in the kitchen around Izzy, who is beaming from ear to ear. Ajay tries to light the candles, but the draught keeps snuffing them out. So someone shuts all the doors and windows. I take a couple of photos of Izzy, her face lit up by the glow of the candlelight, but it's hard to move, we're so squashed together. A kid jostles against me, trying to see the cake, and suddenly I'm overwhelmed by a wave of panic. My chest feels compressed and I'm finding it hard to breathe. I'm worried that I'm going to have an attack of claustrophobia.

'I need the toilet,' I mutter, though nobody is listening, and I push my way through the throng of people and escape upstairs to the tuneless singing of 'Happy Birthday'. On the toilet I breathe deeply the way I was taught by Dr Lopez. *Hold it together*, I tell myself. *You can't afford to have a breakdown here. You've got to stay professional.* With trembling fingers, I open the packet of beta blockers and swallow a couple, washed down with water from the tap. Then I splash my face with water and, feeling a little calmer, I make my way across the landing. I stop at the end and look up at stairs that lead to the attic bedroom. The door is slightly ajar, and I'm seized by curiosity. Is that the room where the accident happened?

I look around and listen to make sure no one is about and then before I have time to chicken out, I climb the stairs, push open the door and peer in.

The room is small and spartan. There's just a single chair, and a bed with a plain white bedspread. The walls are white, as is the built-in wardrobe. But I'm not really interested in the furniture. My eyes are drawn to the large window and the view of the close. The mock-Tudor latticework reminds me of the bars on a prison window and I shiver. *This must be the window Kate fell from*, I think with a chill. It's quite large but it's high up. You would have to be standing on something to fall out. I wonder what Kate was doing when she fell? Adults don't simply tumble out of windows for no reason.

I find myself sucked further into the room towards the window. Pressing my forehead against the glass pane, I look across the close at Mum and Dad's house. From this angle, I notice that there's a slate that has come off the roof, the grass has grown wild and the hedge needs trimming. My parents used to be so house-proud, but I suppose it's been difficult for Dad to keep everything up as well as take care of Mum. Once again, I feel a twist of guilt in my gut. Maybe when I move, I should try to find a house close to home so that I can help if he needs it.

Someone will notice I'm missing soon. I should go back downstairs and join the party. But I can't move. I'm rooted to the spot. Instead, on impulse, I climb up on the window seat, unlatch the window and slide it open. Leaning out, I stare down at the concrete below. The drop must be at least eight or nine metres and looking down, I feel dizzy and sick. What did it feel like when she fell? I wonder. How long did it take? What was going through her head? Did she even have time to think?

I jump as I hear the door opening behind me and someone says, 'What the hell are you doing?'

Chapter Six

Ajay is standing in the doorway. His face is partly obscured by shadow and it's hard to read his expression, but he sounds angry and I suppose he has every right to be. I would be, if I found someone snooping around in my bedroom.

I flush scarlet and slide the window closed, stepping down hurriedly from the window seat.

'Oh . . . er . . . yes. I'm sorry,' I stammer, thinking rapidly. 'I needed the loo and the main bathroom was occupied, so I came up here to use the en-suite. I hope you don't mind.'

He steps forward into the light and I see that his expression is not just angry, it's furious. It crosses my mind that he might actually hit me.

The expression is there for just a second then it returns to normal, bland and polite.

'I see,' he smiles. 'Well, you're missing the cake. It really is very good. Why don't you come and join us?'

Downstairs someone pours me a glass of champagne and I knock it back quickly. I need to steady my nerves. I'm mortified by what just happened. What must Ajay think of me? He must think I'm some kind of ghoul, with a morbid interest in his wife's death – and I guess he wouldn't be far wrong.

A wave of self-loathing washes over me as the alcohol kicks in. *What's wrong with me?* I glance over at Ajay. He's talking to his mother and father who are leaving. He's talking in a low voice and keeps looking over his shoulder at me. Is he telling them where he just found me, nosing around his room? I refill my glass and take another large gulp, closing my eyes. I should probably get out of here soon. People have started leaving anyway. Kids are trailing balloons and party bags.

'Well, I'll be off now,' I say to Ajay as he waves goodbye to Miriam and Adriana. 'I'll email you the photos.'

'Wait.' Ajay grabs my arm. 'Don't go yet. You don't have my email address. Anyway, I'd like to see the photos now.'

He's slightly drunk, I realise, and he's slurring his words. I'm not much better. The wine has gone to my head and, mixing with the beta blockers, it is making me feel quite dizzy. Everything seems fuzzy and soft-edged and the room is swimming in front of me.

'Oh.' I pretend to look at the time on my phone. 'I really need to get back soon . . .' I tail off, realising I can't think of a good reason why.

'I'm just going to put Izzy to bed. Can you just wait one minute? We haven't had the chance to have a chat yet,' Ajay says.

'OK.'

'Take a seat in the living room. Help yourself to another drink.'

Oh shit, I think. Now everybody's gone and we're alone, he wants to confront me about what I was doing upstairs in the bedroom. I pour myself a drink, drain the glass, then head into the front room, trying to think of a plausible excuse to give for why I was looking out of the window upstairs.

The basic structure of the living room is the same as when Holly lived here but the decor is completely different. Where there used to be an old brown carpet there's now an expensive-looking wooden floor and in place of the old fish tank there's a modern-looking fireplace. There are a couple of tasteful black and white photographs of giraffes and lions on the wall, and above the fireplace there are photos of Izzy and a woman who I assume must be Kate.

I resist the urge to examine those pictures more closely. The last thing I want right now is for Ajay to walk in and find me snooping again. So I sit on the sofa and stare upwards, thinking about Holly to distract myself. Like everything else in the room, the ceiling is now state of the art and elegant. There's a simple fall ceiling with a border of recessed light fixtures glowing softly. There used to be a chandelier, I remember, and I'm transported back to another summer, the early 2000s, listening to Britney Spears, 'Oops I did it again', playing on Holly's CD player while her parents were out.

'Have you ever thought about what it would be like to walk on the ceiling?' I asked dreamily. I was lying on the floor with my feet on the sofa staring up at the chandelier.

'What? No, not really.' Holly was at the window, her jeans hanging low over her skinny hips. She wasn't really paying attention. She was too busy watching Howie, home from university for the holidays, mowing the front lawn.

'Oh my God. He's taken his shirt off now,' she said, practically hyperventilating with excitement. 'Come and look, Jess.'

'Er, no thanks. That would be weird.'

'Oh yeah, I keep forgetting he's your brother. He's such a babe, though, don't you think?'

'You wouldn't think that if you had to smell his farts,' I shrugged.

'Ew! Yuck,' Holly laughed and flung herself down on the floor next to me. 'I don't believe you. I don't believe that he farts – or if he does, I think they smell like roses.'

We both cackled with laughter and rolled around clutching our bellies.

'Seriously, though,' said Holly, pausing for breath, 'do you think I stand a chance?'

Privately I doubted it. Howie had brought home a succession of posh, beautiful girlfriends. Women his age. I didn't think he'd be interested in a skinny little thirteen-year-old like Holly, but it seemed mean to say that, so I just shrugged and grinned mischievously. 'I don't know. I can ask him if you like. I could tell him you think you're in love . . .'

'Don't you dare!' she squealed, trying to cover my mouth. 'Please, Jess, promise you won't, or I'll tickle you to death.'

'All right, all right, I promise,' I conceded, shrieking and giggling as she tickled me.

I smile sadly thinking of Holly. We were so close for a while. Then we fell out. I can't even remember why. And we never made up before she and her family moved to Scotland. I've tried to contact her a couple of times in recent years, but she must have married and changed her surname because I haven't been able to find her on social media.

'Well, that was quick,' Ajay smiles, coming in carrying another bottle of wine. 'Izzy was out like a light. All that partying must have worn her out.'

He tops up my glass before I can refuse. Not that I would have anyway. I take another large swig and perch on the edge of the sofa.

He sits next to me and I show him some of the photos on my camera, but neither of us is really concentrating

61

and we talk about other things: Izzy's school, films we like, food we don't. We drink more wine and get into more personal topics: what it was like for Ajay growing up Indian in a predominantly white area and what it was like for me living in Madrid. I steer clear of the last few months, of course.

Our conversation is so friendly, and we seem to have so much in common that I've almost forgotten about what happened earlier until, during a pause in a discussion about Catalonia, Ajay suddenly blurts, 'You know what I said earlier, upstairs—'

'I can explain,' I interrupt. 'I went upstairs because I needed the loo and then I got distracted by the roof of my parents' house, there are a couple of tiles missing . . .'

He waves his hand. 'It's OK,' he says expansively. 'Actually, I wanted to apologise to you. You must have thought my reaction was a bit strange. It's just that . . . I don't know if you know, but my wife died recently.' He clears his throat. 'She fell from the window in that room, so you see . . .' A look of raw pain flits across his face and I think that he must have loved his wife very much.

'My God, I'm so sorry,' I say, doing my best to look shocked. If he knew that I already knew about her death, my behaviour would be unforgiveable.

'Yeah, well,' he says bitterly, draining his glass. 'Life goes on.' He stands up and walks to the mantlepiece.

'This is her,' he says, picking up a photo and handing it to me.

I hold the frame in my hands and gaze into a pair of sultry, cat-like eyes.

'She's beautiful,' I say honestly. In fact, beautiful doesn't do her justice. She's stunning, with a sort of lithe sexiness that shines out of the photograph. But there's a slight curl to her lip and a hardness in her eyes that makes me wonder whether I would have liked her if I'd known her.

'Yeah, she was.' Ajay frowns. 'Beautiful inside and out. I know that's a cliché but in her case it was true.'

For just a moment, I wonder if he's playing a part – the part of the grieving husband, saying all the things he's supposed to say. I remember what his mother said about her not being a good person and what Miriam said about her being brilliant and wonder who is closer to the truth.

'She liked photography too, like you. She took those. He points to the photos of animals on the wall. It's where we met, in South Africa on a sabbatical at a game reserve. We had both just qualified as vets.' He sighs and takes the picture from me and lays it flat on the mantlepiece. 'It makes you realise how fragile life is, how one minute someone is so vibrant, so alive. The next minute they can be gone, without warning' – he snaps his fingers – 'just like that.'

'You said she fell from the window?' I venture, supressing a shiver.

63

'Yes, there was a pigeon's nest in the gutter. She was leaning out trying to clear it. She'd asked me to do it the day before, but I put it off . . .' He laughs bitterly. 'If only I'd done it when she asked me, she'd still be alive.' He drops his head into his hands.

'You can't blame yourself,' I say softly.

'Can't I?' he looks up, his beautiful eyes bloodshot with unshed tears and alcohol. He sounds almost angry.

'No, how could you have known that would happen? I mean, it's a chance in a million.'

'Yeah, well . . .' he says, waving his hand and knocking over a glass. I watch the glass tumble to the floor and the wine spill onto the carpet. Neither of us try to clear it up. The room is swaying slightly. I'm really drunk, I realise. How have I allowed myself to get this drunk? I should go home. But I can't move.

'Where was Izzy? Was she here when it happened?' I ask.

He shudders. 'No, thank God. She was at school. Can you imagine if she'd seen that?'

I shake my head.

'I think that was the hardest part,' he continues, 'telling Izzy her mum was dead. She couldn't understand why her mummy wasn't coming home. She cried in bed every night for a month. She still has nightmares.'

His eyes well up with tears. I can feel his grief swamping me. It's heavy in the air.

'I can't imagine how hard that must be,' I say. My own eyes are filling with tears. I find myself reaching out and touching his arm. It's intended to be a comforting pat, but somehow, I end up folded in his arms. Then I'm not sure who makes the first move, but we're kissing clumsily, drunkenly. And I can taste the alcohol in his mouth. For a moment his mouth is hard and urgent against mine and I'm lost in a haze of alcohol and lust. Then the next thing I know, he shoves me away roughly and I stagger back against the sofa.

'I'm sorry,' he blurts. 'I can't. I just can't.'

He looks at me with an expression I can only describe as horror. And then, to my mortification, he flings his head into his hands and sobs as if his heart will break.

Chapter Seven

I wake up with a massive hangover and the sense that something really bad has happened. My mouth is dry. It tastes stale and bitter and my head is pounding. There's the usual feeling of shame and self-loathing but it seems more intense this morning. *Why the hell did I drink so much?* I think, as I stagger to the bathroom. Staring at my even paler than normal face and trying not to throw up, yesterday comes back to me in a wave of humiliation.

I kissed Ajay Chandry, my parents' neighbour – a man I've known for less than twenty-four hours, a man whose wife has only just died. What was I thinking? I groan out loud as I remember the expression of horror on his face when he pushed me away. Then the way he crumbled in front of my eyes afterwards. I don't think I've ever seen an adult cry with such abandonment. Poor man, he's only just lost his wife and here I am shoving my tongue down his throat – at his kid's birthday party too. Who does that?

What's wrong with me? Only yesterday I was thinking I could make a go of it here, make new friends, build a reputation as a photographer. Now it looks as though I've fucked it all up already.

I go to the window and rip open the curtains. The clouds of yesterday have lifted without bringing any rain or relief from the heat, and the weather is already hot even though it's only half past nine in the morning. I want to go back to bed and lie under the fan but the pain in my head is throbbing.

Downstairs my mother is sitting at the kitchen table, steadily swallowing her way through the pills Dad has put out for her on a dish, and Dad is reading the Sunday paper, slurping at his tea.

'Have you got any painkillers?' I mumble.

'Maybe,' says Dad. 'They'll be in that cupboard.'

I rummage through the medicine cabinet, bottles of medicine, plasters and packets of pills spilling out. There are several that are out of date, but I know it's pointless telling Dad. He refuses to throw anything away.

'What's this?' I ask, reading a random packet.

Dad folds up his newspaper and sighs. 'It's a painkiller I got when I pulled my back. But it's very strong. You can't take that. There must be some Nurofen in there.'

'Oh, yes, here it is,' I say, teasing a packet out. I open it and wash a couple of tablets down with a glass of water. *I ought to eat*, I think. Carbs are good for a hangover. Even though I feel nauseous, I pour some cereal into a bowl and splash milk over the top.

'Do you want some, Mum? What cereal would you like?'

'Oh.' She looks helplessly at my dad. 'I don't know. What cereal do I have, Brian?'

I survey the selection of cereals in the cupboard. 'There's shreddies, muesli, cornflakes or porridge. You always used to like porridge with hon—' I break off because Mum is looking more and more panicked. She scratches her head. 'Um, I don't know. What should I have?'

'You usually have cornflakes,' Dad intervenes firmly. 'But first you have to write in your diary, remember? The doctor said.' He reaches for a spiral notebook covered in pictures of butterflies and a pen, and places them in front of her.

'The doctor recommended she keep a record of what happens every day to aid her memory,' he explains.

'We went shopping yesterday,' he says to Mum, opening the notebook to a blank page and writing the date at the top. 'And Polly popped around for a cup of tea, remember?'

'Oh yes, that's right.' Mum sucks at the end of her pen and starts writing. 'What else did we do?' I can see the strain on her face as she tries to recall, and I feel a wave of love and admiration mixed with pity for this determined woman. She's fighting this thing as hard as she can. Of course she is. Mum has always been a fighter.

After a few minutes she closes it with a sigh. 'I feel tired, Brian. Can I stop now?'

'Yes, OK, love.' He pats her hand patronisingly.

As if she's a child, I think, suddenly angry. *As if she can't make a decision for herself.*

But Dad looks tired and his eyes are ringed with grey. He's doing the best he can. I've been so wrapped up in my own problems that I've forgotten how difficult this all must be for him. Not only is he slowly losing the love of his life, watching her disintegrate in front of his eyes, but over the past couple of days, I've realised that Dad barely gets a minute to himself. Mum has become so dependent on him. On the one hand, she can still do most physical tasks for herself, but on the other she gets anxious when Dad is gone for too long because she forgets where he is.

I pour Mum some cornflakes then sit at the table nursing a coffee, staring at the cereal and deciding I really can't bring myself to eat it.

'How are you, Dad?' I ask.

'I've been better,' he says. 'My back's been bothering me lately. We're getting old, I'm afraid,' he smiles sadly. He does look old. It's time for me to start looking after them instead of the other way around.

My head is still killing me. But it's self-inflicted and I

know it'll be better when the painkillers kick in. 'Why don't you go and have a lie-down? I can take care of things here. I can look after Mum,' I say.

'I don't need looking after,' Mum snaps crossly. We both ignore her.

'It's all right, Jessie, I'll be all right. I know you've got things you need to do.'

'How about I do some shopping at least? I'm going into Aylesbury to the estate agent's. I can easily visit the supermarket on my way back.'

'All right then,' Dad agrees. 'I'll write you a list.'

It's a relief to have a reason to get out of the house. I only wish I could break free from myself too – just step out of my skin and emerge like a beautiful butterfly. But I know that I'm the one person I can't escape. I'm trapped with myself, whether I like it or not. Wherever I go, I'm always there, sabotaging myself – doing stupid things like snogging a man whose wife has just died or destroying my boyfriend's expensive wooden floor.

Chapter Eight

I'm the only person my age on the bus into Aylesbury. Apart from a couple of listless teenagers lolling at the back, it's full of pensioners with bus passes. I sit at the top, in the front, like I used to with Holly and Alice when we were kids, and the bus rattles through estates of uniform red-brick houses and past empty school playgrounds. The branches of trees whip the windscreen. It's hot inside the bus and there's a faint smell of body odour. My head is still throbbing, and I'm trying not to feel closed in. I'm trying not to think of the Metro in Madrid – that journey home last month, squashed between two businessmen in suits, screaming and crying to be let out. Matteo reluctantly getting out a stop early, dragging me along the platform, his face like thunder.

The bus pulls up and disgorges its passengers. I

scramble out and head across the covered bridge to the mall. They've done their best to make it a pleasant environment. There are comfy-looking seats and bean bags strewn around as well as a nice new cafe that sells drinks in jars with paper straws. But they can't disguise the fact that shops are shutting down all over the place and you still get the impression of a place in terminal decline. How can Aylesbury compete with online stores and all the out-of-town shopping centres?

The estate agent is blonde and bubbly. Her name is Paula and she's very hopeful that she can find me something I'll love within my price range. We arrange to view some properties tomorrow. Then I head outside, past the betting shop, towards the statue of John Hampden. I'm near the bank when I hear my name called.

A tall, fair-haired woman is standing near Greggs and waving at me frantically.

It's Alice. Older, thinner. She's dyed her hair and cut it short. But I recognise her straight away and feel a rush of affection as she bounds across the street and wraps me in fragrant arms. Then she steps back and looks at me, her head tipped to one side.

'Oh my God, Jess, is it really you?'

'Last time I checked,' I laugh.

'Well, you look great.'

'Why, thank you, darling. It must be all the botox.' I pout and flick my hair.

'What, really?' She peers at me, unsure whether to believe me.

And I laugh. 'What do you think, Ally?'

She laughs too and shakes her head. 'You haven't changed.'

'Neither have you. You look fab too,' I say sincerely. She's wearing grey culottes and a chiffon top that would probably make most people look dumpy, but on Alice it looks stylish and sophisticated.

'Well' – she looks at her watch – 'do you have time for a coffee with an old friend?'

'Sure, why not?'

The coffee shop isn't busy, and we find a table by the window overlooking the entrance to the mall. I sip an Americano, watching a woman pushing a pram through the doors and an elderly couple shuffle out arm in arm.

'How are Tommo and the kids?' I ask. Alice and I have been in regular contact and I know that she's got two children now – two little girls, Isla and Scarlett.

'Oh, they're OK. They keep me busy. You know what it's like . . . ballet lessons. Temper tantrums . . .'

I don't know, I think with a twinge of regret. It's funny, when we were teenagers, Alice was always the one who said she never wanted to marry or have kids, whereas I had thought I'd have at least three by now. I had wanted to have kids with Matteo, but he always put it off. Thank God he did, I reflect, or who knows what kind of mess we would be in now.

'Anyway, I've got a bone to pick with you,' Alice is saying, smiling. 'What I want to know is, why didn't you tell us you were back?' She tears a sachet of sugar and pours it into her coffee.

'Oh,' I flounder. 'I've only been here a few days. It's been manic.' It's not the whole truth. The truth is, I realise that I haven't contacted my old friends because I've been avoiding the inevitable questions about Matteo and my life in Madrid.

'And before that?' Alice frowns slightly. 'I haven't heard from you since Christmas. I sent you loads of messages. You never answered. I've been worried about you.'

'Things have been . . . difficult for the past few months,' I say. 'Matteo and I . . . we were having problems.'

'Oh well. You're here now. I've missed you,' she smiles warmly. I've missed her too, I realise. I hadn't realised how much I'd been isolated by Matteo – how he slowly separated me from all my friends. For a second I contemplate confiding in her the whole, awful truth. But I'll save that for another time, I think. I don't want to bring her down. I want to be like Paula, the estate agent, funny, bubbly and optimistic.

'So, how long are you back for?' she says. 'Is Matteo with you?'

'We've split up.'

Her eyes widen. 'Oh, I'm sorry.'

'Don't be,' I shrug. 'It's for the best. He was an arsehole.'

She gives me a searching look then laughs. 'OK, I won't be sorry. I never liked him much anyway.'

'Now you tell me,' I smile. 'Why didn't you tell me at the time?'

'I don't know. Would you have listened?'

'Probably not,' I admit. I think back to when I first met Matteo, how obsessed I was with him and I wonder now how much of the attraction was Matteo and how much was because he represented an escape from my life here.

There's a moment's silence as I look down at the people slouching or scurrying into the mall.

'So, what's the gossip?' I say. 'What's been going on since I've been away?' I'm trying to steer the conversation away from Matteo – away from Spain.

Alice frowns and looks at her fingernails. 'I know something must have happened. Oh yes. Holly's had a baby boy.'

'Holly?' I say, surprised. 'As in Holly Thompson?'

'Yes, but she's not Holly Thompson now, she's Holly Hargreaves. She married a couple of years ago, but surely you know that?'

'No, I lost contact with Holly years ago.' I'd assumed that Alice had too. I thought Holly had cut off ties with all of us from our old gang, and I'm surprised and a little hurt that she's been communicating with Alice all this time.

'Where does she live now? What's she doing?' I picture Holly – sharp, scrappy little Holly – and feel a wave of nostalgia.

'She's still in Scotland. She's a doctor now, would you believe?'

I laugh. 'She always did like biology. Do you remember she was the only one of us who could dissect that frog?'

Alice nods and smiles. 'It made me feel quite sick,' she says.

'Do you have an address for her?' I ask. 'Or contact details. I'd like to write to her.'

Alice looks embarrassed. She hesitates a minute then says, 'Sure . . . I'll message you them.' Then she looks out of the window. 'Oh, and Sean White is living in Wendover now. He's good friends with Tommo. Actually, I'm surprised you haven't bumped into him yet.'

Sean White. I haven't thought about him in years. I remember another hot, sultry summer. The summer of 2004, in the sixth form – playing *GTA* in his cramped bedroom, drinking cider in Wendover Woods, experimenting with sex on the damp ground under that old oak tree.

'Oh my God. Sean White. How is he?'

Alice grimaces. 'Not too good at the moment actually. His girlfriend died recently.'

'I had no idea,' I murmur.

'No, well, it wasn't exactly public knowledge.' She leans towards me over the table and lowers her voice. 'Only Tommo and I knew about her. She was married.'

'I see.' It doesn't surprise me. Sean was always a bit of a player. 'Was it serious?'

'Oh yes,' Alice nods. 'She was going to leave her husband. But it was complicated. She had a little girl about Isla's age.'

A little girl, I think.

Alice shivers and leans in. 'It was a real shocker. She fell from her bedroom window and broke her neck.'

I grip the table, swamped by a wave of dizziness.

'What was her name?' I ask, though I already know the answer.

'Kate Chandry. Why?' Alice frowns. 'What's wrong? Are you OK? Did you know her?'

'Not exactly. She lived opposite my parents in Holly's old house. I know her husband. He's their neighbour. I took the photos at his daughter's birthday party just yesterday.'

Alice claps a hand to her mouth. 'I had no idea they lived there. You must promise not to say anything to him about Sean. I probably shouldn't have told you.'

'It's OK. I won't say a word,' I reassure her. 'I don't know him very well. I only met him the other day.' I stare into my coffee cup, trying not to think about last night.

'Ajay told me she was clearing the gutter when she fell,' I say.

Alice shrugs and then gives a little shiver. 'Let's change the subject. It gives me the creeps.'

We talk about mutual friends and Alice's husband and children for a while, until Alice looks at her watch and exclaims, 'Oh no! Is that the time? Well, much as I'd love to sit here and chat all day I've got to go and pick up the kids.' She makes a face. 'But why don't you come to our house on Saturday? Tommo's brother and his wife are coming for a barbeque. I could use the moral support.'

After Alice leaves, I head to the supermarket and wander around the aisles, picking up the items on Dad's list. I know it's not healthy for me to obsess about Kate and Ajay, but I can't help thinking about what Alice has just told me – that Kate Chandry was having an affair, with Sean White of all people. Alice said that Kate had been planning to leave her husband. What if she'd told him she was leaving him? How would he have reacted? He would have been furious, of course. I imagine a blazing row, a tussle. I close my eyes as an image of Ajay pushing his wife barges into my head. Maybe they were standing close to the window at the time. It could have been an accident. I think about him standing behind me at the window and a spasm of fear and revulsion seizes me. Could Mum have been right? Could he have killed her?

When I get home, I spend what's left of the day designing and ordering business cards. Then I read up online about how to set up shop as a photographer and attempt to build my own website. But it's more complicated than I thought, so I decide to leave it for another time. Instead I upload the pictures I took at Izzy's party and start editing.

Surprisingly, some of them haven't turned out too bad. I think my favourite is the first picture I took of Izzy, of her opening the present. She's set slightly to one side of the frame, the light from the window illuminating the side of her face, capturing her excitement as she rips off the paper, and the image is slightly blurred, creating a feeling of movement and energy. I scroll through the other photos and find a colourful shot of a group of girls on the lawn and the close-up I took of Isobel on the swing. She's staring pensively out at the grey sky. It's a good picture but there's something I don't like – something wrong, something that makes my stomach churn with anxiety. I zoom in and realise what it is that's making me uneasy. It's the bruises on her arm. Peering closely at the screen, the feeling of uneasiness grows. When the bruises are enlarged like this, their shape reminds me very much of fingers.

Chapter Nine

The next morning, I wake up late, feeling worn out after a night of fractured sleep and troubled dreams. In one dream I found myself in the bedroom at the top of Ajay's house. There were lots of people crowded inside and the window was wide open. A girl was leaning out and I was trying to warn her of the danger, but someone jostled me, so I fell against her and she plummeted out of the window. When I ran outside and turned over her body, I saw that it was Anna Maria, her face stained with tears.

I get out of bed, those awful last few months in Spain replaying in my head on a loop and a dreadful tightness in my chest. I take my depression medication and a pill for anxiety and, feeling a little calmer, I wash, dress and make my way downstairs.

I find Mum sitting at the kitchen table, staring at her

watch. Dad is out. I know that from the large note in marker pen pinned to the fridge.

GONE TO THE CHEMIST'S. BACK IN TEN MINUTES. JESS IS UPSTAIRS IN BED.

It's the perfect opportunity, I think, *to quiz her about the accusation she made against Ajay, without Dad here to read too much into my curiosity.* If he thinks I'm taking what she said seriously, he might start to believe that Matteo's right and I really am crazy after all.

'Mum,' I say casually, opening the fridge, looking for the butter. 'You know what you said at dinner the other day?'

She blinks at me. One eyelid has thick blue eyeshadow and mascara on and the other has none. It makes her look like a demented clown.

'What did I say, darling?'

I hesitate. I don't want to distress her unnecessarily, but I need to know the truth. It's been eating away at me all night. 'You said that you saw our neighbour push his wife out of the window, remember?'

'I said what?' She looks at me aghast.

'You said that he killed her. You warned me that he was dangerous.'

She shakes her head vehemently. 'I don't think I said anything of the sort. Why are you saying such horrid things?' She looks around wildly, her hands trembling. 'We'll ask Brian. Where's your father? He'll know what all this is about.'

81

'He's not here. He's popped out to the chemist's. I'm sorry, Mum, I shouldn't have said anything. I think I got mixed up.' I feel terrible for upsetting her. Me and my big mouth. I sit next to her and rub her arm gently, trying to soothe her. 'I was just talking nonsense, like normal. Ignore me.'

She smiles at that and seems to calm down. 'Well, we all talk nonsense occasionally, don't we?'

I put some bread in the toaster and Mum goes back to fiddling with her watch.

'There's something wrong with this damn thing. I can see the hands, but I don't know what they mean. Jessica, come and see.'

'It's ten fifteen,' I say, leaning over her shoulder. I check my phone. 'It looks fine to me. Just a minute out. My phone says ten sixteen.'

'Really?' She gives me a sly look as if I'm teasing her then she looks at her watch again. 'Oh yes. I see it now.' She runs her hands through her thin, thistledown hair. 'Oh gosh, I really am losing my marbles, aren't I?'

'Nonsense, Mum, you're fine.' I kiss the top of her head.

'Don't lie to me, Jessie,' she says crossly. 'I know it's happening. I can feel a little bit slipping away every day. A little piece of me. Poof! Gone.' She clicks her fingers. 'I'm scared.'

I blink back the tears that suddenly spring up in my eyes. Mum was always so feisty and adventurous. She was the one who laughed away my fears when I was a little girl and encouraged me to be brave. It's hard to see her reduced to this fearful, quivering old woman.

'Why are you scared, Mum?' I ask, trying not to show my emotions. I need to be strong now for both of us.

'Because I know what happens next. I know what I will become. I don't want to be that old woman sitting in a chair in an old people's home. Dribbling and talking nonsense. You won't let that happen to me, will you? Just shoot me if it comes to that.'

'That's a long way off,' I say, hoping that it's true. Inside I feel like a coward. I remember watching a clip of an old woman's hundred and tenth birthday. She was sitting there all hunched and shrivelled like a living mummy, just repeating, 'I want to die,' over and over. And all her friends and relatives were just laughing at her, brushing off what I guess were her genuine feelings. Am I doing the same to my own mother by refusing to acknowledge what we both know is true? That the inevitable end of this disease will be horrible and degrading? But I can't bring myself to talk about it. What's the point anyway? I don't want to upset her any more than I already have.

'Would you like a cup of tea?' I ask with an attempt at brightness.

'That would be lovely, darling,' she smiles, pacified once more.

'I'm getting old sans eyes . . . no teeth . . . Oh, how does it go?' She breaks off, frustrated. 'You know that speech in Shakespeare – the one about the seven ages of man? Where does that come from?'

'I don't know. I can look it up on my phone if you like.'

'It's from *As You Like It*,' I say after a quick search. 'Part of Jaques' "All the world's a stage" speech. Did you ever act in that?'

She brightens up immediately. She loves talking about her days in the theatre. 'Oh yes, I played Rosalind. There was a very lovely boy who played Orlando. Now, what was his name?' She chews her lip. 'Warren, that was it. Oh, he was gorgeous. It was while I was at the Royal Shakespeare Company.'

'Really?' I say. I'm fairly sure Mum never acted with the Royal Shakespeare Company, but the doctor has told Dad not to contradict her when she has false memories. And if it makes her happy, why shouldn't she imagine she was a star in her youth? So instead I make her tea the way she likes it, milky with two sugars, and I sit down at the table next to her. *I haven't always been the best daughter*, I think, *but maybe I can make it up to her now*. All she wants is someone to talk to her, to listen to her stories. Is that so hard?

'I didn't know you were with the RSC,' I say.

'Oh yes,' she smiles. 'I played opposite Olivier, you know.'

'Olivier? As in Lawrence Olivier?' I say sceptically.

She doesn't answer. She's staring down at her tea suspiciously. She sips it very cautiously. Then she starts violently and spits it out.

'Oh sorry, Mum,' I say, alarmed. 'Is it too hot? I can add some more cold milk if you like.'

She flaps her hand. 'No, no, it's not too hot. Sit down, Jessie. I have to tell you something.' She looks over her shoulder and then leans forward, lowering her voice.

'It's poisoned,' she whispers.

I stare at her aghast. Can she be serious?

'Mum, it's not poisoned,' I say firmly. 'I made it myself. I poured the water from the tap and put the teabag in myself.'

I pick up the cup and take a sip myself before she can stop me.

'No, don't!' she cries out so urgently that she almost convinces me there's something wrong with the tea. But it tastes completely normal, if a bit too milky for me. I take another sip. 'Look. It's fine, Mum. I'm not dead yet.'

She looks at me, smiling slightly as if I'm trying to trick her. 'Little Johnny thin,' she says apropos of nothing. 'He killed her, you know? He said it was the fishing boy, but I know it wasn't.'

'What are you talking about? What fishing boy?' I ask, my heart sinking. Some days I think Mum is absolutely fine, then the next, like today, it seems as though she's really losing it.

She just taps her nose and then picks up the tea. 'You think this tea's OK, do you?' she asks.

'Yes, Mum,' I say firmly. 'No one is trying to poison you. Unless you think I am – for your millions. Can't wait for my inheritance.' I try to make a joke. But it falls flat.

'No, not you, Jessie. You were always a good girl,' Mum says seriously. 'But I know too much, you see. He's worried I'm going to spill the beans.'

I stay silent. I don't want to encourage her in this line of thinking. I know all too well where this kind of paranoia can lead.

Chapter Ten

'You didn't tell me Sean was going to be here,' I say.

It's Alice's barbecue. We're in her open-plan kitchen and I'm helping her chop salad. I try not to let my irritation show, but I can't help feeling ambushed. When Alice invited me, she told me it was going to be a small affair, just her and Tommo's brother and sister-in-law. For some reason they've decided to add my ex into the mix.

Alice smiles slyly. 'We didn't know he was coming until last night. Tommo bumped into him in the pub,' she explains. 'Anyway,' she says, scraping the tomatoes into the bowl, 'he needs cheering up. You know, I told you about his girlfriend.'

I look out of the French windows at Alice's kids who are bouncing on the trampoline and at Sean, who is tending the barbecue and talking animatedly to Tommo. I try to work out the last time I saw him. It must have been ten years ago, just before I dropped out of college. We hooked up for one night. 'A quick shag for old time's sake,' as he so romantically put it.

'You should go and say hello,' says Alice, following the direction of my gaze.

'Yeah, maybe you're right,' I agree. Speaking to him will only get more awkward the longer I put it off. So I pour myself a drink for Dutch courage and head outside.

It's spotting with rain, a fact which everyone seems to be doing their best to ignore, and Sean looks up as I walk towards him. Running his hands through his dark brown hair, he gives me a familiar, lazy smile.

'Hello, stranger,' he says. I look into his sleepy, cool-cowboy eyes and I'm transported back fifteen years. 'Well, well, well, the traveller returns,' he says, flipping a burger on the griddle. 'How are you, Jess?'

'I'm OK. You? You haven't changed much.'

It's true. He hasn't changed. He has more laughter lines, maybe, and his chest is broader, but he still looks like the Sean I remember – the one with the dimples that drove all the girls in our year wild. I think about what Alice told me about him and Kate. *He doesn't look heartbroken*, I think unkindly. In fact, he looks as pleased with himself as I remember. But then perhaps he's just hiding it well.

'Nor have you – you're looking pretty damn fine,' he

says, looking me up and down with a flirtatious grin. *No, not heartbroken at all*, I think. But I don't get to deliver the pithy put-down that's on the tip of my tongue, because at that moment there's a crack of thunder and rain starts pummelling down.

'Well, that's fucking typical!' exclaims Tommo with gloomy humour. 'The day we decide to have a barbecue is the one day it decides to rain. It said it was going to be sunny all day on the forecast.'

We help him rescue the burgers and food and dash inside before we get drenched.

Alice gives us towels and we dry our hair, laughing. Then we all bustle around trying to salvage the meal until Alice orders us all out of the kitchen. The children run upstairs to their bedrooms to play and Sean follows me over to the window seat where I sit with my plate of food in my lap and another Mojito in my hand. I'd meant to lay off the booze, especially after the fiasco with Ajay the other night, but seeing Sean here has weakened my resolve.

'So, how was Spain? Madrid, right?' he asks.

'That's right.' I'm surprised and flattered that he's taken enough of an interest in my life to know that, and I hate myself for feeling that way. Why should I care what he thinks? 'Spain was good,' I say. 'But I'm glad to be back in the rain.'

He laughs his slow, lazy laugh. 'Yeah, great, isn't it? Good old England. Do you remember when we went to Cornwall and it rained the whole week?'

A week in his aunt's caravan. The rain drumming on the caravan roof as we lay in bed. The first time I ever had sex. There must have been a break in the rain at some point, because I remember lying together in the long grass above the cliffs and him writing on my belly in biro *Sean was here* and me giggling as the nib of his pen tickled my skin. For weeks afterwards, I tried not to wash that spot. What an idiot I was.

'I do remember,' I say tersely.

'Hmm.' His eyes hold mine for a fraction too long. But I look down at my drink, because I remember other things too. How he told me he loved me in Wendover Woods, and then the very next day I walked in on him snogging Natasha Harvey at a party.

I look at Alice, who is fussing around in the kitchen. She catches my eye and winks. 'That all seems like a long time ago,' I say.

'Yeah, I suppose it is.'

'What are you doing now?' I remember he always wanted to be an actor. He was good too. He could have made it. 'Are you still acting?' I ask.

'I go to amateur dramatics. But my job is in property. Living the dream,' he smiles ironically.

'You're an estate agent? Maybe you can help me then,' I

say without thinking. 'I'm looking for a flat in the Aylesbury area.'

'You are?' he smiles. 'Does that mean you're back for good then?' He leans towards me, his amber eyes intent, and I look away. I'm not about to be sucked into all that again.

'It looks like it. I want to be close to my parents. My Mum has early-onset dementia.'

'I'm sorry.' He gives me that look he gives. The one that seems to say I understand you perfectly and I'm totally on your side. 'I always liked your mother,' he says. 'The little I knew of her.'

I bite my lip thinking of the way he used to flirt and joke with her.

'You two look like sisters,' he used to say. 'And you're the younger, more beautiful sister, of course.' And she would hit him with a tea towel and chase him around the kitchen. 'Go on with you, you silly boy,' she would say. But I could tell that she loved the attention.

'It's OK,' I say. 'She's not too bad really. Not yet. I mean she's still herself . . . if you know what I mean.'

He nods. 'I do.'

'It's just she gets things muddled up.'

Sean nods again and looks out of the window. Then he turns back to me, changing the subject. 'I can certainly help you find a flat. What exactly are you looking for?'

'One or two bedrooms. It would be nice to have a garden. Something inexpensive. I'm living off savings at the moment.'

'You haven't got a job yet?'

'Not exactly. I'm setting up my own photography business.'

'Ah, yes, I remember you were always into photography,' he grins wolfishly. 'I've still got some of those pictures from that summer. Do you remember?'

I cringe. I do remember. We took some black and white photos of both of us naked. I hope he means the photos I took of him and not the ones he took of me. Is it too late to ask for them back?

We talk about his family. His sister who's had six kids from three different fathers – the latest apparently is in prison for dealing drugs – and about his brother who is training to become a pilot.

'Anyway, what about you? What about the guy you were with in Spain?'

'Matteo? Oh, that's all over.'

There's a silence as I think about what Alice told me the other day.

'I was so sorry to hear about your girlfriend . . . Alice told me . . .' I tail off lamely. A fly buzzes around our food and Sean brushes it away, his eyes suddenly blank.

'Yeah, well, she wasn't officially my girlfriend. No one

really knew about us, except for Tommo and Alice. She was married to someone else, you see. Ajay Chandry. You must know him. He lives opposite your parents.'

'Yeah, I know him a little,' I say, deliberately vague.

'I think that was the most difficult part,' he says with a deep sigh. 'After she died, I couldn't explain to anyone why I was grieving. I couldn't even go to the funeral even though I'd been seeing her for two years.'

Two years, a long time for an affair, I think. A long time for the news of their affair not to filter through to Ajay. Wendover is a small place and, in my experience, gossip spreads quickly.

'That must have been tough,' I say out loud, trying to sound sympathetic.

He winces and nods. And for the first time I see a flash of what looks like genuine pain on his face. *Maybe he really cared about this woman*, I think. Instinctively I reach out to touch him; to comfort him. But my hand drops by my side. Given our history, too much physical contact could be misinterpreted, or could lead to a place I don't want to go again.

'Yeah,' Sean says, blinking. 'We were going to get married too.'

'You were?' I say, pretending to be surprised.

'Yeah. She was going to finally leave him. We'd made plans. We were going to travel together . . . She was going to tell him about us just before she died.'

'Do you know if she did tell Ajay?' I ask.

Sean shrugs. 'I don't know. It doesn't really matter now, does it? We've both lost her.'

'I don't think she told him,' I murmur, more to myself than to Sean.

'Why? What makes you say that?' Sean looks sharply up at me.

'I spoke to him about his wife just the other day. I got the impression he didn't know. He seemed to really love her. He gave me the impression they were happily married.'

Sean's eyes darken with anger. 'That's complete bullshit,' he says. 'They were having problems even before I came into the picture.'

'What kind of problems?'

'Oh, all sorts of things. He's not a very nice man, Jess. He made her life a misery. He was very controlling and jealous, and he was unfaithful to her.'

I try to square this with the man I met the other day who seemed so devastated by his wife's death. 'Was he ever violent?' I ask.

He looks startled. 'No, not to my knowledge – though I wouldn't be surprised.'

I stare down at my drink. Tommo has made the Mojito strong and it's going to my head, loosening my tongue.

'Don't you think it's a bit odd, the timing of her accident?'

'What do you mean?'

94

'I mean, she was planning to tell him she was going to leave him for you. Then next thing you know, she falls out of a window and breaks her neck.'

Sean stares at me. Then he laughs. 'Are you serious? You mean, you think . . .' He shakes his head. 'No, much as I don't like the man, I don't think he killed her. There was nothing suspicious about her death. She was alone in the house when she fell.'

'It's just that . . . my mum said something the other day. She said she saw him push her.'

Sean stares down at his shot glass. He looks thoughtful.

'But you said yourself your mother has dementia,' he says. 'You don't actually believe her, do you?'

'No, I suppose not,' I say. Do I believe her? The idea is growing inside my head like a mushroom cloud. But I'm careful not to show Sean. I've made accusations before and it ended up with me in Dr Lopez's office and nearly being sectioned. I'm not going to make the same mistake again.

'No, of course I don't believe her,' I say.

Chapter Eleven

The rain is easing off by the time Sean drops me outside my parents'. He kills the engine and looks up at Ajay's house, giving a deep sigh.

'This is the first time I've been here since she died,' he says.

I follow the direction of his gaze. The house stands stoically, its rain-darkened walls revealing nothing. The windows are black, and there's no car parked outside. There's no of sign of movement inside. *Is Ajay at home? I wonder with a shiver. Could he be watching us now?*

'I'm sorry, I should have thought . . .' I say out loud. 'It must be hard for you.'

'It's OK,' he shrugs. 'I had to come back here sooner or later. In a way, it's therapeutic.'

'What was she like?' I ask. I'm trying to build up a picture of Kate Chandry but so far I've received so many conflicting descriptions that I can't seem to get a handle on her.

'Um . . .' Sean clears his throat. 'She was amazing, honestly. Wild, unpredictable, sexy. Brutally honest. I don't think I've ever met anyone quite like her . . . except maybe you . . .' He reaches over and grasps my hand.

I'm shocked into silence. Is he actually coming on to me? Now? After just talking about how sad he is about his ex? It's a totally inappropriate time. I disentangle my hand from his and clear my throat.

'Well, thanks for the lift,' I say primly, unbuckling my seat belt.

He grins at me, enjoying my discomfort. He always liked to provoke a reaction of any kind. 'No problem, Jess. I'll give you a ring about that flat.'

'Yes, thank you,' I mumble, getting out of the car and bolting for the door.

Mum has nodded off in the living room watching *Last of the Summer Wine*, so I creep past, trying not to wake her. I'm looking for Dad. There's so much on my mind. I need to talk to someone. I need to talk about Sean and Kate, their affair and all the dark suspicions swirling around in my head. Mum was always the one I went to with problems. But Mum is clearly out of the question. There's a risk that Dad will take whatever I say as evidence of my precarious mental condition, but right now I'm willing to take that risk.

I find him in the conservatory reading the paper.

'Did you have a good time?' he asks, peering at me over the top of the page.

'Yes, thanks. It was nice to see Alice and Tommo and all their kids again.'

'Good,' he says, and the newspaper goes up again.

I sit down and flick through the magazine, reading an interview with a famous actress. Dad clearly doesn't want to talk. A trapped bee buzzes around, flinging itself at the glass ceiling. The window ledge is a graveyard for dead insects. I open the door and nudge the bee out with the magazine.

'Sean was there too,' I say.

Dad looks up reluctantly from the article he's reading.

'Sean?'

'Yes, you remember Sean White?'

'Oh, him.' Dad's tone is contemptuous. 'Yes, I remember. I remember you spent about a week crying after he left you for some other girl.' He places the newspaper on the table next to him. 'What was he doing there?'

'He's really good friends with Tommo, Alice's husband.'

'Oh,' Dad snorts. 'Well, I hope you're not thinking of starting anything with him again?'

'No, of course not.'

'Good.' He picks up the paper again. Conversation over as far as he's concerned.

'He told me something really strange, though.'

Dad sighs and folds up his newspaper. 'Oh?'

'He said that he'd been having an affair with Kate Chandry.'

Dad frowns and then nods slowly. 'That makes sense. I saw a strange car parked outside a couple of times while Ajay was away. I suppose it could've been his. Does he drive a BMW?'

'I don't know. His car's black.'

'Yes, that's right. A black BMW. Poor Ajay. I always thought Kate was a bit . . .' He shrugs. 'Oh, I don't know. You shouldn't speak ill of the dead, I suppose.'

'She was planning to tell Ajay,' I say. 'She was going to leave him. Sean says they were planning to get married.'

'Really?' Dad looks surprised. 'Well, there's no accounting for taste.'

I take a deep breath. 'Don't you think it's a bit suspicious? She tells him she's leaving him for another man and the next thing you know is she's dead.'

Dad sighs impatiently. 'It's not a joke, Jessie.'

'I'm not joking. I mean . . . I'm not saying he killed her on purpose. Maybe it was an accident . . . maybe they got into a fight and he pushed her.'

Dad has an incredulous look on his face. 'Don't you think

the police would've got involved if anything untoward had gone on?' He flaps his hand dismissively. 'Anyway, it's not possible. He wasn't even there. He was at work that morning.'

I can see he's not buying any of it, but it's too late to back down now.

'That's what he says. But how do you know? How can you be sure?'

'Because I was the one who phoned to tell him,' Dad snaps. 'That's why.'

I'm stunned into silence.

'So it was you who found her?' I say after a few moments. 'You never told me.'

Dad shakes his head. 'No, I didn't find her. Polly at number six was the one who found her. But she didn't have Ajay's number, so she asked me to call him and tell him what had happened. Honestly, if you'd have heard him or seen him, Jessica, you wouldn't be thinking such nasty things about him. It was obvious he was in shock. The man was completely devastated.'

'But you saw her . . . That must have been horrible.'

He closes his eyes. 'Yes. I went to see if there was any-thing I could do, but she was already dead by the time I got there. It's something I'd rather not have seen.'

'Did you ring Ajay's work number or his mobile?' I ask. 'I don't see—'

'Well, he could have been anywhere, couldn't he? If he

was on his mobile. You've only got his word for it that he was at work.'

Dad tuts crossly. 'I'm sure the police checked his alibi. Look, these are real people with real lives, Jessica. You can't just go about making wild accusations.'

'I know. You're right.' I feel close to tears. I'm beginning to realise that I've made a big mistake talking to Dad. He's looking at me with an expression I've seen before and I don't like it. I got that look from Dr Lopez a couple of times and saw it on Rachel's face just before she told me I should leave the Academy.

'Are you OK, Jessica?' he asks more gently.

'I'm fine,' I smile brightly. 'I just have an overactive imagination, that's all. You know what I'm like.'

He doesn't smile back. 'How are your sessions going with the therapist?'

'Good. I'm fine, honestly, Dad.'

He sits back and sighs. 'Are you sure?'

'I'm sure. You don't need to worry about me.'

'Good. Because you need to focus on resting and getting better, not on obsessing about the neighbours. I've got enough to worry about with your mother. I don't want to have to worry about you too.'

'I know. I'm sorry.'

Is he right? Am I getting sick again? I can feel the darkness closing in on me and I'm scared of it – I'm scared of feeling so out of control again. I must stop thinking about Kate Chandry. It's not healthy.

But lying in bed at night, images force their way into my mind – violent, frightening images. Ajay screaming at Kate. Ajay with his hands squeezing her neck, shoving her roughly towards the window. I picture the moment she falls, her mouth wide open in a silent scream and the impact as she hits the ground. Did it hurt when she fell? Or did she die instantly? I shudder as I picture her lying in a tangled heap, her neck broken, Ajay standing over her, Izzy running out of the house crying.

Izzy. What if she's in danger too? I think about the bruises on her arm and I feel sick. What if he did that to her? I need to do something to protect her.

No, no, no. I turn over in bed, pummelling the pillow. *You've been here before, remember. At the Academy.*

I put my headphones in and listen to the *Moonlight Sonata*, turning up the volume to drown out the voices in my head. It's a habit I got into in Spain, listening to this piece of music as I go to sleep. It's weird how much I love it. But from the very first time I ever heard it played, I had a strange feeling of peace – like coming home. It works its magic now, and I can feel my heart rate dropping as I lie back and let the slow, soothing music roll over me, until I finally drift off to sleep.

Chapter Twelve

A noise wakes me in the middle of the night, and I lie in bed, my heart hammering. The darkness squeezes itself around me, and a feeling of dread grips me. I sit up and listen. But there's nothing, just the usual night sounds. The gurgle of the water pipes, the low hum of traffic from the road. *It was just a dream*, I think, curling up and hugging my pillow.

But then I hear it again. A quiet but distinct rustling downstairs. My first terrified thought is that it's an intruder. And yes, there it is again. Not a rustling this time but a low scraping, the sound of a drawer opening and a muffled thump. *You're imagining it*, I tell myself. *This is an auditory hallucination, like you had before – like the child crying under the floorboards.* The thought that my psychosis is coming back is even more frightening than the idea of an intruder and I press my hands over my ears, burying my face in my pillow.

But someone is definitely in the kitchen, moving around. There's the sound of the tap being turned on, the pipes settling and water running.

Of course! It's not an intruder or my psychosis, I realise. It's just Mum or Dad fetching a glass of water from the kitchen. I lie back, closing my eyes. Everything is OK.

Then there's a low whine like a door closing. *Shit!* What if Mum's gone walkabout in the middle of the night again? I need to stop her. She could hurt herself. I clamber out of bed and pull on a long T-shirt. Then I pad across the landing and run downstairs. Opening the front door, I peer outside into the darkness. But the close is still and silent. *Maybe she's already out on the road*, I think. So I put the door on the latch and dash out in my bare feet across the close and onto the main road. The street is deserted, no one about in either direction. She couldn't have got so far in such a short time, could she? As I head back, I notice the lights are on downstairs in Ajay's house, and I wrestle with the irrational idea that Mum's there.

Back inside, I climb the stairs trying to think what to do. I'll have to wake Dad and let him know she's gone AWOL. I don't want to disturb him, but I can't think what else to do. Their bedroom door is slightly ajar. I push it gently and peek in.

Dad is lying in bed snoring gently, and to my surprise and relief, Mum is sitting on the edge of the bed, in her nightie and slippers, clutching a small jewellery box in her hands.

'Mum, are you OK?' I whisper, my eyes adjusting to the darkness.

'Jessica.' She blinks at me, startled. 'What are you doing up?'

'I heard noises downstairs. I thought it was . . . It must have been you.'

'It wasn't me,' she says firmly. 'I just got up to go to the toilet.'

'What are you doing with that box?' I ask.

She looks down as if she's only just realised that she's holding it.

'Oh. I don't know.'

'Shall I put it away for you?'

'Oh yes, darling, that's a good idea.' She climbs back into bed and I slide the drawer in the dresser open as quietly as possible and slip it inside. Dad turns over and grumbles a bit in his sleep, but he doesn't wake up.

'Night, Mum,' I whisper.

'Night, darling,' she says, peering at me over the top of the covers. There's something about her expression. If I didn't know better, I'd say she looked guilty.

So it was Mum I heard, I think, standing at the top of the stairs. Or was it? She said she just went to the toilet. Has she forgotten already or was I mistaken about where the sound was coming from? Whatever I heard, I'm wide awake now. I'm not likely to go back to sleep anytime soon. I go

105

back downstairs, make myself a cup of tea and wander into the living room. Opening the curtains, I stare out of the window at the close lit up by a dim orange street light. The lights are all off now at Ajay's house, the windows as dark and inscrutable as ever.

I shut the curtains just in case there's someone outside looking in and I search around for signs of a break-in. As far as I can tell, nothing has been touched. Just one of the drawers in Mum's desk has been left slightly open. I tug it out and examine the contents. There's not much in there. Stationery, a few cards Mum keeps in a box and her diary – the one the doctor advised her to keep.

I turn on the lamp, sit in Dad's armchair and flick through the pages.

Most of the entries are about what she's eaten and the weather, written in Mum's difficult to decipher, wavering hand.

Monday, 22nd May. It was warm and sunny today. I went to the park. We had fish and potatoes and broccoli for dinner and afterwards we watched Call the Midwife *on TV.*

Tuesday, 23rd May. Today it rained in the morning. Brian bought a new iron to replace the old one.

It carries on like this – lists of simple, innocuous facts. I suspect a lot of them have been dictated to her by Dad. I look at the first page. She's been keeping it for a while, since 1st January this year.

It suddenly occurs to me that she might have recorded the day Kate Chandry died. So I flick through the entries until I find one dated 15th June.

We went to Milton Keynes shopping centre. It was very crowded. We had a cup of coffee and a slice of carrot cake in Costa Coffee. The woman across the road had an accident.

That's all. *The woman across the road had an accident.* I'm not sure what I expected, but surely something more than that simple, unrevealing statement. She hasn't even mentioned that she died.

I turn the page, and flick through the rest of the diary to the back, feeling frustrated. I'm about to put it back in the drawer and head to bed when I notice something. Maybe it's nothing, but it's a very nice notebook, not the kind you would want to spoil, and yet, the last page of the book has been ripped out.

Chapter Thirteen

When I wake up the next morning, sunlight is already streaming in through the window and I can hear Mum laughing downstairs. I feel exhausted, totally drained already, and the day is only just starting. Reluctantly, I crawl out of bed and pull on a T-shirt and a pair of shorts.

I follow the sound of laughter and chatter downstairs to the conservatory and freeze in the doorway.

'Ah, here she is,' says Dad with a note of reproof. 'Do you have any idea how long you've been asleep, Jess? It's nearly eleven o'clock.'

I don't answer. I'm momentarily at a loss for words because Ajay is there, ensconced on the sofa sipping tea, and Izzy is sitting cross-legged on the carpet sifting through a box of Howie's old Lego and Playmobil. What the hell are they doing here?

'Um, I didn't sleep well last night,' I mumble.

Ajay half stands up and smiles at me eagerly.

'Hi,' he says, and Dad throws me a warning glance that says, *Don't you dare embarrass me*. He obviously hasn't forgotten what I said yesterday and maybe he's worried I'm going to accuse Ajay or make a scene. There's nothing Dad is more afraid of than people making scenes.

'Hello,' I say to Ajay as politely as I can. 'How are you?' I run fingers through my hair, wishing I'd bothered to brush it, and look around at the four of them. On the face of it, it's a very normal sight: an elderly couple entertaining their neighbour and his daughter.

'I was going to wake you,' Dad says, 'but Ajay insisted we let you sleep. He's been waiting for ages.'

Ajay flushes. 'I just popped in to say hello. I was just wondering if the photos were ready, that's all. It's not important if they're not . . .'

The photos, of course. I'd almost completely forgotten about them.

'Oh, yes, I've narrowed it down to about fifty shots,' I say, trying to sound professional. 'Would you like to come and choose the ones you like?'

'Sure.'

He follows me into Dad's study where I fire up his old computer and find the file of photos, while Ajay examines the cricketing trophy on the windowsill and the picture on

109

the wall of Mum and Dad in Crete. He stands close behind me as I click on the photos, so close I can feel his breath on my neck, and my hand trembles slightly as I move the mouse.

'I'll fetch you a chair,' I blurt, my voice sounding unnaturally high. *Calm down, Jessica. You need to behave like a normal person*, I remind myself as I carry a chair from the living room and we sit side by side, heads bent over the computer.

'These are all great. You're an artist, Jessica,' he says as we scroll through. And, despite everything, I feel a rush of pride. It's true they have turned out well, much better than I'd expected. Maybe I've found something I can actually do after all.

'I love this one,' he says, jabbing his finger at the picture on the screen. It's of Izzy holding a bunch of balloons. She's on her tiptoes and from the angle I've taken it, it looks as if she's about to float off into the air.

'What about this?' I ask nonchalantly. We've reached the photo of Izzy on the swing seat. 'I can Photoshop out the bruises if you like.'

I look at him surreptitiously and hold my breath, watching for a reaction.

A muscle in his cheek twitches but otherwise nothing. His face wears the same benign expression it always does.

'Um, maybe,' he says. 'I like to think of myself as a

110

warts-and-all kind of guy, but I suppose Izzy doesn't want to be reminded of how she got those bruises.'

My hand freezes on the mouse. 'How *did* she get them?' I ask as casually as I can.

His thick black eyebrows knit together. 'It was some kid at her summer school. A boy in her class. Little shit.' He grins. 'I wanted to go and kick his teeth in, but Izzy's teacher didn't think that was a good idea.'

There's no reason to think he's lying. But, on the other hand, I have no reason to believe he's telling the truth either.

'Kids can be horrible to each other,' I say, feeling sad. Cruelty always makes me sad, especially cruelty to young children. 'Izzy's such a sweet girl too.'

He lifts his shoulders. 'Yeah, well, she has her moments. I'm not sure if I'm too soft on her sometimes. She's turning into a spoiled little madam. I let her get away with murder . . .'

An unfortunate choice of words, I think, avoiding his eyes. The word hangs in the air and he shifts uneasily as if he's suddenly aware of what he's just said.

'She seems like a lovely, well-behaved little girl to me,' I say out loud. And he laughs. 'You haven't seen her have a temper tantrum . . .' I look at him and his eyes hold mine. They're difficult to read.

'Well.' I push back my chair and smile professionally. 'I'll get these to you ASAP.'

Ajay doesn't move. He takes a deep breath. 'About the other night, at Izzy's party . . .'

'Yes, I'm sorry about that,' I say swiftly, my cheeks burning. 'I just had too much to drink. I'm on medication and I think the booze and the pills didn't mix well.' I laugh awkwardly.

He doesn't smile. 'It's me who should apologise. I should explain.'

'There's no need to explain anything,' I say hastily. 'I completely understand. It was too soon after—'

'No, it's not that.' He looks away. He seems to be struggling with some complicated emotion; his eyes are dark and troubled. 'I used you and that's not fair.'

'Used me?' I repeat, nonplussed.

'Yes, I used you . . . as a kind of revenge.'

'Revenge?' I'm even more confused.

'Revenge against my wife.' He laughs a hollow-sounding laugh. 'It sounds stupid, I know, to take revenge on someone who's dead, doesn't it?'

'Um . . .'

'You see, what I told you the other day was a load of bullshit. My wife and I, we didn't have a good relationship. We hadn't – not for a couple of years. She was having an affair.' He stares out of the window at his house, his eyes dark and angry.

'Oh.' I try to look surprised. I'm trying to ignore the humiliation I'm feeling. Of course, I should have known.

He didn't kiss me because he really wanted to. He kissed me as a kind of twisted revenge against his wife.

'Let's forget about it. Pretend it never happened,' I say. Just another thing to add to my list. I've become quite good at erasing history.

He smiles and stands up, holding out his hand. 'Good idea. Friends?'

Not exactly, I think. But I nod and shake his hand.

He goes to fetch Izzy and say goodbye to my parents. Then at the door I ask on impulse, 'You didn't hear anything last night, did you?'

'Like what?'

'Like a car or, I don't know, anything out of the ordinary.' I look down at Izzy who is standing a short distance away, petting a cat, and I lower my voice. 'I think someone broke into our house. I don't want to say anything to Mum or Dad. It will only freak them out.'

'Oh my God,' Ajay exclaims. 'Was anything taken?'

'No, I think I scared them away before they got the opportunity.'

'Well, thank God for that.'

'Yes.'

'Your parents should have an alarm installed. There've been a lot of burglaries in Wendover lately.'

'I'll tell them. But you know what these old folks are like. They don't like anything new.'

'Mine are the same,' he laughs. 'See you soon.'

I watch him amble across the road, Izzy skipping at his side. Why did he change his story? Why now? Did he see me and Sean the other day and realise that Sean must have told me about the affair? When he gets to his front garden he turns and waves. *On the spot where she died*, I think, feeling sick. He's standing on the spot where Polly found his dead wife and he's waving cheerfully.

I wait for Ajay and Izzy to disappear inside. Then I run upstairs and pull on a pair of flip-flops.

'I'm just popping out for a minute,' I call out to Mum and Dad. And I'm out of the door before they have a chance to ask me where I'm going.

Chapter Fourteen

Polly opens the door and blinks at me in surprise from behind thick-rimmed glasses.

'Jessica!' she says, after a couple of seconds. 'For a minute there I thought you were your mother. You've grown to look so much like her.'

I'm not sure how to respond to this comment. It's not exactly a compliment, as Mum must have been nearly forty when we moved here. But it turns out I don't need to say anything because Polly ushers me inside, chattering away without pausing for breath.

'Come in, come in. Your father told me you were back. Are you here for good now? I must say, I bet they're happy you're back. I think your father could use the help now with your mother in the state she's in.'

'Mmm.' I nod guiltily, thinking how little I have actually

helped him and how I won't be able to do much, now I'm moving.

I follow Polly into a bright, airy kitchen with plants on the windowsill and various inspirational messages pinned to the walls and the fridge such as *Work for a cause, not for applause*, and *Don't tell God how big the storm is. Tell the storm how big your God is.* There's a delicious smell of baking filling the kitchen as Polly slips on a pair of oven gloves and stoops, pulling a steaming cake out of the oven.

'I've just made a chocolate cake for my grandson,' she says, placing it on the table. 'He's coming around this afternoon. Do you want some?'

'Oh, no thanks. Save it for him.'

'Well, if you're sure. A cup of tea then?'

'Yes please, that would be lovely.' I perch on a kitchen chair and watch her fill the kettle. She's in her sixties, slim and straight-backed with no nonsense, steel-grey hair. She's an unlikely sort of friend for my mother as they're so different, but they have been friends for as long as I can remember.

'Well, it's lovely to see you, Jessica,' she says. 'It's amazing to see you grown into a young woman. I always think of you as a little girl. You and your friend from across the way, what was her name?'

'Holly.'

'Yes, Holly. Whatever happened to her?'

'She moved to Scotland.'

She pushes her glasses up her nose. 'Oh yes, that's right. And Howard? How's he?'

'Oh, he's fine – planning his next mountain climb.'

She's too polite to ask but I can tell she's wondering why I'm here. I don't want her to know the real reason because she might think I'm ghoulish or, worse, crazy, so I pretend I'm here to promote my business. I take out one of the cards I made the other day and hand it to her.

'I don't know if Mum told you, but I'm setting up my own photography business and I'm just going around the village handing these out, seeing if anyone's interested.'

Polly turns the card over in her hand.

'Jessica Delaney photographer,' she reads. 'My, my, these look fancy.' She smiles at me kindly over the top of her glasses. 'You remember Elizabeth, my younger daughter? You used to babysit for her sometimes. Well, she's getting married soon. They've been looking for a good photographer. I'll be sure to give it to her.'

'Thank you,' I say. 'That would be great.'

'How is your mother, by the way?' she asks after a pause. 'I haven't seen her for a while. I've been so busy with Elijah, my grandson. My daughter-in-law has got a new job and I have to look after him four mornings a week. It's exhausting. I'm getting way too old for running round after a three-year-old.' She pauses for breath. 'I'm sorry, I do tend to rabbit on, don't I? How's Jean?'

'She's not too bad, all things considered,' I say carefully. 'She's OK most of the time, except she has these weird delusions. Like, the other day she thought Dad had stolen her watch and . . .' I pause before deliberately ploughing on. 'She claimed she saw the guy next door push his wife out the window.'

Polly blinks at me. 'You mean Ajay and Kate? Whatever put that idea into her head?'

'I don't know. Maybe she saw something on TV. She mixes up reality and fiction sometimes.'

'Yes,' she nods. 'That'll be it, I expect.' She stands up and begins drying cups. 'That poor man. You know he doted on her? And that little girl,' she winces. 'It just doesn't bear thinking about. She's only a couple of years older than Elijah.'

'Dad told me you were the one who found her?' I venture tentatively.

She nods. 'Yes, that's right. I was just in the living room, writing an email to my friend Margaret, who lives in Swindon, when I heard a scream and then an awful thud. So I went to look outside and that's when I saw her, just lying there . . .' She shudders. 'I knew she was dead straight away. Her head was at a strange angle and her eyes were all blank and staring, but I called the ambulance anyway just in case. My poor old hands were shaking so much.'

'Did you look up at the window?'

'No.' She considers this. 'No, I don't think so. After I called an ambulance I went straight to the door and rang the doorbell. I thought Ajay was in, you see. I'd forgotten he was at work.'

I lean forward. 'What made you think he was in the house?'

She looks surprised by the question. 'Um . . . I'm not sure. I think maybe I thought I'd heard his voice a bit earlier in the garden, but I must have been mistaken. It was probably someone on the canal path. You know, it runs along the back of our houses. People's voices carry sometimes, especially when they're coming home for the pub. It can be a real nuisance. Anyway, this person was shouting and cursing away' – she purses her lips disapprovingly – 'so I should have known it wasn't Ajay. He's always such a nice, polite young man.'

My mind is working rapidly. What if she did hear a voice from the house and not the canal? What if there was someone in there with Kate that morning?

I take a sip of tea and then ask carefully, 'Did you mention the voice you heard to the police?'

She looks mildly affronted. 'No, why should I? They only asked me about how and when I found her. I think I told them everything they needed to know.'

'Are you sure it wasn't Ajay you heard?'

'Yes, of course, dear,' she says with a slight edge to her voice. 'He was at work, like I said.'

'How do you know that?'

'Well, when your father rang him at work he was there.'

So she really has no proof he was at work, I think, any more than Dad does. He could have been in the house upstairs for all they know. Would they have heard the phone ringing from outside? I don't think so. But I can see Polly's patience is wearing thin, so I change the subject.

'Were you good friends with the Chandrys?' I ask, trying to sound conversational.

She sips her tea. 'Not really,' she says. 'They only moved here a few years ago. I invited Kate to bring Izzy to come and play with Elijah a couple of times. I thought it would be nice for them to get to know each other. But she always made some excuse. Kate Chandry kept herself to herself. She was a bit strange and standoffish really. Not at all like Ajay. Now, he's a lovely, friendly young man. He's been round several times to help me with things about the house. When the boiler broke and my computer needed fixing. All the things that Bill used to do.'

She starts talking about her husband, Bill, who died a year ago of pancreatic cancer, and then moves on to her son and grandson and various friends and acquaintances in the village and at her church. It's about half an hour before I manage to make my excuses and leave.

It's starting to rain again, a slow steady spit, as I leave Polly's house carrying a portion of the cake she's insisted on giving me. I let myself into the house and pick up the mail on the floor. Mum is in the living room, snoozing in front of the TV, and there is no sign of Dad. I creep past her upstairs to my room and sit on the butterfly bedspread I chose when I was about fifteen. I think about what Polly said. If there was anything suspicious about Kate's death, the police would have been all over it. They would have almost certainly checked Ajay's whereabouts when the accident happened. *But then again*, says a little nagging voice at the back of my head, *if they didn't have any grounds for suspicion, why would they bother checking his alibi?*

There's just a small part of me that can't let go of the feeling that he's involved in his wife's death somehow. I need to know for sure. Should I go to the veterinarian clinic and ask if he was there that day? How likely are they to give me that kind of information?

Then I remember. I'm not sure why I didn't think of it before. At his house the other day, Howie said that Lara was doing work experience at the Wendover clinic – with Ajay.

I take out my phone to ring Howie, but he doesn't answer. So I pick up Dad's car keys from the dresser in the hall and I go out to the garden.

Dad is digging up weeds, He stops when he sees me and leans on his spade.

'Hi, Jessica. I wondered where you were,' he says vaguely.

'Dad, can I borrow your car?'

Chapter Fifteen

Bella is on the doorstep, growling at me and snapping at my heels.

'Jessica, hi,' Vicky says, scooping the dog up and flushing faintly. Someone is bellowing inside the house. I think it's Brandon.

'I'm afraid you caught us at a bad time,' she says apologetically. She looks tired. There are dark circles around her eyes and her hair is not quite as perfect as usual. 'Our au pair is on holiday and Brandon's having a bad day.'

She leads me to the kitchen where Brandon is lying on the floor, creating a sort of snow angel out of cereal hoops and bawling at the top of his lungs. He stops crying and sits up when he sees me. Picking up a cereal hoop, he pops it in his mouth, giving me a speculative look.

'Oh Brandon, you naughty boy,' Vicky wails. 'What have

you done now?' There are multicoloured hoops scattered all over the polished tiles and an empty cereal packet has been tossed into the corner. Bella trots in and starts snuffling them up enthusiastically.

'He doesn't like the new cereal I bought him,' Vicky explains, pushing Bella out of the way and picking up the broom. 'Brandon, that was very naughty,' she says, sweeping the hoops into a pile. 'If it happens again, you'll have to go to your room.'

Brandon picks up a cereal hoop and flings it at her. 'No! I won't!' he shouts. 'You stupid bitch!' and he storms out of the room.

I find the dustpan and brush under the sink and help Vicky clear up the rest of the hoops.

'I'm sorry about that, Jess,' she says. 'I don't know what's got into him today. We're going to get him assessed soon. I don't think this behaviour is normal for a five-year-old, do you?'

I'm not quite sure what to say. I don't want to offend Vicky, but he does seem like a bit of a nightmare.

'I don't know,' I say. 'What does Howie think?'

Vicky sits down at the kitchen table and rakes a hand through her hair. 'Oh, Howie doesn't think there's a problem. But then Howie's not the one who has to deal with him every day. He doesn't know how bad he can be. He's completely uncontrollable sometimes. He's

123

even been kicked out of summer school for hitting other children.'

'He hits other children?'

She nods ruefully. 'One of the parents complained that he'd been bullying their daughter – that he left bruises on her arm.'

I'm tipping the last of the cereal into the bin and my hand slips and I drop the whole dustpan inside, as I make a sudden connection in my head. 'It wasn't little Izzy Chandry, was it?' I ask, rooting around for the pan.

'Yes, that's right. Oh God, Ajay hasn't been complaining about him to you, has he?'

'What? No, it was just a passing comment. Don't worry,' I try to reassure her. But I'm not really thinking about Brandon anymore, I'm thinking about Ajay and Izzy. I feel an intense relief to know that he wasn't lying about her bruises after all. I wonder if he knows that Brandon is my nephew and, if so, why he didn't mention it.

'I'm sorry. Can I get you a drink?' asks Vicky, putting away the broom. 'Howie's not here at the moment. He's at the office, I'm afraid.'

'Actually, it's Lara I really wanted to speak to.'

'Lara?' Vicky looks surprised.

'Yes, it's about . . . her work experience.'

'Well, she hasn't come down from her room all morning. But I'll give it a try.' She heads out of the room and a few minutes later appears with Lara trailing behind her, rubbing her eyes sleepily. She's dressed in a baggy black T-shirt and black leggings, and her pink-tipped hair doesn't look like it's been washed. Even so, she looks beautiful.

'Hi, Jess,' she says, giving me a sweet, sleepy smile. Then she rounds on Vicky. 'What's up with Brandon? Why was he making all that racket? I was trying to sleep.'

'I'm doing my best,' says Vicky wearily. Then with a rare hint of acid she adds, 'You could come and help for once.'

'Why don't you just give him a bag of sweets or something? That'd keep him quiet.'

'The dentist said—'

'Oh, fuck the dentist,' says Lara. 'They're baby teeth. They're going fall out soon anyway.' She flicks her hair, pulls out a packet of cigarettes from her back pocket and lights one, staring at Vicky defiantly.

'No smoking inside,' Vicky says weakly.

'Oh Jesus fucking hell,' Lara says and she flounces out to the garden.

It's not difficult to see where Brandon gets his colourful language from. I'm amazed that Vicky lets Lara speak to her like that, and I wish for her sake and Lara's that she would grow a backbone. *But it's not my business*, I tell myself. I've never had kids and I've no idea what it's like. It must be doubly difficult for Vicky, I think, as she's not actually Lara's mother.

I follow Lara outside and find her sitting on a bench hunched over her cigarette and scrolling through her phone.

'Do you mind if I sit here?' I ask.

She smiles ruefully. 'No, you go ahead. Sorry about that, Jess. It's just Vicky. She's the worst. She winds me up so much.'

'Why do you give her such a hard time?'

'I don't know.' Lara stares gloomily at the garden. The lawn slopes down to a line of trees, the start of the woods. 'She's so dumb and she never stands up for herself.'

'All the more reason to be nice to her, surely?'

I'm beginning to feel really sorry for Vicky, which is strange because I've always been a little jealous of her and Howie. I always imagined they had such a perfect life. Now I'm starting to realise all is not perfect in paradise. And I know it's not a nice thing to admit but I can't help feeling a tiny bit of satisfaction about that.

'She's just so fake, all the time,' Lara says. 'She tries to act like my mother and she's not. She swans around like she owns the place just because she's married to my dad. She only married him for his money.'

'You don't know that,' I say, wondering vaguely if it's true.

'Don't I?' She digs viciously into the grass with her toe. 'Anyway, Vicky said you wanted to talk to me. What about?'

I hesitate, realising what I'm about to ask is going to sound strange. 'I want to ask you something.'

'Yeah?' she flicks ash onto the lawn.

'Your dad told me that you've been doing some work experience this summer at the vet's in the village.'

'Yes, that's right. I thought I wanted to be a vet, but now I don't know. It's so competitive and I'm just not sure I'm going to get in.' She hunches over and glares at the grass.

I probably should assure her that she's very bright and will almost certainly get the grades she needs, but I'm still annoyed about the way she spoke to Vicky, and besides, I'm eager to get to the point. 'Were you working there in June?' I ask.

'Yes. I started in the middle of June. Why?'

'Do you think you would remember if Ajay Chandry was working on a particular day?'

'Ajay?' she looks surprised. 'I expect so. He's almost always there. Even after his wife died. He keeps coming in even though Samantha, the other vet, has told him to take some time off.'

I lean forward, twisting my hands together. 'Do you know if he was there on the day his wife died?'

I hold my breath as Lara drops the cigarette on the grass and grinds it under her heel. 'Yes, of course he was.'

I exhale slowly. 'You're certain? How can you be sure?'

'I'm sure because I remember him getting the call. He came into the waiting room. His face was white as fuck, and he said that his wife had had an accident and he had to go to the hospital.'

'I see.' I absorb this slowly. *So that's that then*, I think. Ajay couldn't have killed his wife because he wasn't there. Mum was talking nonsense after all. I feel a strange mix of emotions. Relief is a big part, of course. But there's another part of me that feels empty and I can't really explain why. My instincts were telling me that Mum really saw something and now it looks as if I was wrong.

'She died instantly, didn't she?' Lara asks, interrupting my thoughts. Something in her voice makes me turn to look at her. She's picking at the flaking paint on the bench. Her beautiful eyes are dark and troubled, and it hits me that underneath all the hostility and bravado she's a deeply unhappy girl.

'Yes, as far as I know . . .' Unease twists in my belly. 'Lara, is there something bothering you?' I ask.

'No,' she says, fiddling with her cuff. She shifts a little and I notice a shallow scratch on her wrist. *Oh Jesus, no*, I think.

'Because you know you can always talk to me,' I say carefully, my words dabbing cautiously, like cotton wool around the edge of a wound that I can't see.

She turns, pushing her hair back from her eyes, and

gives me a frankly appraising look. She opens her mouth and for a second I think she's about to tell me something. Then she bites her lip.

'Thanks, Jess, but I'm OK,' she smiles.

We sit in silence for a while. Lara picks at her sleeve. I look up at the sky at an aeroplane far above and a red kite wheeling over our heads, searching for prey.

You have to stop this now, I tell myself. *You've been here before, remember? There's nothing wrong with Lara. She's just a normal teenage girl. A little bit moody maybe but who isn't when they're seventeen?*

'Do the police think that it was an accident?' she asks unexpectedly. 'I mean, they don't think she killed herself, do they?'

I sigh. 'I don't know, to be honest.'

'I wouldn't blame her if she did commit suicide.' She laughs bitterly. 'I mean, she hung out all the time with Vicky. I should've thought that would be enough to make anyone want to kill themselves.'

'Lara, that's a horrible thing to say,' I murmur, shocked.

'Yeah, well, that's me. Horrible.'

'You're not horrible, you're just—'

'Just what, Jess?' she asks, grinning wryly.

I don't answer. I'm too busy thinking about what she just said about Vicky.

'I didn't know Vicky was friends with Kate.' I try to

remember if Vicky has ever mentioned that she knew her. I'm pretty sure she hasn't. 'Were they close?' I ask.

'Quite close, I think. They used to go to the gym together. Vicky's obsessed with looking toned.' Her lip curls in disdain.

'She didn't say.'

Lara shrugs. 'Yeah, well, that's Vicky for you. She keeps secrets.'

'Really, like what?'

'Oh, you know . . .'

'No, I don't. That's why I'm asking you.'

She flaps her hand impatiently. 'Oh, she's just a stupid cow, that's all. What do you care?' She stands up. 'Sorry, Jess, but I'm going out in a bit to meet some friends. I need to go and get ready.'

'Lara, wait. I care about you. I mean, I know I haven't been around much, but I do care. I want to make sure you're OK. You are OK, aren't you?'

'Me? Yes, I'm OK.'

'That scratch on your wrist . . .'

She glances down at her wrist.

'Oh that,' she smiles. 'It was Bella. She's a vicious bitch,' she laughs, 'in more ways than one. Don't worry, Auntie Jess, I'm not about to top myself.'

'You would tell me if there was something wrong?'

'Course I would.'

I watch her mooch away inside, not feeling entirely satisfied. I remember very clearly what it's like to be that age – and that's why I'm worried.

'Is Lara OK?' I ask Vicky, who's in the kitchen loading the dishwasher.

She closes the dishwasher, pours us both a glass of homemade lemonade and comes to sit opposite me at the kitchen table. 'I don't know,' she sighs. 'She won't talk to me. You might have noticed our relationship is not the best.' She gives a small, tinkling laugh. 'And to be honest, I haven't got time to worry about her. I've got enough on my plate with Brandon.'

'It's just I noticed a scratch on her wrist . . .'

'Oh that.' She waves her hand dismissively. 'That was the dog.'

'Are you sure?'

'Yes, I saw it happen. I think Lara was testing out some of the things she'd learned at the clinic and Bella objected. I can't really blame her.'

'Oh.' I feel relieved. Once again, I'm finding drama and misery where there is none. What's wrong with me? Why do I always have to imagine the worst?

'What were you two talking about?' Vicky asks, flushing delicately. 'I mean, it's none of my business if you don't want to tell me.'

131

'We talked about a few things,' I say vaguely. I take a sip of lemonade, thinking about what Lara told me. 'I didn't know you and Kate were friends?'

Vicky nods. 'We met at a spin class. There's a bunch of us from the gym who go for coffee and stuff, but we weren't all that close.'

'What was she like?'

She frowns thoughtfully. 'She was complicated. The life-and-soul-of-the-party type. She seemed tough on the outside, but I think she had a soft side too.'

I think this is the most believable and thoughtful description I've heard of Kate so far, and I wonder if Vicky was actually closer to her than she's letting on.

'Did you know she was having an affair?' I ask.

She looks startled for a second and then she nods. 'Yes, it was an open secret. Everyone in the village knew. But how did you find out?'

'I met up with him the other day at a friend's house – the guy she was having an affair with. He used to be . . . he was an old school friend.'

She stares at me. 'Small place, isn't it?'

There's a short silence as Vicky chips at her nail polish. 'I keep thinking about that day – the day she died,' she says. 'I keep wondering if I could've done something different.'

'What do you mean?'

'Well, I was with her that morning.'

'You were?' I say, surprised.

'Yes, we met up for a coffee after drop-off, just the two of us. Kate only stayed about an hour. She said she had a doctor's appointment. But . . . I think she was probably lying.'

'Why?'

'It might seem like a small thing,' she says, twisting her hands together. 'But Kate didn't usually wear a lot of make-up. That morning, though, she had it plastered on, false eyelashes and everything.'

'So, you think . . .'

'I think she'd arranged to meet him – the guy she was seeing.' She tips her glass and looks broodingly inside. 'I keep thinking I should've persuaded her to stay and have another coffee. If she had stayed, maybe she'd still be alive now.' She puts her glass down and gazes at me, her eyes filling with tears, which she dabs at delicately with a tissue.

'You can't think like that,' I say. 'How could you have known what would happen? How could anyone have known?' Inside, my mind is racing. If Vicky is right, Kate wasn't alone that morning.

I think about what Polly said about hearing shouting in the garden. And a new suspicion uncoils in my belly, making me nauseous. Could it be that the person she overheard was Sean?

Chapter Sixteen

The front door slams, making us both jump, and Howie breezes in.

'Jess! What are you doing here?' he exclaims, dumping his briefcase by the door and kissing Vicky lightly on the cheek.

She smiles up at him. 'We were just talking about Kate Chandry and Sean White.'

'Oh that.' He rubs his hands together. 'Juicy gossip, eh? Everyone in the village knew about them. Luke used to do their garden for them sometimes. He saw him coming and going all the time.' He flops onto a chair and loosens his tie. 'Didn't you use to go out with Sean White for a while, Jess?'

I grimace and blush as Vicky looks at me curiously. 'Just for a few months in the sixth form. It was all a long time ago.'

So, Luke worked for the Chandrys, I think. Everybody knows everybody in this village. How could Sean and Kate ever have expected that their affair would stay a secret?

'Why don't you stay for dinner?' Howie asks me as Vicky pours him a lemonade.

'Oh no, I'm OK,' I say hurriedly, catching Vicky's expression. She's got enough on her plate without having to worry about cooking for me. 'I'd better get back. I said I'd make tea for Mum and Dad. I'd like to just have a quick word with Luke before I go.'

Luke is in his room painting Warhammer figurines with his headphones on.

I tap him on the shoulder before he hears me. 'Oh, hey, Aunt Jess,' he grins, removing his headphones.

'These are good,' I say, picking up a fierce-looking warrior with a large, spiky sword and complicated-looking armour. There's quite a lot of detail on there and I'm genuinely impressed by his handiwork.

'I sell them on eBay,' he smiles. 'You can make quite a lot of money. With this and all the gardening I do I'm going to have enough to fund my diving trip to the Maldives.'

Wouldn't Howie pay for him? I would have thought he'd have more than enough money. But then, maybe he figures it's good for Luke to be independent. It's never good to have everything handed to you on a plate, I suppose.

'Oh yes,' I say, trying to sound casual. 'Your dad said you help out with people's gardens. He told me you do the Chandrys' garden.'

'That's right,' Luke says, returning to his painting. I perch gingerly on his unmade bed. 'Did you ever see Sean when you were there? Sean White?'

'A few times.' He peers closely at the base of the figure he's working on, the tip of his tongue poking out in concentration. 'I know they were sleeping together, if that's why you're asking. I heard them arguing once.'

I'm immediately alert. 'About what?'

He shrugs. 'I'm not sure.'

'You weren't there on the day she died, were you?'

'No.' He puts the Warhammer warrior down and stares at me with a mixture of surprise and curiosity. 'What made you think that?'

'I was just wondering if you saw or heard anything.'

'Nope, sorry.'

'What was she like? Kate Chandry?'

'I didn't really know her. But she seemed nice. She always paid on time and sometimes she gave me a drink and a biscuit.'

I can't help smiling at that. It's so typically Luke. Positive and practical.

At home, after tea, I check my phone. There are three

messages. One from Miriam who has seen the photos of Izzy's birthday and wants me to photograph Adriana. And one is from Elizabeth, Polly's daughter, saying she would like to see my portfolio of work.

It's a great opportunity. She wants me to be her official wedding photographer. This could be the start of something. Feeling excited, I message her back immediately, suggesting a time to get together.

The third message is from Sean, saying that he's found a real gem of a house, at a great price. I agree to meet him tomorrow. I'm thinking about what Luke told me – about how he heard Sean and Kate arguing and how Vicky had the impression that Kate was going to meet him that morning.

I try to brush these thoughts aside. I was wrong about Ajay. Am I wrong about Sean too?

Chapter Seventeen

I wake up feeling good. Last night, for the first time in a while, I dropped off to sleep without thinking about Kate Chandry or about Matteo and all the awful things that have happened. It's time to stop thinking about the past. Time to focus on the future. Optimism wafts in on a beam of sunshine and I hop out of bed, pulling back the curtains, inhaling the smell of damp mown grass and looking up at the fresh blue sky. It's early in the morning and the garden is stirring with life. Somewhere a pigeon coos, and I watch as a squirrel scrambles up a tree, digging its claws into the bark, and a sparrow hops onto the bird table. It tilts its head and pecks at the breadcrumbs Dad has left out. There's so much beauty in the world, if only you look for it. Why don't I notice it more often?

I shower, humming the *Moonlight Sonata*, and dry myself

in front of the mirror. Then I slip into a pretty green summer dress and tie my hair up in a no-nonsense knot. *I look good*, I think. I look like someone with a purpose. This is the start of my new life. The new positive, successful Jessica – home-owner and photographer and possibly, eventually, a teacher again. This version of Jessica doesn't need a man to make her life complete. She's independent and confident and she doesn't take any shit from anyone. After I've brushed my teeth, I automatically root in my washbag for my pills. I take one out of the packet and stare at it for a few seconds. Then I toss it into the bin. I don't need them. They just make me sleepy and blunt the edges. I want to see all the edges. I want to keep a clear head dealing with Sean today.

I drive to the address that he's given me, a house in an estate on the outskirts of Aylesbury. As I turn into the estate, suspicion nudges its way into my head again. Was Kate really on her way to meet Sean that morning? And if she was, what transpired between them? I turn into Green Lane. Do I really know what Sean's capable of? I already know he has a violent temper. That sunny charm of his can disappear in an instant when he's crossed. I witnessed it once, when we were dating. Another guy was chatting me up in the pub and he punched him in the nose. He was lucky to get away without a charge of assault. At the time

I wasn't shocked; I was flattered. I thought it was a sign of how much he liked me. But that just goes to show how young and stupid I was.

But why would he fight with Kate? They were in love, weren't they? She was going to leave her husband for him. Unless . . . Luke said that he heard them arguing, didn't he? What if she'd decided not to leave Ajay after all? I think of Sean with his large but delicate ego and his sense of pride. How would he have reacted?

I pull up outside a small terraced house and see him waiting outside holding a clipboard. He's wearing a suit and tie, the jacket straining over his broad shoulders, his hair smoothed down.

'Good morning,' he grins at me, flashing his dimples. 'Well, don't you look lovely today? That's a very nice dress.'

'Oh, this? This is old,' I say, hoping he doesn't think I put it on for his benefit and wondering if, subconsciously, I did. I hope not because that would be pretty messed up given my suspicions about him. *No, I didn't*, I reassure myself. *I put it on for me, not for him. I put it on because I wanted to feel confident. And I do*, I tell myself. *I feel really confident.*

'Well, you look great,' Sean smiles. Then he switches to his professional persona. 'I think you're going to really like this place. It's very, very good for the price.'

Inside the house, my newly found self-assurance wavers. The living room is tiny and dingy and I have that familiar, panicky feeling of being shut in. Sean is too close. He seems bigger and more muscular than I remember, and I'm suddenly all too aware that he could easily overpower me if he wanted to.

'Hmm,' I say, looking around, trying to ignore my misgivings and focus on the house as a potential purchase. The place smells damp and there's a sagging purple sofa and signs of mould on the ceiling.

'It'll be really nice with a lick of paint,' says Sean optimistically. 'And it comes with all the furniture.'

'Yeah, well, that's an advantage,' I say, wearing my sarcasm like armour.

And he laughs. 'OK, OK, it's not in the best condition but you've got to admit the price is amazing for a two-bed.'

He's not lying. It's very cheap, and upstairs is a slight improvement on downstairs, even though the bathroom looks like it hasn't been refitted or cleaned since the last century. I don't look too closely at the bedroom because I don't want to be alone in there with Sean, but a quick glance tells me all I need to know. It's small but serviceable.

Downstairs the kitchen isn't too bad. There are relatively new-looking countertops, a clean hob and a washing machine. There's even a dishwasher.

Sean unlocks the back door and we step out into a walled garden. The grass is knee-high. Bushes and trees have grown wild; trailing plants curl like tentacles. There's a gnarled old tree weighed down by apples, fruit scattered on the ground beneath it.

'So, what do you think?' he asks.

'Um. It's good for the price,' I say. In truth, impractical though it is, I really love the garden and am already imagining myself taming the weeds, planting a small vegetable patch and growing some herbs in the flower beds.

'It's got a lot of character, hasn't it?' he says. Then he pats his breast pocket because his phone is ringing. 'Sorry,' he says. 'I'd better take this.'

'Hi,' he says, answering in a low voice and moving away from me into the kitchen. I walk up to the apple tree and pretend to be absorbed in inspecting the fruit. It's laden with small, rotten-looking apples. I pick one that doesn't look too bad, rub it on my jacket and take a bite. All the time I'm straining to hear what Sean says. His voice carries out of the open window. I can't catch it all, just a few shreds of the conversation.

'Really?' he's saying. He sounds a little impatient. 'No. I'm sorry, I didn't see them. I've been so busy with work . . . Yes, of course I do, you know I do. Look, I can't talk now. I'm showing a house. But I'll make it up to you, I promise.'

His voice drops to a whisper and I don't hear what is said.

'Sorry about that. That was my boss,' he says, coming back outside, folding up his phone and slotting it into his pocket.

It was a strangely intimate tone to use with his boss, I think. Has he found someone else already – so soon after Kate's death? It's entirely possible, I think, knowing Sean as I do.

'Well, what do you think?' he says again. 'I have a couple of other properties I can show you before you make a decision.'

'No, I don't need to see anymore. I really like it. I'll take it,' I say decisively.

'Really?' he looks taken aback. 'Well, that's great.'

'We should celebrate with a drink,' he says as we step outside.

'Don't you have to work?'

'No, my boss is out of the office at the moment. So, while the cat's away . . .' He grins and closes the door, locking it behind him.

'I thought you said your boss just phoned you.'

'What?' He gives me a weird look. 'Yes, he did. From Majorca. He's a nightmare. A real control freak. He can't just trust us to get on with it while he's away.' He rolls his eyes. I think he's doing his best to convince me he doesn't like his boss. Perhaps he's trying too hard.

'So how about it?' he grins at me. 'I feel like we've got so much catching up to do. We barely scratched the surface the other day. I want to hear all about Spain – about everything.'

'All right,' I smile back automatically. *I can quiz him about Kate*, I think, or maybe he'll let something slip.

I follow Sean's car to a quaint old pub called The Trout. Sean orders a beer for himself and insists on buying me one too. Then we carry them out to the garden and sit at a wooden table overlooking the canal.

'So, tell me everything,' he says, cupping his chin in his hands and gazing at me with his amber eyes – those eyes that give you laser-like attention and make you feel as though you're the only person in the world. I think about how those eyes used to make me melt but how, now, they leave me completely cold.

'What do you want to know?' I ask.

'Everything. All about Spain, what you're doing now. Everything.'

But I'm not interested in discussing Spain with Sean. I want to talk about Kate Chandry. I have to know if he saw her that morning – the morning she died. The suspicion is eating away at me.

'I saw Ajay the other day,' I say tentatively, tearing at the edge of a beer mat.

'Oh?' he frowns.

'And I found out that he was at work the day she died. My niece worked with him. She was there at the time. So he couldn't have had anything to do with her death. You were right. My mum must have just been confused.'

'Yeah, well, just because he didn't kill her, doesn't mean he didn't make her life a misery.' He looks broodingly into his pint glass. 'I would have treated her right. We were going to go to Thailand for a honeymoon. We were going to get a place together with a room for Izzy. We had it all planned out.' He rubs his eyes and squeezes a tear out.

He's faking, I think coldly. 'It must've been hard for you when you found out she was dead,' I say, tipping my chair back and watching him through narrowed lids.

He nods. 'It was the worst day of my life, to be honest.'

I take a sip of beer, letting the cold, bitter liquid roll around my tongue, and look at him over the top of my glass. 'How *did* you find out?'

'Ajay told me. I rang her phone a few days later, and he answered.'

'That must have been an awkward conversation,' I say sceptically.

'Not really. I told him I was a friend.'

'And he believed you?'

He shrugs. 'Who knows? Does it matter?'

I stare out at the canal – at a moorhen ducking its head under the water in the reeds on the far side and a man walking along the towpath with his dog.

'When was the last time you saw her before she died?' I ask.

He gives a sad smile. 'It was a couple of days before.' He rubs his nose as if he has an itch. 'We met up at Wendover Woods. We had a spot there where we used to meet near the old hill fort.'

I hold my breath. He must mean the same place we used to go together. Is it possible he's forgotten? Because I sure as hell haven't. I remember every detail. I remember lying on the dry dead leaves, my skin pimpled with goosebumps in the cold air, his weight on me, his breath in my ear. I remember him laughing afterwards and picking off the bits of old bark clinging to my back.

I'm angry that he could forget something that was so significant to me. *You remember what's important to you*, I think, and I was clearly never very important to Sean. But then I already knew that.

Maybe it's because of my anger that I find the courage to say what I say next.

'That's weird,' I murmur, 'because my sister-in-law was good friends with Kate and she told me that Kate said she was going to meet you that morning – the morning she died.' It's a lie, of course. Vicky didn't say that definitively, but I want to see his reaction.

There is a reaction. So swift you could almost miss it, but it's certainly there, a slight widening of the eyes, a twitch of the head. 'Well, she must be mistaken,' he says smoothly, unaware that he's given himself away.

'It's funny,' I say. 'She was quite sure.' My hands are trembling under the table, but I refuse to let this go.

His eyes roll in his head as if he's thinking. Then he claps his head. 'That's right, we did arrange to meet up, but then she cancelled at the last minute. It was something to do with the garden, someone was coming to trim the hedge, I think.'

It's not true, I feel it. Why would she cancel a meeting with her lover just because someone was trimming the hedge? Anyway, Luke was their gardener, wasn't he? And he already told me he wasn't there at Kate's house that day, so Sean must be lying.

Sean rubs his chin and looks at his watch. 'Oh crap. I need to go. I'm showing a house in Great Missenden at twelve o'clock.' He stands up abruptly and smiles at me, but the smile doesn't quite reach his eyes this time. 'I'll email the landlord about the house and be in contact,' he says. Then he pecks me on the cheek and walks away. I watch him wend his way around the tables, stopping to say hello to someone, his face a mask of genial politeness.

He was there, I think. He met Kate Chandry that morning. I'm almost certain of it. He met her, but did he push her? He's certainly no saint, and his morals – especially where women are concerned – are questionable, but he's not a killer, is he? A few days ago, the idea would have been laughable. So why do I feel so uneasy now?

Chapter Eighteen

Mum is standing amongst my luggage in the hallway, watching me drag a suitcase down the stairs.

'What's going on?' she says. She looks alarmed and bewildered. She rubs her head until her white hair is sticking up around her head like a halo.

'I'm moving today, remember?' I say. 'Howie and Luke are picking me up in about an hour.'

'Oh yes,' Mum answers vaguely. Her cardigan has been done up on the wrong buttons and, once I've deposited the last suitcase by the doorway, I undo the buttons and rearrange them.

'Well, that's it, I think,' I say, kissing her on the cheek. 'I think I deserve a cup of tea now. Do you want one, Mum?'

'Ooh, that would be super, darling.' She plonks herself down in the living room and I bring her tea in the chipped mug that she likes, and we sit together sipping tea and staring out of the window at the rain. Mum picks up her book – the Jilly Cooper she has read about a million times – flicks through the pages and turns it over, reading the blurb on the back as if she's not quite sure what it is.

She glances over her shoulder and frowns at the cluttered hall.

'So, you're moving out today, are you?' she asks.

'Yes, I've found a new house just outside Aylesbury.' I don't tell her we've had this conversation about five times already over the past couple of days.

'Well, I'll certainly miss you, darling.'

'I'll miss you too.' I reach over and embrace her thin shoulders.

She pulls me closer and kisses me firmly on the head a few times. 'I love you, Jessie,' she says and as I pull away, I notice her eyes are filling with tears. I feel a lump in my throat. It feels as if we're saying goodbye for the last time.

'I'm not going far, Mum. Less than half an hour away,' I smile, blinking back tears.

But Mum's face is still pinched with worry. 'There's something I want to give you before you go,' she says. 'I should have given it to you a long time ago but . . .'

'Oh, Mum. Don't be silly. You don't have to give me anything.'

'Yes, I do,' she nods firmly. 'It's in our bedroom. If you go to the drawer in my dressing table, you'll find my jewellery box. Could you fetch it for me, darling?'

'That's really sweet of you, but I don't want any of your jewellery.'

'Just do as you're told for once,' she snaps, as if I'm a child again.

I sigh and head upstairs. I knock on the door, but Dad is in the shower and doesn't hear me so I just go in. The small, decorative enamel box is in the top drawer where I placed it a few nights ago, along with a hairbrush and a manicure set. I pull it out and carry it downstairs, placing it on the coffee table in front of her.

'What's this?' she asks, looking at it like she's never seen it before.

'It's your jewellery box, Mum,' I explain patiently. 'You asked me to fetch it for you.'

'Oh, yes. That's right. I know, no need to treat me as if I'm gaga.'

She opens it up slowly and tugs out a silver necklace with a swallow pendant with diamond-encrusted wing tips.

'Oh, it's all tangled, Jessica,' she says, distressed.

I spend a few minutes teasing out knots. Then I hold it up and twist it around, the diamonds catching the light.

'It's beautiful,' I breathe. 'How come I've never seen you wear this?'

'When would I have the occasion?' she says. 'Besides, it's

not really mine. Here.' She presses it into my hands. 'It's yours, Jessica. I want you to have it.'

'But it's yours, Mum,' I protest, handing it back. 'I can't take this. It's too valuable.'

If I'm honest, I'm half worried that if I take it, Mum will forget she's given it to me and then accuse me of stealing it like she accused Dad of stealing her watch.

She places the pendant back in the box, closes the lid and then hands it to me, her lips pressed together in a firm line. 'I want you to have it. I want you to have the whole box.'

'The whole box? Mum, you're crazy. What about Vicky or Lara? They might want something.'

'No, it's for you,' she says. 'Now, don't argue with me, Jessica.'

'Well, thank you,' I say, weakening. I'm too tired and preoccupied with the move to quarrel with her. I imagine Vicky probably has enough jewellery of her own, and I can always let Lara pick a few things out later if she wants.

Mum rests back against the chair, looking satisfied.

'You will look after it, Jess, won't you?' she says. 'There are lots of memories stored in there.'

'Of course I will. I'll treasure it.'

She gazes out of the window at something beyond the rain, tapping her fingers on the armrest.

'There's something you should know, Jess,' she says, suddenly turning to me and gripping my arm. 'Something I haven't told you, but I should've. I should have told you a long time ago and I'm sorry.'

'What?' I say, feeling slightly alarmed.

She stares into my eyes with such intensity that I'm afraid of what she's going to say. Then she gives a loud groan and flings her head into her hands. 'May God forgive me,' she cries.

Her words seem to come straight out of a nineteenth-century drama and are so incongruous in our twenty-first-century living room that I almost smile. 'Forgive you for what, Mum? You've done nothing wrong.'

'Oh, you don't know the half of it.' She stares wildly around the room. 'I've done something really terrible. Will you forgive me, though?'

'Of course. It's OK, Mum. Don't upset yourself.' I stroke her arm. My tone is calm and gentle, but inside I'm afraid and I'm suddenly unsure if I want to know what she's done. 'You don't have to tell me, though,' I say.

She shakes off my hand.

'No, I do have to tell you,' she almost wails. 'Please listen to me . . .'

'OK, OK.' I try to sound soothing. 'I'm listening.'

She takes my hand and opens her mouth. 'I . . .' she begins, but then she breaks off abruptly and turns to look at the hall. And I turn too and see Dad standing there in the doorway.

'Your carriage awaits,' he announces. 'Are you ready to go, Jess?'

'Sure.' I notice that Howie and Luke have arrived and are in the hallway carrying my stuff out to the car. I stand up reluctantly. I should probably give them a hand.

Dad glances at Mum, who is breathing unevenly.

'Are you OK, Jean? You look upset.'

Mum doesn't answer him. She gazes into the distance, her eyes suddenly blank.

Chapter Nineteen

It's been a few days now since I've moved into my new place and I'm doing OK. I've been reducing my medication slowly, like you're supposed to, and I haven't noticed any adverse effects. I've been keeping up with my sessions with Claire, and I've been learning some techniques to deal with depression and, so far, it seems to be working.

It feels good to be in my own place, independent at last, and I've been so busy sorting out the house – cleaning, painting the walls, getting rid of the old junk that the previous tenants left behind – that I haven't had time to worry too much about Mum or brood over what happened to Kate Chandry.

It's Saturday afternoon, I've been painting the living room and Howie has popped round on the spur of the moment to see how I'm settling in. I'm surprised and touched that he's bothered. Howie and I have never been all that close. When we were kids there was such a big age gap and he spent half the time away at boarding school. We saw each other in the holidays, of course, but even then, he was so much older that he mostly ignored me or treated me like an annoyance. Now, though, we have the opportunity for a fresh start and maybe, with goodwill on both sides, this will be the beginning of a new, more intimate brother–sister relationship.

'You know you've got paint all over your face?' he laughs as I show him into the living room.

I touch my face self-consciously. 'I'm sorry there's nowhere to sit at the moment,' I say, pulling the sheet off the sofa.

'It's OK,' he shrugs. 'I'll help you with the painting if you like.'

'Are you sure?' I say, surprised. 'Won't Vicky wonder where you are?'

'She's gone to visit her sister. It's good to get out of the house. Lara's in one of her moods . . .' he sighs. 'I don't know what's wrong with her lately.'

'Is she OK? The other day when I came around, she seemed . . . I don't know . . .'

Howie grimaces. 'She's just a teenage girl. You were a moody cow too when you were that age, don't you remember?'

I do remember and that's why I'm worried. I know there's a genetic component to depression and I'm afraid that she could have inherited my temperament.

'How's Mum been lately?' asks Howie, picking up a roller and creating a vertical stripe of white down the centre of the wall. 'Has she come out with any more stories of murder and mayhem in the village?'

'Not really,' I say coolly. I don't really like the way he asks, like it's all a bit of a joke. Howie always takes everything too lightly. There's no denying there is a funny side to Mum's illness, I suppose, and there's a thin line between humour and tragedy. But right now, I can only see the tragic side – the fact that this wonderful, vibrant woman is disintegrating in front of us. Maybe Howie notices my tone because I glance across and find a more serious and thoughtful expression on his face than normal.

'She's been really troubled lately, though,' I add, thinking of the conversation we had just before I left. 'There's something preying on her conscience. I don't know whether it's something real or imagined.'

'She didn't tell you what it was?' Howie dips the roller in the paint.

'No. We got interrupted and then, when I asked her about it later, she didn't remember.' I pick up a brush and start painting the edge of the wall along the skirting board, thinking about how distressed she was.

'Mmm,' says Howie. 'I don't think it's anything to worry about. She's probably just confused. You know the other day she told me she had tea with the queen.'

This time I can't help laughing. 'I'm not so sure all her stories are completely crazy, though,' I say.

'Oh?'

'They sometimes make sense when you know the context. It's just that she gets the time and the place all mixed up.'

Howie gives me a sceptical look. 'Yeah, well, maybe you're right. She's getting worse, though.' He stretches to reach the high parts of the wall. 'I don't know how many times I've offered to pay for a home, a really nice one, but Dad won't hear of it.'

'He doesn't want to lose her. Besides, if she was moved somewhere new, I don't think she'd cope very well.' Mum is mostly operating on habit now and if she was taken away from everything familiar to her, I think she'd be completely lost.

We paint in silence for a while and, with Howie's help, I soon have two walls covered in gleaming white emulsion. Already the room looks much brighter and cleaner. We stop for a rest and a drink, sitting in the garden at my new table.

'Your garden needs a bit of work,' Howie comments. 'I could get Luke to come and help you if you like.'

'That would be great. I'll pay him, of course.'

'No need. It's good practice for him. What else is family for?'

He's interrupted by his phone ringing loudly in his pocket. 'That's probably Vicky,' he says. He takes it out and looks at the screen. 'Oh, it's Dad.'

He holds the phone to his ear, and I can tell right away that there's something wrong. It's the way his whole body suddenly stiffens, and his voice takes on a tone I've never heard him use before. He sounds intently calm as if he's containing some strong emotion.

'Yes . . . Oh, I see . . . yes,' he says.

'What is it?' I ask.

He nods. 'It's Mum,' he whispers to me, holding the phone away from his ear.

My heart lurches. 'Is she OK?' I ask urgently.

But he doesn't answer. He's still listening to Dad. 'Yes, OK. Do you think we should come?'

'Is she OK?' I persist. I'm trying not to panic. But I'm afraid now that something is very wrong.

Howie takes a deep breath when the phone call ends. 'That was Dad. He's at the hospital with Mum. Apparently, she overdosed on her medication. I said we'd meet him there.' His voice is calm, but I notice, as he puts his phone back in his pocket, that his hands are trembling.

'But she's OK, right?' I can hear my voice breaking, already fearing the worst.

'What?' Howie picks up his car keys. 'Yes, I think so. But Dad wants us there. I think we should go right away.'

'Just how much of an overdose was it?' I ask as we speed along the Aylesbury road to the hospital.

'I don't know. He didn't go into details.'

Howie breaks sharply as a cyclist pulls out from a side road. 'Shit! Fucking idiot,' he snarls. I don't think I've ever seen him so rattled and I'm scared. Howie is almost never rattled. Nothing phases him. I pick at the white paint on my fingers, trying to control my breathing. *She's going to be OK*, I tell myself. She's got to be. Anything else is unthinkable.

When we arrive at the hospital, we dash in through the main entrance and spot Dad straight away, sitting waiting for us in the foyer. He looks lost and alone, staring at the polished floor like he wants to dive into it.

'Hey, Dad,' says Howie as we approach. Dad looks up at us and blinks. It's as if he doesn't know who we are for a second and I'm reminded strangely of Mum.

'Where's Mum?' Howie demands. 'Has she come around? Can we see her?'

Dad just stares at him, appalled. Then his shoulders slump and my heart plummets.

'I'm sorry,' he whispers. 'They tried but there wasn't anything . . .'

'You mean . . . ?' My voice comes out thin and far away.

There's a loud ringing in my ears and I'm having trouble breathing.

Dad nods. 'She passed away a few minutes ago. She didn't recover consciousness.'

A crack opens in my skull, blackness pouring in. I'm hearing the words, but they make no sense. Mum can't be dead. She just can't be. I sink to the floor, sobbing, regressing years in the space of a few seconds. I'm a child again. All I want is my mother and she's not here.

Chapter Twenty

'I don't get it,' says Howie, pacing up and down the room. 'Don't you always put her pills out for her, Dad?'

It's a few hours later and we've talked to various doctors and nurses and now, finally, the doctor in charge.

Dad nods vaguely. He looks around the room as if he doesn't quite know where he is. The shock seems to have completely floored him and it's as though he's aged years in the space of a few minutes.

The doctor, a woman in her forties with frizzy blonde hair and tired eyes, smiles sadly at us. 'We can't be entirely sure until we do the post-mortem,' she says. 'But we suspect that it wasn't the Alzheimer's medication, at least not on its own. It was more likely to have been combined with opioids of some kind.' She flicks through her notes. 'Was she on any pain medication?'

Dad shakes his head. 'No.' Then he looks around suddenly, clutching his chest as if he's been shot. 'But I was prescribed Tramadol for my back a few months ago. I only took one because it made me sick.' He looks round wildly at me and Howie. 'Could she have taken them by accident, do you think?'

The doctor rubs her eyes. 'Possibly. But let's not jump to any conclusions. We need to wait for the results of the post-mortem.'

'And how long will that be?' Howie asks. His voice is quiet but full of suppressed rage. The fact that we had to wait so long to speak to a doctor is proof to him that they mismanaged Mum's treatment. I imagine he is already thinking about suing the hospital for malpractice. He lives in a world where someone is always to blame – where lives and emotions can be measured financially.

'They won't be ready for a few days because we have to wait for test results,' the doctor answers calmly, giving an apologetic little shrug. There's a short silence. We're all shell-shocked, I guess. I can't think of anything to say. There *is* nothing to say. My mother is dead, and nothing will change that. I've lost her forever. I grip my chair, trying to hold on in a world that seems to be crashing around me.

'Is there anything else you need to know?' the doctor asks at last.

And we shake our heads and shuffle out of the room, feeling like survivors of a tsunami.

Howie screeches out of the hospital car park and drives dangerously fast along the road back to Wendover. 'Fucking hospital,' he fumes, glaring out of the windscreen. 'That doctor was worse than useless.'

Nobody answers him. As far as I could see, the doctors and nurses were doing their best and were all very polite and sympathetic. But it's the way Howie is. He always reacts to pain with anger. It's his way of dealing with it, I suppose. We all have different coping mechanisms. Dad seems to have drifted off into his own world and sits in the passenger seat staring out of the window at the cloudy sky, whereas I sit in the back seat, overwhelmed by another wave of tears, as if I can somehow wash out the pain that is raging inside me.

We arrive at Dad's, a sorry, bedraggled threesome, and shuffle into the house.

I stick on the kettle and make three cups of tea that we just sit and stare at in silence. Mum is still everywhere. Her cardigan is draped over the back of the chair, a single white hair clinging to the sleeve. Her empty pill box is on the table next to her reading glasses and the Jilly Cooper she was reading, the corners worn because she's read it so often. On the fridge in large capitals is the note Dad left for her:

I AM AT TOWN HALL FOR MEETING. CALL 0798 6247003 IF YOU NEED ME, BRIAN.

'I shouldn't have left her on her own,' Dad murmurs to himself, banging his head with his fist. 'If I hadn't been at that damn meeting . . .'

I know I should reassure him, tell him that it's not his fault, but I can't speak. I feel as if I'm alone on an island, and Dad and Howie are far away from me, stranded on their own islands, separated by a gulf of grief.

I sip my tea with a shaking hand and look at the whorls and patterns in the pine wood table. I've never really noticed them properly before, but right now everything seems strangely clear and outlined, like the first time I got contact lenses. It's the shock, I suppose.

Dad stands up and paces the room. 'I don't know what to do. I don't know what to do,' he mutters.

'It's OK, Dad. You don't have to do anything,' I say.

He slumps back down in the chair, gripping his head and moaning. 'I just don't understand . . .'

'Understand what, Dad?' I ask.

'How did she manage to take so many pills? She must have taken a lot, don't you think?'

'I don't know,' I say, taking a tissue and blowing my nose. 'Let's just wait for the post-mortem. I can't think about it now.'

'It's no good. I have to know,' blurts Howie, pushing

164

back his chair abruptly and yanking open the medicine cupboard. He pulls out the box of medicine and empties it onto the kitchen table.

'Why do you keep all this crap? Half of it is out of date,' he lashes out at Dad, as he trawls through the half-empty medicine bottles, plasters, tubes of creams and packets of pills. 'It's fucking ridiculous.'

Dad doesn't defend himself. He just visibly shrivels, as if he's retreating into a shell.

'There's no need to take it out on Dad,' I say weakly, and Howie looks surprised. He's not used to people challenging him. 'No, you're right, Jess,' he admits and sighs. 'I'm sorry, Dad, I'm just not in a good place at the moment.'

'None of us are in a good place, son.' Dad looks lost in his own world. Again, I get the weird reminder of Mum. It's almost as if a part of her spirit has entered him.

'There's no sign of the Tramadol or her Alzheimer's meds,' Howie says at last, putting the medicine box back with a sigh.

'They must be here somewhere,' says Dad, getting agitated. 'I know I had at least two packets.'

'Are you sure you didn't throw them away?' I ask.

'Positive.'

'Well, they must be somewhere.'

Howie strides over to the sink, pulls out the black bin bag and empties the contents onto the floor. Amongst all the other rubbish, the empty cheese wrappers and tissues, he finds what he's looking for: three packets of pills, all completely empty.

'Shit,' he says slowly, fishing them out and placing them on the table in front of us.

Dad slumps into the chair. He's breathing heavily and his face is ashen. 'I should have locked the cupboard.' He rubs his face with his hands. 'Why didn't I put a lock on the cupboard?'

'You couldn't have known, Dad,' Howie says. But he continues rummaging through the debris on the floor and picks out several small silver pill packs.

'Betaloc,' he reads. 'What are these?' he asks.

I stare at them in horror. I must have left them when I cleared out my room. But I could have sworn I'd packed them away before I moved.

'They're beta blockers,' I whisper. 'They're mine. I take them sometimes for anxiety.' The room is spinning, and I feel sick. Mum must have taken my pills. I didn't think it was possible to feel any worse, but I do. Guilt twists in my belly like a maggot.

'I don't understand.' Howie rubs his face in his hands. 'Why would she take all these tablets?'

'Maybe she thought it was Nurofen?' Dad looks up, willing us to agree with him. 'She was complaining of a headache this morning. She could've taken one then forgotten she'd

166

taken it, then taken another and . . .' He tails off, looking distraught.

Howie paces the room. 'Shit, shit, shit,' he rages. 'Why didn't the doctor warn you this could happen?'

There's a heavy silence. Nobody says what I'm sure we're all thinking – that maybe it wasn't an accident, that maybe she took them deliberately. I think about what she told me the other day: *I don't want to be that old woman sitting in a chair in an old people's home, dribbling and talking nonsense. You won't let that happen to me, will you? Just shoot me if it comes to that.*

Did she decide to take matters into her own hands before it was too late?

'I should never have left her on her own.' Dad is crying now, his face buried in his hands, his whole body shuddering. I stare at him. I don't think I have ever seen him cry before in my life.

'She was having such a good day,' he says pleadingly. 'She seemed fine, almost her old self. I was only gone a couple of hours and I asked Polly to check in on her.'

I take his hand. It's cold and bony in mine.

'It's OK, Dad. You couldn't have known. None of us could.'

Chapter Twenty-One

The next few days pass in a blur of grief – grey and hopeless. I'm back sleeping at Dad's, ostensibly to take care of him, but mainly because I'm not sure I'll be OK on my own. I concentrate on practical tasks such as ringing Elizabeth and cancelling the wedding photos I was due to take. She's very understanding, even though it's only a few days before the wedding, and it will probably be very awkward for her to find another photographer at such short notice. I text Miriam too, asking if we can arrange to take the photos of Adriana another time. Then I set to sorting and cleaning the house. I hoover and dust and tidy in a whirlwind of frantic activity. It's as if I'm being chased by demons and, if I stop, they'll catch up with me. I can feel it closing in on me – that awful gnawing feeling of dread and despair I had when I was in Madrid.

I'm cleaning the countertops in the kitchen when I notice a small pile of white powder between the microwave and the fridge, along with crumbs from the toaster. It's tiny and insignificant and I'm about to wipe it up, but something stops me. What is it? Flour? Sugar? Not sugar, the grains are too fine and irregular. I dip my finger in it. Some of the powder sticks to the tip and I raise it to my nose and sniff. There's no discernible smell so I lick it cautiously. It tastes bitter. *Pills*, I think, *crushed-up pills*.

I stare at it. I've watched Mum taking her tablets lots of times. She always swallows them whole with water. Why would she start crushing up pills . . . unless she meant to take a large amount and wanted to make them more palatable by adding them to food or drink? She must have intended to take them.

Or someone else wanted her to.

I can't help remembering what Mum said about her tea being poisoned. What if she was right about someone meaning her harm?

No, no, no. I hit my head, trying to dislodge the thought. It's crazy. Matteo was right. I'm crazy. I need help. That's how it starts with these random paranoid thoughts. Soon I'll be hearing voices again and I'll end up a drivelling wreck like I did in Madrid. I need to start taking my medication again. Maybe I should ring Claire Matteson and make an extra appointment for a therapy session.

My hands are shaking as I pick up the phone and call her number. But the line is busy, and I hang up. *You're delusional; you don't need Claire to tell you that*, I think firmly as I brush the powder into a dustpan and then tip it into the bin.

I wish I could dispose of my thoughts so easily. But the idea has burrowed its way into my head, and I can't get rid of it. As I scramble some eggs for tea, Mum's voice reverberates in my mind. *I know too much*, she said. *He's worried I'm going to spill the beans.* At the time I dismissed it as the dementia talking, the ramblings of a confused old woman, but now, in light of her death, it seems to take on a new significance. What if she was speaking the truth? What if she told someone that she'd seen what had happened to Kate Chandry? And what if that person was the wrong person?

'Something's burning,' says Dad, sniffing as he appears in the doorway.

Shit, the eggs. Smoke is billowing from the pan. How could I not have noticed? I leap up and snatch the pan off the heat. The eggs are burnt black at the bottom. There's no salvaging them.

'It's OK. I'm not hungry anyway,' says Dad, drifting in and sitting at the table.

'We have to eat,' I say firmly, looking in the cupboard for something else. 'How about some baked beans?'

I stand over the pan, stirring slowly as the beans bubble. *Focus on practical things*, I think. *Just focus on getting through the next few hours.* I can't afford to lose it right now. Dad needs me. Of course Mum wasn't murdered – I'm crazy to even consider it. *She wasn't murdered and she didn't kill herself. She wasn't murdered. She wasn't murdered.* I repeat these words over and over in my head like a mantra, until I've almost convinced myself that they're true.

Chapter Twenty-Two

For one second when I wake up this morning, my mind is blank, and I feel nothing. Then the awful truth comes hurtling back, crashing into me and taking my breath away. *Mum is dead.* She overdosed and some of the drugs were mine. A cocktail of grief and guilt swills around inside me. A world without Mum just doesn't seem possible. She's always been there, a fundamental part of the fabric of my life, and now that fabric is being torn apart. All that unconditional love gone forever. It's too much to bear. I *can't* bear it. All I want is to go back to sleep. I want to be enveloped in blissful nothingness again, just for a while.

But it's only a matter of minutes before the doorbell rings downstairs – a long, insistent *dring*. I wait a minute to see if Dad will answer, but he doesn't. So, reluctantly,

I push back the covers, pull on a pair of jeans and shuffle downstairs to open the door.

Ajay is standing in the doorway, clutching a large bunch of white flowers. He's wearing sunglasses, so I can't see his eyes, but I can hear the sincerity in his voice when he says, 'Jess, I heard about your mother. I'm so sorry.'

'Thank you,' I say, taking the flowers and burying my head in them, inhaling their sweet, cloying scent. I don't want to break down in front of him.

'She was so kind to me when Kate died. They both were.'

'Yes,' I say. I'm waiting for him to go. It's nice of him to bring the flowers, but I don't really want to talk to anyone right now. I want to be alone. But he doesn't move. He just stands there smiling awkwardly and shuffling from foot to foot.

'Is your dad about?' he asks at last.

'I'll see if I can find him. Come in.' I stand back reluctantly to let him in.

Ajay waits in the living room while I search for Dad. In the kitchen I put the flowers in a vase and find a note on the table which says, *Have gone to the registrar's office. Back soon, Dad.*

I pick up the paper and head back to the living room. 'He's not in. I'm sorry,' I say. Ajay has taken off his sunglasses; his green eyes are full of compassion, and I can't look at them or I know I'll break down and sob like a baby.

'I'll tell Dad you called,' I say, ushering him towards the door. He hesitates in the doorway, turning to me.

'If you ever need to talk about anything, you know I'm here,' he says, pressing my hand. His eyes lock on mine.

And for a brief, crazy moment I consider confiding in him. I imagine what it would be like to tell him everything – how good it would feel to share the burden of my suspicions. I open my mouth. Then I close it again. It's hopeless. What can I say? *I thought my mother saw someone kill your wife and last night I almost convinced myself for a moment that he had murdered my mother to keep her quiet?* It sounds ridiculous and melodramatic. He would probably think I was crazy. I'd end up being mentally poked and prodded by doctors again. I came so close to being sectioned in Madrid. If Matteo had had his way, I almost certainly would have been.

'You know, after Kate died, I think I went a little crazy for a while,' Ajay says, as if he's just read my mind. Does he know? Does he know about what happened in Madrid?

'Crazy in what way?' I ask warily.

He frowns. 'I started imagining all kinds of things.'

I inhale sharply. Is this a trick to get me to confess to my own delusions? 'What kinds of things?' I ask.

'Like, I could hear her voice, and once I thought I saw her standing at the end of my bed talking to me.'

I shiver. 'What did she say to you?' I ask.

He smiles sheepishly. 'I don't know. It was never more

than an indistinct murmur. Anyway, it was probably just a dream. I mean, I don't really believe in ghosts, do you?'

'I don't know,' I say. 'I don't think so.' I think of Madrid, of the child's voice I heard under the floorboards. The logical part of my brain knows that was just the psychosis, but another part of me – a more visceral part – still clings on to the idea that she was real. I remember the woman at the end of my bed that I used to dream about as well. What if she wasn't a dream but a spectre of some kind?

Ajay looks bashful, as if he's suddenly remembered that he hardly knows me, and that he might have shared too much. 'Anyway, I'm just across the street if you need me,' he says, putting his sunglasses back on. 'Anything at all. I mean it.'

He sounds sincere. And I have a weird feeling of being connected to him somehow, as if he understands what I'm going through, but I doubt I will actually take him up on his offer.

'Thank you,' I say. 'I appreciate it.'

Just as Ajay is heading out of the door Dad pulls into the driveway. They stop and chat for a moment and then Ajay raises his hand to me and ambles across the close.

'That was nice of him to come,' Dad says, after Ajay has left.

'Mmm,' I murmur, giving him a searching look. Thank God he seems to have pulled himself together a little this morning. He's washed and shaved for what I think is the first time since Mum died; he's wearing a clean shirt and he seems more purposeful. He's been busy organising things and he shows me the death certificate he's obtained from the registrar's office in town.

'That's it?' I say, holding it in my hand. It doesn't seem real. This single sheet of paper, simply recording the date, place and cause of her death. It seems such a small thing to signify something so momentous as the death of such an amazing woman. *It's not enough*, I think indignantly. *A piece of paper isn't enough. It should be a book. It should be a whole library of books.*

'It means we can organise the funeral,' Dad says.

'Why don't I go to the funeral director's now and start the ball rolling?' I offer, eager to get it over with, and glad of an excuse to escape from the house, from the heavy atmosphere of grief.

Dad struggles to his feet. 'I'll come with you,' he says.

I glance at him anxiously. His efforts this morning seem to have exhausted him, and despite his smarter appearance, I notice that there are huge, dark circles under his eyes.

'No, you stay here. You look tired, Dad,' I say. 'You should go and have a lie-down. I can do this by myself.'

'You're right, Jessie,' he nods, patting me on the shoulder and sighing. Then he turns and climbs wearily up the stairs like a man twice his age.

*

I'm just grabbing my jacket to go out when the doorbell rings again. This time it's Polly, with a freshly baked quiche.

'It's mushroom,' she says briskly. 'I hope you like mushroom. You just need to heat it in the oven for twenty minutes or, if you prefer, you can eat it cold.'

'Come in,' I say, taking the quiche to the kitchen and cramming it in the fridge along with all the other pies and lasagnes cooked by Dad's friends and neighbours. How we're ever going to eat it all I don't know.

Polly follows me into the kitchen.

'Oh Jessica.' She hugs me warmly, then holds me at arm's length, her eyes welling up. 'How are you?'

'I'm OK.'

'And your father?'

'He's resting at the moment,' I say. 'He's not so good. It's like he's lost himself the past couple of days.' As I say the words, it occurs to me that this would have been an accurate description of Mum too, in her last few months.

Polly winces. 'I wanted to speak to him, to say how sorry I am.'

'I'll pass the message on.'

Polly hesitates. 'I wanted to talk to him face to face if I could,' she says, taking a deep breath. 'You see, I feel responsible in a way.'

'Responsible?' I stare at her, surprised.

'Yes. Your father asked me to check in on her while he

was out. And, of course, I did. But only once. It was at about eleven o'clock. She didn't invite me in and I didn't like to intrude. I just asked her if she was OK and she said she was fine. I'm afraid I took her word for it.' Her voice quavers and she brushes away a tear. 'You see, I assumed your father had already come back, but I must have been mistaken.'

I grip the kitchen table. 'What made you think he was home?' I ask carefully.

'Um . . .' She looks confused. 'I think it was because I heard Jean laughing and talking, before she answered the door – though I suppose it must have been the TV. And then when she came to the door, I could've sworn she said, 'We're fine.'

'*We're* fine?' I repeat. I can feel my spine tingling.

'That's what I thought.'

'What kind of mood was she in? Did she seem sad or . . . afraid?'

'No, nothing like that. She seemed in high spirits, happy. Like I said, she was laughing . . .' Polly chews her fingernail thoughtfully. 'In fact, I would describe her as more than happy. She was almost giddy. She had flushed cheeks and bright eyes . . . Oh my Lord, do you think that was the effect of the drugs? Maybe she had already overdosed?'

'No, I don't think so,' I try to reassure her. I'm still thinking about that '*We*'. *We're fine.* 'Did you see anyone leaving later?' I ask.

If she thinks this is an odd question, she doesn't show it. She just frowns, trying to remember. 'I did notice someone walking across the close, away from your house, about half an hour later. A young man.'

I lean forward. My heart is racing, my mind scrambling to make sense of it all. So there *was* someone with her that morning. Maybe my suspicions last night weren't so crazy after all. 'Can you describe him?' I ask abruptly.

'Well, he was wearing a jacket with the hood up, so I couldn't see his face. He looked as if he was in a rush and I remember thinking maybe he was up to no good. He had broad shoulders and he walked with a kind of swagger like that chap in all the Westerns, what's his name?'

'John Wayne?'

'Yes, that's the one. But I don't understand what you're driving at. Do you think this man, whoever he was, was visiting your mother?'

I shake my head. 'No, probably not,' I lie.

'Oh.' She gives me an odd look, tilting her head to one side. 'Well, I won't take up any more of your time, Jessica. I'll come back when your father's up to visitors. Please let me know if I can do anything for you. Anything at all. And let me know when the funeral is.' She rubs her eyes and stands up stiffly. 'Jean was such a good friend over the years,' she says, hugging me again. 'She was always so kind and always so much fun. You should be proud of her.'

'I am. Thank you.'

'God bless you, my dear.'

I watch her cross the close. She turns and waves as she reaches her house and I lift my hand and then close the door firmly behind me.

A few seconds later, the phone buzzes in my pocket. A number flashes up. It's Claire.

'Oh, hi, Jessica. This is Claire Matterson,' she says. 'You called me yesterday.'

Shit. 'Oh yes. I'm sorry, I was going to make an appointment, but I think I've changed my mind.'

'Oh. Are you sure? Because I could fit you in tomorrow at three o'clock, if you wanted?'

'I'm sure.' Last night I thought I was going insane, but I can see more clearly today, and I know I'm not crazy. I'm sad, yes, depressed even, but I'm not delusional. Someone was here the day my mum died. My suspicions are valid, and I don't need to discuss them with Claire.

'Well, don't hesitate to contact me if you—'

'Yes, thank you.' I press end call, cutting her off.

Chapter Twenty-Three

I walk briskly along the canal towards the funeral director's, trying to work off this awful, dark energy inside me.

But I have to carry on. Whatever happened, I have to
make sure that Mum gets the funeral she deserves. She
would have wanted that.

I stop in the village at the funeral director's and find out
that the crematorium is booked up for over a week. We
agree on a date next Monday. At least, I think, that gives us
plenty of time to organise everything. I'm making my way
back through the village when I spot Sean up ahead of me,
on the other side of the road. There's something about the
way he's walking that catches my attention. He's sauntering
down the road in that slow, unruffled, new-sheriff-in-town
way he has.

Swaggering. That was the word that Polly used. I stop

dead in the centre of the pavement, causing an old lady to swerve past me and tut loudly. Could it have been Sean that Polly saw in the close the morning Mum died? A chill runs down my spine at the thought. He's been connected to two 'accidents' now. That can't be a coincidence. He knew that Mum said she saw someone push Kate because I told him. If he was mixed up in Kate's death, it would've given him a motive to silence my mother, wouldn't it?

Gripped by horror, I watch him take some money out from a cashpoint in the wall. Then, keeping a discreet distance, I tail him down the street. There's an objective part of me that knows this is not the behaviour of a normal well-balanced person. It's not normal to suspect your friend of murder and what I expect to gain by spying on him, I have no idea, but I can't help myself. I seem to be propelled by something out of my control.

As he stops to chat to a man in a suit, I pretend to look in a shop window, watching his reflection in the glass. The man is middle-aged, plump and balding. I don't think I've ever seen him before. He laughs and slaps Sean on the arm. Then they say goodbye and carry on in opposite directions. And I continue to follow Sean, crossing the road when he goes into a bookshop and diving into the charity shop next door.

'Can I help you?' asks the shop assistant pointedly. My behaviour probably seems weird to her as I'm just standing and staring through the window, waiting for Sean to come out of the bookshop.

'Oh, no thank you,' I smile sweetly. I pick up a china dog and feign interest. 'How much is this?' I enquire. But I don't wait for her answer because at that moment Sean emerges from the shop opposite with a book under his arm. I place the dog back on the shelf and hurry out onto the street. He's moving rapidly now – in a rush – and I need to run a little to keep up. I'm slightly out of breath when he suddenly turns into the car park behind the library and catches sight of me behind him.

'Jessica!' he exclaims. 'What are you doing here?'

I freeze and look into his eyes. My heart is racing with anger and fear.

'Oh, I thought it was you,' I say as casually as possible. I look down at my hands, which are trembling, and I stuff them in my pockets, hoping he hasn't noticed.

'Yeah, it's me,' he grins, spreading his arms. 'Where've you been, Jess? I've been trying to call you, but you never answer your phone.'

'Well, I've been a bit preoccupied lately.' I give him a direct stare. It's a challenge. 'My mum has just died.'

But perhaps you know that already.

He blinks at me with what appears to be genuine shock. I'm not convinced. Sean was always a good actor. At school he was the lead in the school play three years in a row.

'Your mother . . . ?' He claps his hand to his mouth. 'But I saw her just the other day. She was fine.'

'Yes,' I say evenly. 'It was quite sudden. She overdosed on her medication.'

'Oh my God.' He shakes his head. 'I just can't believe it.'

'That makes two of us.'

'Jess, I'm so sorry.' He places a hand on my arm, and I stare at it as if a poisonous snake has just crawled up my sleeve. He pulls away. 'When did it happen?'

'Two days ago.'

'Really?' he looks shocked. 'What time?'

'Sometime between two thirty and six o'clock. Why?'

He puts his hand to his head. 'Jesus, oh my God, I was there, at your house.'

I chew my lip. This admission throws me. I didn't expect him to own up to it so readily. 'You were?' I say.

'Yes, I came to drop off some paperwork for the house.'

'And? Did you speak to my mother?' I hold my breath.

'No. I rang the doorbell, but no one answered. Oh my God.' Sean's eyes are wide; he bites down on his finger. 'Do you think she was there?'

'She must have been,' I say coldly. I'm thinking about what he said about coming to see me. It doesn't make sense. I think I've found the hole in his story. 'Why did you try to find me at my parents' house,' I ask, 'when I'd already moved into my new place?'

184

He doesn't miss a beat. 'Oh really?' he says. 'I thought you told me you were moving this weekend.'

That's right, that is what I said, I realise. I'd originally intended to move in after I'd done all the redecorations, but I'd changed my mind. So what he says is quite plausible, and I suddenly doubt myself. He could be telling the truth after all.

'How is the new place anyway?' he asks.

'What? Oh, OK.'

My anger is dissipating slowly, leaving me deflated and very tired. What am I doing? I feel so confused. Yet again I'm leaping to conclusions without any hard evidence and I suddenly see how ridiculous I'm being, trailing him down the street as if I were in some second-rate spy movie.

'Did you see or hear anything at my parents'?' I ask half-heartedly. 'Were there any cars parked outside?'

'Nah, I don't think so. I didn't really notice. I was in a hurry. Tommo was waiting for me in the car down the street. We were on our way to football practice.' He looks at his watch. 'Listen, Jessica,' he says, 'I've got to go and show a house now, but we should go for a drink soon. How about Saturday? Are you free?'

'Um . . . I'm going to be busy with arranging the funeral.'

He frowns. 'Oh, OK. Some other time then. I'll call you, OK?'

I don't answer. As he leaves, I notice the book he's

carrying under his arm. It's a book of love poems with gold lettering and red flowers on the cover.

'Doesn't look like your type of book,' I comment. 'Who's it for?'

He glances down at the book. 'Well, that just shows you don't know me very well, Jessica,' he grins. 'It is for me. I'm a romantic soul at heart.'

Like hell you are, I think, watching him head to his car. I'm certain that book isn't for him. It's probably for some poor, unsuspecting woman he's trying to seduce.

Once a liar, always a liar, I think as I take out my phone and call Tommo.

Tommo answers with his usual breezy, 'Yep?'

'Quick question,' I blurt. 'Did you and Sean go to football practice last Saturday, and did you stop off at my house to drop something off?'

'Sure,' he says. 'Why?'

'How long were you waiting for him?'

'I dunno. It can't have been more than a couple of minutes. By the way, Jess, um, er . . . Alice told me about your mum. I'm really—'

'Thanks,' I say, cutting off his clumsy attempt at sympathy. 'I'll see you at the funeral.'

I switch off my phone and make my way home, along the Aylesbury road, head bowed, thinking hard. It seems like Sean was telling the truth for once. If he was only a couple of minutes at my house, he wouldn't have had time to administer an overdose. It seems my suspicions about him were unfounded after all. He's a liar but he didn't kill my mother. He couldn't have. Could I have been wrong about everything? I was so sure before, but it seems I've let my imagination run away with me again. There was no cover-up. No murder.

Chapter Twenty-Four

Over the next few days, there's a lot to organise and I don't have time to brood or to wallow in grief or suspicion. Together with Dad and the funeral director we work out a programme of service. And with the funeral booked in just a few days, I set about informing all Mum's friends and relatives.

Sitting in Dad's study, a photo of him and Mum in Crete beaming down at me, I work my way through her address book, crossing people off as I go. Each time I tell someone and hear the shock and sadness in their voice, it becomes more real to me. My mother is dead. I'm never going to see her again. And another hairline crack appears in my heart.

Most of her friends are local – people who live in the village or who belong to amateur dramatics. And it strikes me, as I'm reaching the end of her address book, that she hasn't kept in contact with any friends from her childhood or early adulthood. Mum was one of those people with disposable friendships, I suppose. With her gregarious nature she made friends easily, and with her fiery temper she lost them just as quickly. But it's still strange that there's no one at all from her earlier life. Surely she must have kept in touch with someone?

I'm putting her address book away in her desk and am about to make myself a coffee when I remember Eve – her best friend at the convent – the one she mistook me for by Hampden Pond. The way that Mum talked about her, I could tell they were very close, and it seems a shame to me that we don't have her address. I think about Alice and Holly and what an important part of my life they were and how, even though I haven't spoken to Holly for years, I would want her to know if anything happened to me and vice versa.

On impulse, I find the email address Alice has given me and I sit down at the kitchen table and write a letter to Holly.

I hesitate a long time about how to start, my finger poised over the screen. And a couple of times I write the first line and then erase it and compose it again.

Dear Holly,
I hope you don't mind me contacting you after all this time.
I got your address from Alice. I hear you're living in Scotland

now and have a baby son. Congratulations!!! I'm still living in Wendover. I went to Spain for a while but that didn't work out.

Anyway, the real reason I'm writing is to share some sad news. My mother passed away a few days ago, and I thought you would want to know. I know how fond you were of her and she was of you. The funeral is next Monday. I don't expect you to come, because Scotland is a long way! But I thought I should tell you anyway. I hope you are well and happy. I often think about all the fun we had at school, and I remember those times with a lot of affection.

Love,

Jess (Delaney)

I read it through, hoping I've got the tone right – friendly and casual, not too pushy. Then I press send.

After I've finished, I spend a while stacking the dishwasher and cleaning the hob, pretending I'm not waiting for the ping of a message on my phone. But it's stupid of me to expect her to reply immediately. Even if she does check her messages regularly, Holly would be caught off-guard by a message after all this time and would need time to consider her answer.

Or perhaps she won't reply at all, I reflect with a dull twinge of pain – we hardly ended on good terms, though I've still no idea why. I just arrived at school one day and she'd moved to a desk far away from me, on the other side of the classroom next to Georgia Brown.

'What's wrong? Why aren't you speaking to me?' I asked at break time, running to catch up with her.

'Just leave me alone, all right, Jess. I don't want to talk to you.'

'But why not? What have I done?'

She turned, hugging her books to her chest, and gave me a look of surprising venom. 'Nothing, Jess. Just leave me alone.' And then she strode away, leaving me perplexed, hurt and angry.

I sure as hell wasn't going to make the first move after that. As far as I was concerned, I'd done nothing wrong and it was up to her to apologise. But she never did, and the next term she left, and I never saw her again.

I wonder if something similar happened between Mum and Eve. It wouldn't surprise me, given Mum's tempestuous nature. I close the dishwasher and switch it on. Then I go back to Mum's desk and fish out her address book. I read through it again, checking I haven't missed anything, but there's no one called Eve in there. *There must be a way to trace her*, I think, feeling frustrated. But I don't have much to go on – just a first name and the fact that she went to a convent school. I don't even know the name of the school. Maybe Dad knows.

*

I find him in the garden, sitting on a bench staring at the hedge, a piece of bread in his hands and a small, whimsical smile on his face.

'Do you know there's a robin that likes to hide under there?' he whispers 'He peeps his head out now and then, but I can't get him to trust me. He'll come about so far, but no further.'

I sit down next to him. *I'm not the only one that has problems dealing with reality*, I think.

'Dad,' I say gently. 'I need your help. I'm trying to invite people to the funeral, and I was wondering how I could get hold of Eve.'

He doesn't answer immediately. He stands up stiffly, breaking the bread into crumbs and throwing them to the bird. Then he turns to me slowly. 'Eve?' he says.

'Yes, Eve. I don't know her second name, I'm afraid. She was a good friend of Mum's, wasn't she? Mum said they were very close when they were at school, but I can't find her in Mum's address book.'

'I've never heard of any Eve.' Dad stoops and tugs out a weed from the flower bed.

'You must have,' I insist. 'She was a good friend of Mum's at the convent.'

He stares up at the sky at an aeroplane rumbling overhead. 'What?'

'What about the convent school she went to? Maybe I

can trace her through them. Do you remember what it was called?'

'Your mother never went to a convent school. She went to a posh private school up north somewhere.'

'Oh,' I say, disappointed and frustrated. Perhaps Eve was a figment of Mum's imagination, like her stint as a Cold War spy and her acting career at the RSC.

'Well, is there anyone else I've forgotten – anyone from Mum's side of the family?'

There's no one to ask from Dad's family. I know that. He was an only child and his parents died a long time ago.

'I don't think so,' Dad says vaguely. 'You know her parents are dead, and you know your mother fell out with the rest of the family a long time ago.'

'Yes, but don't you think we should let them know all the same?'

'Maybe. But do you think your mother would really want them there after the way they treated her?'

'I suppose not,' I admit.

Even so, I decide to put a notice of her death in the newspaper.

I keep it simple – a few lines at the back of the *Yorkshire Post*. I remember Mum saying that her family came from that part of the world.

It is with the saddest regret that we announce the death of Jean Mary Delaney on 26th July 2019 in Wendover, Buckinghamshire. The funeral will be held at St Peter's church on Monday, 3rd August at 11 a.m.

Donations can be made payable to the Alzheimer's association. No flowers, please.

It's a long shot. But you never know. Somebody might see it.

Chapter Twenty-Five

The day of the funeral arrives, and I sit shell-shocked in the crematorium, listening to the speeches, trying not to break down completely, while Mum's friends talk about what a valued member of the community she was, and Howie tells funny anecdotes, which make everyone laugh and cry.

After the funeral everyone drives in convoy from the crematorium to my brother's house, where we gather in the large living room. He's organised a huge, lavish buffet, way too much food for the modest turnout. He's hired waiters and waitresses dressed in black, and even booked a violinist who is playing some soulful classical piece. I try to believe that all this extravagance is his way of demonstrating his love for Mum, but I can't help wondering what the use of his money is now, and why didn't he spend more on her when she was alive? Isn't this just Howie once again showing off how wealthy and successful he is?

But I'm being mean and petty. Mum would've loved it – she always loved luxury and opulence – and that's the most important thing. I know she would have also wanted me and Howie to support one another. So I swallow my feelings and go and congratulate Vicky and Howie on a very well-organised event.

'Do you know who the violinist is?' Howie gives me a gratified smile.

I shake my head, and he names a musician I have vaguely heard of.

I murmur something to show how impressed I am and then look around the room at the small huddle of people assembled. There are about forty altogether: some are business associates and friends of Howie's and a handful of Mum's friends from the village and amateur dramatics. I don't know half the people here. The only people I know well are Alice and Tommo, who have turned up for moral support, and Mum and Dad's neighbours from the close, including Ajay and Polly, who are deep in conversation. Lara and Luke are here too, along with Brandon, who is sitting in the corner kicking his legs, looking unusually subdued and uncomfortable in a mini suit and tie. Luke is talking to one of Mum's friends, obviously charming the pants off her, and Lara is hanging out near the buffet necking champagne. She's wearing a very skimpy black dress which barely covers her backside. She's got a nose ring too, which must be new. She looks pretty and edgy and completely oblivious to the fact that she is drawing the eye of all the male waiters and many of the guests.

'Has Lara had her nose pierced?' I ask.

Vicky follows the direction of my gaze with a frown. 'Yes,' she says with a shudder. 'I think it's hideous, don't you? Sometimes I think she only does these things to annoy us.'

At that moment Lara, who must be more drunk than I realised, knocks over a tray of champagne and falls to the floor laughing hysterically.

'Right, that's it,' Howie says, his face like thunder. 'I'm not going to let her ruin Mum's funeral.' He strides over to the bar, hisses something in her ear, grabs her roughly by the arm and frogmarches her outside.

'The rebellious teens have hit her with a vengeance, I'm afraid,' Vicky says to me, watching them leave. 'We're at our wits' end. She's completely out of control. She goes out all the time and doesn't come back till the early hours. God knows who she's with.' She lowers her voice. 'I think she might be taking drugs.'

'Most teens go through a rebellious phase.' I think about myself as a teenager – how after school I turned down an offer from a good university and moved in with a man more than twice my age. I remember how furious my dad was. He felt that I was throwing away all the opportunities he'd given me. He begged me to reconsider but, of course, I didn't listen. It took me three years to finally figure out he'd been right and to pack up my bags and head to art college.

'Yes, but it feels like more than a phase with Lara.' Vicky looks at her hands. 'She seems so angry all the time. I really don't know what to do with her.'

'What about Louise?'

Vicky flicks her hand dismissively. 'Oh, she's no help. She likes to undermine me and Howie at every turn. And anyway, Lara has refused to go back to living with her. She wants to stay and finish her exams here.'

'Have you thought about . . . ?'

I break off because Sean walks in from the dining room and whatever I was going to say is swept clean from my mind.

'Jesus, who invited Sean White?' I mutter under my breath.

I no longer think that Sean had anything to do with Mum's death, but I'm worried about what will happen if Ajay sees him. It doesn't help that he looks more than usually pleased with himself. I watch him as he scans the room, his eyes finally landing on me.

'What is he doing here?' I plaster a smile on my face as he approaches our table, and I let him plant a kiss on my cheek, resisting the urge to wipe it away with my hand.

He shakes Vicky's hand and gives her a charming smile. Vicky smiles back absent-mindedly and mutters something about checking on Lara before wandering off and leaving us on our own.

'You OK? How are you holding up?' he asks me and, before I can stop him, he's wrapped me in his arms and is holding me in an unnecessarily long embrace.

'I've been better,' I say, breaking free. From across the room I can feel Ajay's eyes on us. He's staring at Sean with what can only be described as hatred, and I hurriedly usher Sean to a seat as far away as possible. The last thing I want at my mum's funeral is a scene.

'I'm really gutted about your mother.' Sean grabs a handful of nuts from the bowl in front of us. 'She was a wonderful lady, a great character.'

'Thank you,' I nod.

'Do you remember before the sixth-form dance when we were dating, and she taught me to ballroom dance in your kitchen?'

I can't help smiling at the memory. Mum at her most flamboyant, whisking Sean around the room, and the expression of pure comical surprise on Sean's face. Of course, at the time, as a self-conscious teenager, I was mortified. But now I realise what a brilliant and unusual soul she was and how much joy and laughter she brought to our lives.

There's a silence. Sean seems preoccupied and I watch Lara slip back inside, looking mutinous, followed by a grim-faced Howie. She heads straight over to Luke and whispers something in his ear and they both laugh.

'It doesn't seem like long ago we were that age,' says Sean, looking at them. 'Those were the days,' he grins at me.

'Were they?'

'We had some good times, didn't we? You and me?'

'And some bad,' I say pointedly, and I stare at him, unsmiling until even Sean, usually impossible to embarrass, starts looking a little uncomfortable.

'Well, if you ever need to talk to anyone, I'm here for you, Jessica. You know that.' He stands up and kisses me on the cheek. 'Excuse me, I just need to go outside for a ciggie.'

I watch him head out to the garden. I'm watching Sean so intently, I don't notice Ajay approach until he's right in front of me, standing over me, holding a plate of food.

'Thought you might like something to eat,' he says. 'Do you like scones?'

'Thanks,' I smile. I don't really feel hungry but it's nice of him to offer.

He hovers awkwardly. 'Is this seat taken?'

'No, you go ahead.'

He sits down opposite me, tapping the armrest of his chair. 'How are you doing, Jessica?'

The way he's looking at me, as if he understands and cares, releases something inside me and I feel a choking in my throat and tears welling up in my eyes. I brush them away. I've cried so much over the past few days. I wanted to try and hold it together for the funeral.

'I'm OK,' I say.

He hands me a tissue. 'It's not OK. It will never be OK. But the pain will get less over time.'

'I don't know.' I blow my nose. 'Maybe it's better this way. You know, with the dementia . . . her condition would have only got worse. She would have hated the long, slow, humiliating decline. She was such a proud woman.'

He nods but says nothing.

'But the truth is,' I continue, filling the silence, 'I miss her so much . . . I would have taken her any way, even if she was only part there. It's selfish of me, I suppose, but I would have taken any shred of her.' I struggle to express what I'm feeling. 'She was always there, you know? I mean, we didn't always get on, but she was a fundamental part of the world for me. It's like the world isn't complete anymore.'

I break off as my body convulses with tears. I don't know how long I cry for, but when I stop Ajay is still sitting there waiting patiently.

'The grief never completely goes away,' he says gently. 'But I think it does get a little easier each day. Some days now I go for hours without thinking about Kate, and then

I feel so guilty. But then I reflect that she wouldn't want me to waste my life feeling sad. And I'm sure your mum would feel the same.'

I nod. I know he's right. Everything Mum ever did was for me or for Howie. She wouldn't want us to be unhappy.

I dry my eyes and look around the room. I know I probably should be circulating but there's something comforting about sitting here in silence with Ajay.

I watch, with a feeling of detachment, as Sean comes back in and heads over to the buffet.

'I didn't know you knew Sean White,' says Ajay, watching me carefully.

'Oh,' I say. 'I've known him since I was fourteen. We went to school together.'

He takes a deep breath. 'I know that I don't really know you very well, and I hope you don't think I'm being cheeky offering you advice, but I like you, Jessica, and I don't want you to make a mistake you would regret.'

'A mistake?' I say, confused. 'Oh, you think . . . ? Me and Sean?' I laugh. 'No, there's nothing between us. Or at least not now. There was once. We dated for a while when we were sixteen.'

'Are you sure there's nothing now?' He looks at me searchingly. 'I know it's none of my business, but that guy is bad news.'

'Yes, I'm sure, and I already know he's no good.'

He looks relieved. 'There's something I haven't told you,' he says quietly. 'I haven't told anyone, in fact. I'm not sure if this is an appropriate time, but I really think you should know.'

I brace myself for what is coming. 'Go ahead, I want to know.'

'OK then.' Ajay lowers his voice. 'You remember I told you before that Kate was having an affair?'

I nod.

'Well.' His face twists with anger. 'It was with Sean White.'

'Oh,' I say, trying to look surprised.

He pushes the food around his plate with a fork. 'She fell in love with him and I hated her for that. But she couldn't help herself. Yes, she was selfish and thoughtless, but at least she was always honest with her emotions and I know that she genuinely loved him.' He winces in pain. 'When she loved someone, she loved them with all her heart. She was even prepared to destroy our family for him but . . .' He breaks off, unable to finish his sentence.

'I'm sorry . . .' I say inadequately.

He balls his hands and continues through clenched teeth. 'But he didn't love her. Not really. He was just playing around. She was just one in a long line of conquests for him. He just took her heart and trampled on it.'

I think about what Sean told me about wanting to marry Kate.

'Are you sure he didn't love her?' I say. I know better than most that Sean can be a bastard but when I spoke to him at Alice's party, I got the impression it was different with her – that he was really in love.

'Oh yes, I'm sure,' he says bitterly. 'After she died, I looked through the messages on her phone. There was one message that stood out. She received it just before she died.' He lowers his voice. 'The message said, and I quote, "Back off, bitch. Sean is mine and you can't have him."'

I absorb this. 'So, Sean was sleeping with another woman?'

Ajay nods bitterly. 'Probably more than one other woman. He has quite the reputation, you know.'

I'm not totally surprised. It fits with what I already know about Sean. I think about the timing of the message. Just moments before falling to her death, Kate found out that Sean was cheating on her. And I draw in my breath, suddenly understanding the possible significance, and the true depth of Ajay's hatred of Sean.

'Do you think that . . . that message had anything to do with . . . her death?' I ask tentatively.

'I don't know.' His head slumps into his hands and when he looks up his eyes are glittering with tears. 'I tell myself it was an accident because I can't handle the idea of anything else. But the truth is, I just don't really know for sure. What I do know' – he rips the beer mat viciously – 'is that

Sean White made her very unhappy in the last few hours of her life.'

'Who was the woman?' I ask. 'The woman who told Kate to back off?'

He shrugs. 'I don't know. Does it matter?'

'No, I suppose not.'

I pick at the scone. It doesn't taste of anything. Is it possible Kate's death was suicide? I mull the idea over. Perhaps she didn't mean to die, just make some kind of grand gesture. Perhaps she didn't know what she was doing – maybe she just wanted to do anything to stop the pain. I can understand that feeling. I've been there myself. It crossed my mind more than once during those last few weeks in Madrid.

Chapter Twenty-Six

'I'm sorry, Jessica,' Ajay says, breaking the silence. 'I don't mean to burden you with my problems again. Not here, not now. I just thought you should know what kind of man he is.'

'Well, you don't need to worry,' I say. 'There's nothing between me and Sean. I appreciate your concern, but I already know what he's like – though I had thought he would have grown up a bit.' And somehow, I find myself telling him all about my break-up with Sean. It all spills out, feelings of hurt I thought were long buried: how I walked in on him kissing Natasha; how he laughed when I confronted him and told me he'd never said we were exclusive.

Ajay listens without speaking, his eyes dark with anger. 'Excuse me,' he mutters when I've finished. He stands up abruptly, brushing crumbs from his trousers, and I watch him stalk away across the room. Too late, I realise with horror that he's heading straight for Sean. I follow him, trying to stop him, but I'm intercepted by a friend of Mum's – an old lady with short grey hair – and I'm forced to watch as Ajay mutters something in Sean's ear. Sean looks up with a gleam of hostile amusement, and they head out to the garden. At least they're taking their argument outside, I think.

'I just had to speak to you before I go,' The old lady is saying. She has a slight northern accent and seems a bit out of breath. 'You must be Jessica. You're the spitting image of your mother.'

'That's me,' I nod and smile. She's one of Mum's theatre friends, no doubt – though she looks more down to earth than most of them. She's not wearing make-up, her complexion is fresh and healthy, her blue eyes bright and full of vitality. She looks like the kind of woman who has lots of dogs and goes for long country walks in the rain.

'The last time I saw you, you were just a baby in a pram,' she says, 'though of course you won't remember me. I'm your mum's cousin, Margery.'

'Oh.' She must be a second cousin, I think, because as far as I know, Mum didn't have any first cousins.

'So how exactly are we related?' I ask. I'm distracted, still thinking about Sean and Ajay. What if they get physical? What if Ajay gets hurt? Should I go out and intervene?

'I'm your Great-Aunt Violet's daughter,' Margery is saying. She seems slightly surprised that I don't know. And I have heard of Aunt Violet but I'm almost certain Mum told me she didn't have any children. 'We haven't been in contact for years, but I saw your notice in the paper and I recognised her photograph.'

'Oh, I see,' I say, though I'm still confused.

'It's a shame your mother isn't here,' Margery continues. 'I always hoped there could be a reconciliation between us all.'

I nod and smile vaguely. What am I supposed to say to that? 'She's here in spirit,' I try lamely. I wish I could believe that was true. I would give almost anything to hear her voice just one more time.

'Mmm, I suppose so,' Margery nods. 'It's such a shame. They were always so close when they were little girls. We all used to go and stay in Wales together, with your grandmother, when we were children. Did Jean tell you?' She looks misty-eyed. 'They were fabulous holidays. Of course, your Aunt Jean always used to make us dress up and act out plays she'd written, and we would play all day on the beach in the fresh air, all by ourselves. There wasn't all that health and safety nonsense and children weren't cosseted like they are nowadays.' She pauses for breath and laughs a little. 'One day we got caught by the tide and Jean had to carry Eve on her shoulders. It was a close shave, but we survived.'

I'm only half listening, still worrying about Ajay and Sean. But one word that Margery says catches my attention.

'Eve?' I say. 'Mum mentioned her recently. She was a school friend, right? Are you still in contact with her?'

She gives me an odd look. 'No dear, *Eve*, your mother.'

She's confused, I think. Dementia runs in families. Why not in ours?

'Jean was my mother,' I tell her patiently. 'You must be mixed up.'

Margery's face blanches. Then she claps her hand to her mouth. 'Oh, my dear, is it possible they haven't told you?' She looks around wildly. 'Oh, me and my big mouth. What have I gone and done?'

'Tell me what?' I ask, a dull unease stirring in my gut.

She shakes her head. 'I can't believe it. I just can't believe it. Where's Brian?' She looks over her shoulder. 'He should have warned me. I need to speak to him.' She spots Dad sitting in the window seat talking to Howie. 'Excuse me,' she blurts, and she bolts over to him.

I watch her go, confused and slightly alarmed, turning over the strange conversation we've just had in my head. *What did she mean, They haven't told you? They haven't told me what? And why did she say your Aunt Jean? Yes, I'm sure that's what she said.*

She's talking to Dad now, waving her hands around wildly, and Dad glances over at me, nodding his head slowly, his expression unreadable. He says something to Margery, and she stands up abruptly, heading out of the front door. From the back garden I can hear raised voices and the sound of something smashing. *Ajay and Sean*, I think vaguely. But I'll have to deal with that later. I'm more concerned now about the weird conversation I've just had with Margery. *Something is very wrong*, I think. It's nudging at the edge of my consciousness – something big, dark and threatening.

With the strange sensation that I'm sleepwalking towards a cliff edge, I stand up and follow her out of the house. I catch up with her as she's unlocking her car.

'What did you mean?' I ask.

'Jess . . .' she starts nervously and turns to face me. A light drizzle is falling, but I don't care. I barely notice. We stand opposite each other in the rain.

'You said they hadn't told me,' I say. 'Told me what? What did you mean?'

She shakes her head vigorously. 'I can't, I'm sorry, Jessica. It's not my place. You need to speak to your father.'

She opens the car door and starts to climb in. 'Wait.' I put a restraining hand on her arm. 'You called my mother "Aunt Jean" a minute ago. Why?'

'Did I? I must have made a mistake.'

'No, you didn't. I know you didn't.'

She sighs deeply and clasps her chin, giving me a searching look. She seems to be trying to decide something.

'It's not right,' she mutters to herself finally. 'They should have told you. It's just not right.'

'They should have told me what?' I persist with grim determination. The big, dark thing is crashing towards me and I'm terrified of what her answer will be. But I *have to* know.

'Come and sit in the car out of the rain,' says Margery. 'We're both getting soaked standing out here.'

'What should they have told me?' I repeat as I clamber into the passenger seat and stare at the rain streaking down the windscreen.

'I just don't understand why they didn't tell you,' Margery removes some things and shoves them on the back seat. There's a blanket covered in hairs and the car smells strongly of dogs. The stench of the car makes me want to throw up. 'I suppose they thought they were sparing you. But it's still not right. You ought to know the truth.'

I say nothing. The big dark thing is getting closer.

'Jean isn't your mother. She's your aunt.'

'No, she's my mother,' I say.

Margery shakes her head slowly. 'Your mother is Eve. Jean's younger sister. Eve Susanna Leyton. She left your father in 1990 and went off to live in Australia with another man. Your father moved in with Jean shortly after.'

The world seems to be folding in on itself. I grip the side of the seat, holding on tight. A part of me wants to dismiss this as the ramblings of a mad old woman but another part of me, a part deep inside, recognises that what she says has the ring of truth.

'Jessica? Jess, dear, are you all right?' Margery is peering at me anxiously, her face swimming in front of my eyes. 'Oh, maybe I shouldn't have told you,' she agonises. 'I'm so sorry. I know this must be a shock to you . . .'

For a moment I can't speak. I'm shaking so much.

'It's a lie,' I blurt. 'Why would you make up something like that?'

But my head is spinning. I think of Mum and the last time I spoke to her. *I've got something to tell you, she said. Something that you should know.*

'It's not a lie, I'm afraid,' Margery says gravely.

I don't answer. I just want to get out of here; I feel as if I'm trapped inside, sinking under a weight of water, and my claustrophobia is kicking in with a vengeance. I grab the handle and wrench open the door.

'Wait. Where are you going?' Margery says.

'Away,' I manage. 'I don't need to listen to your bullshit anymore.'

Margery sighs. 'You don't have to believe me if you don't want to, but I can prove it to you, if you give me the chance. Wait!' She scribbles something on a piece of paper and presses it into my hand. 'This is my phone number,' she says. 'Ring me if you want to talk.'

I clutch the paper tightly in my fist and stumble out into the rain as Margery starts up her car and drives away. Automatically, I walk up to the front door and I stand there with my finger hovering over the bell as the rain lashes down on me. But the thought of going back in there with Dad and Howie and all those people after what I've just heard makes me want to scream.

Chapter Twenty-Seven

I get into my car and drive blindly out of the gate. I have no idea where I'm going. I'm just driving. The rain blurs my windscreen and, as I veer round a sharp bend, a car hoots loudly, swerving out of my way, and I only just manage to avoid ending up in the hedge. I don't care. What does it matter? My whole world is falling apart.

I reach Wendover and at the bottom of Coombe Hill, I park in a layby and sit in the car, my hands gripping the wheel, trying to steady my breathing. I'm thinking furiously. I want to believe that Margery lied or that she's confused, but there's no denying that what she told me makes a warped kind of sense. There are things that shift and fall into place: the fact that my parents didn't stay in touch with anyone from before we moved here, the small number of baby photos of me and Howie with

Mum and the way they were so reluctant to talk about the past.

And there's that dream of the woman standing at the end of my bed. Is it possible that it was a memory of my real mother?

The rain eases off and I climb out of the car and head up the hill, striding up the slippery chalk path. If what Margery told me is true, then everything has been a lie. My whole life has been one huge fabrication.

Why didn't Mum tell me? Why didn't any of them tell me? Because Howie must have been in on it too. If our mother left when I was nearly three, then he would have been a teenager. There's no way he didn't know. My disbelief morphs into anger. Deep anger. I feel so betrayed, by Dad, by Howie, but by Mum most of all. And the worst thing is that there's nothing I can say to her. I can't confront her or demand an explanation, because she's dead and I can never talk to her again.

About halfway up I skid on the slippery chalk path, my foot sliding, and I steady myself by grabbing on to a tuft of grass. As I do, I notice a rabbit lying in a ditch. Its fur is wet and matted, its legs spread out uselessly behind it. It's twitching. It looks as if its back is broken, I think. Should I kill it – put it out of its misery? I look around for a rock to smash into its skull. But I can't find one and, even if I could, I'm not sure I would be able to go through with it.

So, feeling like a coward, I leave it and continue to scramble up the path.

I reach the top of the hill and stand looking down at the rain-soaked landscape. I don't know what to do. I can't go back to the funeral. I just can't. I don't want to face Dad and Howie. And I can't go back to stay at Dad's. I can't bear to spend another night under the same roof as him, not after what Margery's told me. I look at my watch. It's only four o'clock. The funeral won't have finished yet, so at least I have time to fetch my stuff before he gets home.

I drive back to the close, let myself in with my key and shove all my things into a suitcase as quickly as I can. Then I head to my house, dive inside and lock the door.

In my half-painted living room, I pace up and down, trying to order my unhinged thoughts. Suddenly, in a frenzy of furious energy, I pick up a tin of emulsion and hurl it across the room. White paint splatters all over the wall and onto the floor. I kick at the tin and scream with rage and grief until I'm all worn out. Then I sink onto the sofa, staring at my handiwork in dismay. I'm losing it. I need to calm down, pull myself together and work out what to do. But what the hell *am* I going to do? What can I do?

I need to speak to Margery, I decide, and I spend a fruitless few minutes searching for my phone before I realise it's inside my handbag, which I've left in the car. When I go to get it, I find the car door unlocked and wide open. But at least my handbag is still on the passenger seat.

Upstairs, I sit on my bed, staring at the piece of paper Margery gave me, at the number she scrawled. If I call her, I'll probably regret it. It's not as though I'm going to find out anything good. There's no good reason for a mother to leave her own child. But the not knowing is worse than the fear. I need to find out the truth.

Taking a deep, shuddering breath, I tap the number into my phone and press call.

She answers after a couple of rings.

'Jessica?' she says breathlessly.

'Why did she leave?' I ask abruptly. No preamble, no niceties.

Margery gives a deep sigh at the other end of the phone. 'I don't really know all the details. You need to ask your father about that. All I know is that there was some man she fell in love with, and she went to Australia with him.'

A man, I think, a bitter taste in my mouth. She left me for a man, for something as simple and tawdry as an affair. I'd hoped for something more complicated. Something tragic and unavoidable.

'Didn't she stay in contact with you?' I ask.

'No, she cut herself off from everyone – all her family, all her friends.'

'Is she still alive?' Hope flares in my chest – hope that's so intense it feels almost like fear.

There's a short silence. 'I wish I knew, Jessica. I'm sorry. I tried to find her for a long time, but with no success. She clearly didn't want to be found.'

'What was the name of the man?' *It's possible that she remarried and took his surname*, I think, and with everything online now, surely it would be possible to track her down?

'I think he was called Michael, but I don't know his second name. Your father would be able to tell you, I expect.'

'Can you tell me anything else? Anything that might help me trace her? Like . . . how old she is?'

'She was five years younger than Jean – six years younger than me. So that would make her . . .' I do a quick calculation. Mum was seventy-three so that would make Eve – my mother – sixty-eight.

'Sixty-eight,' I say.

'Yes, that's right.'

Sixty-eight is still young, I think, after I end the call. There's every chance my real mother is still alive. Feeling a small, tremulous hope, I snatch up my keys, get back in the car and head to Dad's house.

Chapter Twenty-Eight

I find Dad in the back garden, sitting in the small summer house just staring into space. He's still wearing his suit from the funeral, but he's taken off the jacket and rolled up his sleeves. He looks tired, hollowed out.

'Ah, Jessica,' he says vaguely. 'Where did you get to? We were looking for you.'

'I just went for a walk, up Coombe Hill.' I plonk myself down next to him and glare at him until he shifts uneasily, not meeting my eyes. He doesn't ask me why I left the funeral. I'm guessing he already knows. 'Well, you missed all the drama,' he says, looking at me sideways. 'Your old boyfriend and Ajay got into a fight.'

'Was anyone hurt?' Despite everything, I still manage to feel a faint twinge of anxiety on Ajay's behalf.

'No, it was all right. Howie sorted them out. A couple of glasses were smashed but that's all.'

I don't answer. I stare at my hands which are trembling, and Dad clears his throat. 'I see you've taken your stuff out of your bedroom,' he says.

'Yes. I've moved back out.'

'Right.'

There's a long silence. Now I'm here, I'm scared to confront him. I'm not scared that he'll deny it all, but that he won't.

'Dad, I need to talk to you,' I blurt at last.

He exhales deeply. 'OK. Well, I don't know about you, but I need a drink. I'm just going to pop inside and get a beer. Do you want one?'

'No thanks.'

That's right, run away, like the coward you are, I think, watching him scuttle into the house.

I tap my fingers impatiently and look around. This summer house was Mum's refuge and there are her personal touches everywhere – a signed photo of Sir Ian McKellen on the shelf, sequined cushions she sewed herself and copies of *The Stage* newspaper and *Woman and Home* scattered about. These reminders of her fill me with sadness and longing for the mother I've lost. *But she wasn't my mother*, I remind myself, hardening my heart. *She was my aunt. My Aunt Jean. She lied to me. She lied to me all my life.*

'There, that's better,' Dad says, returning with a bottle of beer. He sits down and takes a long swig. 'What did you want to talk about, Jess?'

I breathe deeply and straighten my back. I can feel the tension in my shoulders and an angry tightness in my chest. This is typical Dad, I think, pretending everything's OK when he's fully aware that it isn't.

'You know what I want to talk about,' I say quietly.

He twines his fingers around the beer bottle and looks out of the window. 'Yes. You spoke to Margery at the funeral, I gather.'

'You told me Mum didn't have any cousins.' My voice is calm but there's a deep well of rage bubbling up inside me.

'No, well, I—' he begins.

'She said something really strange,' I interrupt. 'Really, really strange. At first I thought she must be crazy but then I wasn't so sure . . . because it seemed to make sense in a weird kind of way.'

'Jess, I—'

'She told me that Jean was my aunt – that my real mother, Eve, left for Australia when I was three years old.'

There's a small part of me that's clinging on to the hope that Dad will just laugh and dismiss this whole thing as crazy.

But he doesn't. He grips the side of the bench, staring at the ground. Then his whole body sags. 'She had no business telling you that,' he says at last.

'But it's true, isn't it?' My heart feels as if it's splitting in two. The anxiety I've felt for the past few hours feels like it's going to overwhelm me.

He nods weakly.

And my whole world comes crashing down. Everything I thought I knew . . . The foundations of my life are built on a lie – a huge fault line of a lie.

'Why didn't you tell me the truth?'

Dad scratches his head. 'We thought it was for the best – me and Jean. We thought . . . I don't know . . .' He struggles to articulate his thoughts. He's never been very good at expressing emotion at the best of times. 'As you know, my mother left me when I was ten. All my life, I've felt that somehow, I wasn't good enough – that she hadn't loved me enough to stay. I didn't want you to go through what I went through.'

I think it's one of the most emotional speeches I've ever heard Dad give. He looks so broken and lost that attacking him feels cruel, but I can't let it go. I can't forget that what he's done is awful, terrible, unforgiveable.

'She was my mother. I had a right to know,' I say. 'You had no right to—'

He shakes his head sadly. 'Perhaps it was a mistake, but we just did what we thought was best at the time. We were just trying to protect you.'

That 'we' again. A reminder that it wasn't just him

that lied to me. It was Mum too. Her betrayal hurts even more. It feels worse than his somehow. I was closer to her. I trusted her more. I pick up one of the sequined cushions and squeeze it to my chest. 'Was shacking up with Jean a way to protect me too?' I say bitterly. 'Jesus, Dad. She was my aunt. My real mother's sister. You realise how fucked up that is?'

He stares at the ground. 'After Eve left, I was devastated. We both were. We both missed her so much. It seemed natural for us to gravitate towards each other.' He waves his hands around his head. 'Oh, I don't expect you to understand.'

'You must have been angry when Eve left with Michael.'

He looks surprised. 'Oh, so Margery told you about him?'

'Yes. Who was he exactly?'

'I never met him. He was from Australia, I believe. That's where they went when they ran off together.'

I nod. It fits with what Margery told me. 'Do you know which part of Australia she went to? Does she still live there?' I ask hopefully.

'I don't, I'm afraid.'

I wonder if it's possible to trace her. 'Do you think she could have changed her name? Did they get married?'

Dad shakes his head. 'She can't have married him. She would have had to divorce me and that would have meant contacting me to give me the divorce papers.'

'And all these years she's never tried to get in touch with me or Howie?' It's surprising how much the rejection hurts, even though I don't remember her at all.

'No.' He shakes his head and smiles at me sadly. 'It's not that she didn't love you. She loved you and your brother so much, but she changed that summer. Something happened to her. I don't think she was in her right mind.' He leans forward and grasps my hand in his. I slide it away.

'What was Michael's second name?' I ask.

Dad chews his fingernail. 'I don't know. I can't remember, I'm afraid.'

'You don't know?'

I find it hard to believe that he doesn't remember. She was his wife. Wouldn't he have made it his business to find out the name of the man she was having an affair with? Perhaps he's just blocked it all out of his mind. Dad is good at doing that. Forgetting things is a talent that seems to run in the family.

'And you have no idea where she is now – or even if she's still alive?' I ask.

'I'm afraid I don't, Jess. I put it all behind me. I've tried not to think about her. Shortly after she left me, we moved here. I couldn't stand living in the house where we were so happy. I couldn't stand being reminded of her all the time.'

There's no point in talking to him anymore. Even if he knows anything, he clearly isn't going to tell me. The anger that's been bubbling away finally rises to the surface. I stand up and I speak slowly and deliberately, watching him flinch as each word hits the mark.

'I think what you've done is unforgiveable. You've lost my trust completely and I don't ever want to see you again.'

And I sweep out of the summer house and through the side gate, slamming it behind me.

At home I make myself a tea to calm myself down and then I switch on my laptop. I spend a couple of hours trawling the internet looking for Eve. I find a couple of Eve Delaneys in the States and one in the UK. There's an Yvonne Delaney that lives in Adelaide, but no Eve Delaney that lives in Australia – or at least none of remotely the right age that I can find.

Most likely she's changed her name. I suppose she could have reverted to using her maiden name – Leyton. But a brief search for Eve Leyton yields no promising results either.

I snap the laptop shut, arching my back and stretching my arms over my head. She must have taken Michael's surname, I think, even if she couldn't have formally married him. Or maybe she just doesn't use social media. It seems unlikely, in this day and age, that she wouldn't leave any trace on the internet, but I'm not really sure of the best way to find her; I'm not even sure if I want to. After all, she obviously wanted nothing to do with me.

But I need to know the truth. I need to know what was

so special about Michael that she could leave her three-year-old daughter for him. Maybe it wasn't him, but me? The idea snakes its way into my thoughts, insidious and persuasive. Even though I know it's illogical, there's a part of me that feels, somehow, I must be to blame – that I'm so fundamentally unlovable that even a mother couldn't love me.

There's no point in thinking that way. I know that. One of the strategies Claire has been teaching me to deal with depression is not to blame myself for things that aren't my fault – to see that some things are out of my control. *It wasn't anything to do with you*, I tell myself firmly. *You were only three years old*. And it was Eve's choice to leave. But why? Why did she abandon us and never even try to contact us? I need to know.

Maybe Howie can tell me something, I think. Even though we were never close, it's hard to believe he would have kept something like this from me. But he must have known. He was fourteen or fifteen at the time Eve left – old enough to be aware of what was going on. I pick up the phone and call his mobile, but it goes straight to voicemail, so I leave a message. Then I switch off my phone and head to bed.

Chapter Twenty-Nine

Watson and Clyde has a black door with gold lettering and, inside, the waiting room is tastefully decorated with plush sage-green carpet and a mahogany desk. There are magazines like *Horse and Hounds* and *Tatler* scattered over the low coffee table. Everything about the place suggests class and money. The door to Howie's office is firmly shut. *Howard Delaney. Senior partner*, says the sign. He's very proud of that title, the fact that he managed to get himself promoted over much older, more experienced, less ruthlessly determined people.

'Can I help you?' Howie's secretary, Zoe, glances up from her computer and smiles blandly. Her eyes take in my trainers which are stained with dirt, my cheap-looking handbag and my hair that I haven't washed or brushed for a while.

I try to ignore the faint look of distaste that crosses her face. 'I'd like to speak to Howard Delaney,' I say firmly. 'Is he about?'

Howie didn't reply to my message and hasn't answered my calls, so I've come here where I can confront him directly.

'He's with a client at the moment,' says Zoe. 'Can I ask what it's concerning?'

'It's personal. I'm his sister, Jessica.'

'I see.' Her expression doesn't change. She looks like a pretty doll. And everything about her is glossy, I think, from her black hair to her bee-stung lips.

She pushes a button with an immaculately manicured nail.

'Hello, yes, your sister Jessica is here to see you,' she says. She pauses as she listens to his reply. 'Right, OK. Will do.'

She looks up at me. 'He says do you want to come back later or meet him at home because he's going to be quite a while?'

'It's OK. I'll wait,' I say firmly, sitting down and taking out my phone. 'Can I have the wifi code?'

Her eyes widen. 'Um . . . sure. Would you like a coffee?'

'That would be great.'

I watch her totter away, restricted by her tight skirt and heels. Her figure is attractively curvaceous and, although Vicky is slender and athletic, I know that Zoe's exactly Howie's usual type. It wouldn't surprise me if there was something going on between them. It's how he and Vicky met after all. She was his secretary while he was married to Louise and it was only when Louise found out about their affair that he came clean and got a divorce. He's had so much practice lying to the women in his life I suppose I shouldn't be surprised that he's lied to me too. But still, I'm angry. And I'm particularly annoyed that he hasn't returned my calls.

I've finished my cup of coffee and am just scrolling through the news when the door bursts open, and Howie bustles out along with a middle-aged man. There's a lot of back slapping and laughter as the man leaves and Howie sees me. A worried frown flits across his face before his features rearrange themselves into his usual hearty grin.

'Hi, Jess!' he exclaims. 'What are you doing here?'

'I need to speak to you privately,' I say tersely. Surely he knows why I'm here? Why is he pretending he doesn't? Dad must have told him by now.

'Sure,' he says, steering me into his office.

'So, what can I do for you?' He sits behind his desk and looks at his watch.

'Don't give me your bullshit. You know why I'm here,' I say. I'm angered by the implication that he doesn't have time to talk to me.

His eyes narrow. 'Yes. You mean about what Margery told you at the funeral?'

'If you mean the small fact that our mother wasn't actually our mother, then yes.'

'Jessica—'

'And don't try to tell me you didn't know. You must have known. You were what? Fourteen or fifteen at the time she left.'

He sighs. 'Fifteen.'

I shake my head. 'I just don't understand it. How could you all keep something like that from me?'

Howie spreads his arms wide. 'I was just a kid. I went along with what Dad and Jean told me. They thought it would be better for you if you didn't know. What you don't know can't hurt you. I think that was the idea.'

I twist my hands in my lap. My anger is slowly evaporating and a wave of sadness washes over me. 'But I think I did know, deep down,' I say. *What you don't know can hurt you*, I think. Half-guessed secrets can damage you more than the plain truth in the same way that hidden reefs under the sea are more treacherous than rocks in open view.

And I feel a sudden deep jealousy. Howie got to know our mother for the first fifteen years of his life, and I didn't. It's not fair. 'What was she like?' I ask.

He lifts his shoulders and frowns. 'She looked a bit like you actually. She had red hair, freckles. Kind of pretty.'

'I mean, what was she like as a person?'

Howie shrugs. 'She was our mother. I didn't really think of her as a person. She was a good mother, though.'

I sigh with frustration. 'What does that even mean? She abandoned us, didn't she?'

'She was a good mother until I was about twelve, but she changed after you were born. She suffered from postnatal depression, I think. That's why Mum – I mean Aunt Jean – came to live with us.'

His words hit me in the gut. So, it was because of me. Of course she couldn't love me. Because there is something fundamentally wrong with me.

Howie misinterprets my silence. 'I know how you feel. I've been so angry with her all my life, but over the past few years I suppose I've reached a kind of acceptance. You can't really blame her. Depression is an illness.'

You don't have to tell me that, I think.

'Did you ever meet the guy she left with – Michael? Do you know what his surname was?'

He looks surprised. 'No. I was at boarding school at the time. Dad didn't even tell me she was gone until I came back for the summer holidays. I think he hoped she would come back before the term finished and I would never have to know anything.'

Yes, that sounds like Dad, I think. *Burying his head in the sand, pretending nothing had happened.*

'She didn't leave a note or say goodbye?' I ask. 'She's never tried to contact you?'

'Nope. Nothing.'

His face twists with sudden anger. 'Jess, I know you don't agree with what Dad did, but really, you got off lightly. Imagine what it's like knowing that your own mother doesn't want you. Doesn't love you.'

Well, I know now, I think, my own anger bubbling up inside me. I repress it. There's no point in taking it out on Howie. We're both victims in this situation.

'And you never tried to contact her? You've never been curious about what she's doing now?' I ask.

'Nope.'

'Someone must know where she went – one of her friends in Cirencester maybe. Was she friendly with any of the neighbours?'

He shrugs. 'I don't know. Like I said, they packed me off to boarding school as soon as they could.'

'What was our address in Cirencester?'

He hesitates, tilts his head to one side. 'Are you sure you want to know?'

'Positive.'

'It was forty-two Church Street,' he sighs and drums his fingers on the desk. 'But you're not thinking of going there, are you, Jess? I'm not sure it's such a good idea, raking the past up like this. If she doesn't want to be found, she doesn't want to be found.'

Chapter Thirty

Maybe Howie is right. Digging too deep is never a good idea. You never know what you might discover. And it's not that I don't have misgivings as I tap the address he gave me into my satnav and head out onto the M40. I have no idea if I'm doing the right thing. But I don't think I could stop if I wanted to. I've started on this course now and I must carry on until I find the truth – why my mother left me. Why I wasn't enough. Why I've never been enough.

The traffic is snarled up on the road around Oxford and the sun is high in the sky by the time I turn off the main road and wind my way through small, picture-perfect Cotswold villages towards Cirencester.

I expected to recognise something, some landmark to trigger a cascade of memories. But nothing seems familiar at all as I drive through the quaint old market town. And even when I turn into Church Street, there's no sudden lightning bolt of recognition.

Number forty-two is a tall, Victorian semi, the stone walls stained dark with age and pollution. The front garden is concreted over, with a large stone bird bath in the centre and a neat border of lavender and other small shrubs. It's pretty in the sunshine – not at all sinister looking – but as I head down the path towards the front door, a feeling stirs deep in my gut and coils its way up to my throat. And I fight a strong compulsion to walk back to the car and drive away.

I don't turn around. Instead, I take a deep breath, plaster a polite smile on my face and ring the doorbell. After a couple of minutes, a woman opens the door. She's alternative looking, with dark hair tied back simply, a nose ring, her face bare of make-up. And she's close to my age, maybe slightly younger. From inside the house I can hear children squabbling and a man telling them off. I swallow my disappointment. I'd hoped for someone older, someone that might remember my family.

'Hi,' I say, forcing a bright smile. 'I'm Jessica Delaney. You don't know me, but I used to live in this house when I was a little girl.' I pause for breath. 'I was just driving through the area and I thought I'd like to see the place, take some photos for my family to see, if you don't mind?'

She gives me a brief assessing stare and then clearly decides that I'm not casing the joint for a burglary because she smiles and says, 'Um, no, of course not. Would you like to see inside?'

'Is that OK? I'd love to,' I say, hardly believing my luck.

'It's fine, if you don't mind the mess. I'm Saskia, by the way.' She ushers me into a small, dark hallway and through to the kitchen. In the kitchen a girl and a boy are sitting at the table doing a jigsaw puzzle and a handsome grey-haired man is wiping down the surfaces.

'This is my husband, Ryan. Ryan, this is Jessica,' Saskia says. 'Jessica used to live here, and she wants to take some pictures to show her family.'

'Oh, I see.' He looks up with polite interest. 'When were you here?'

'Oh, a long time ago,' I say. 'It must have been . . .' – I do a quick calculation – '1990 when we left.'

It must all be stored somewhere in my brain, I suppose. But right now, I'm drawing a blank.

'Do you want to take a look at the garden?' Saskia asks. 'It must have changed a lot since you lived here.'

I nod and follow her out through the conservatory.

The sunlight blinds me for a second as I step outside. When my eyes adjust, I make out a long narrow garden with balls and scooters lying around on the lawn. There's a vegetable patch and a shed at the end.

'How much have you done to the garden?' I ask.

She smiles. 'We haven't had time to do much but the

couple that lived here before us completely redid it. The only feature that might be the same as when you were here is the sundial.'

'Sundial?'

She leads me to part of the garden divided from the rest by a low hedge. There's a circular patio with benches around it and in the centre there's an old stone sundial.

I stare at the sundial thoughtfully. It's ornate and unusual. Instead of the normal triangular-shaped pointer, the gnomon is a small statue of a boy fishing, his rod casting a shadow to indicate the time.

'It's beautiful, isn't it?' says Saskia. 'It's one of the original features of the house, close to a hundred years old. At least that's what the estate agent told us.'

I study it carefully. I have no memory of it, but there's something about it that I feel is important – something nudging at the back of my mind. I walk around it, taking snaps from various angles. 'For my father,' I say to Saskia, and she smiles and nods.

'Do you want to see the rest of the house?' she asks when I'm finished.

'That would be great, if you don't mind,' I say. 'I'd like to see if I can remember which room was my bedroom.'

The staircase is narrow and uneven. As I climb, with Saskia close behind, the heat builds and the feeling of unease I had before returns and grows stronger.

I stop on the landing, confused.

'Anything seem familiar?' asks Saskia.

I shake my head.

'There are three floors. Maybe it's right at the top of the house.'

We go up the next flight of stairs and I grasp the banister, pausing to catch my breath when I reach the top.

'This is it,' I say with sudden conviction, stopping outside a door on the right. Along with the certainty, the feeling of apprehension tightens in my chest – inexplicable and visceral.

'It's my son's room. Go ahead and take a look,' says Saskia. She laughs lightly. 'I apologise for the mess in advance.'

I push the door open. There are football posters and pictures of wrestlers on walls and the bed has a WWE duvet cover. Lego is strewn across the carpet along with lots of books that have just been tossed onto the floor: *Goosebumps*, *Diary of a Wimpy Kid*, *Percy Jacksons*. But I'm not really interested. I'm focused on one thing: the wardrobe door next to the bed.

Something bad is happening and I don't know what it is.

My breathing has become shallower. I feel dizzy and afraid. All I know is that I need to open that wardrobe and see what's inside.

'Can I just . . . ?' I say. And without waiting for a reply I tug open the door.

Inside there are boys' clothes – shorts, T-shirts, trousers, jackets, a football kit. I push them to one side and reveal what I already knew was there.

A small white door about a metre wide, bolted shut.

'Oh, you've found our secret cupboard,' says Saskia.

Without waiting for her permission, I slide the lock open and peer inside. There's no light and I can't see much, just a few dark shapes and a strangely familiar musty smell fills my nostrils.

'It's an interesting feature, isn't it?' Saskia continues. 'I believe it used to be a passageway that ran along the back of all the houses, but they bricked it up a long time ago. Our boys love it. They sometimes use it as a den, though I worry about how solid the floor in there is.' She gives a little laugh.

I can't answer. My chest feels as if it's about to explode and my heart is racing. I close my eyes and I'm trapped in the darkness, pounding on the door for someone to let me out. The air is thick with dust and I feel as if I'm choking.

'Are you OK?' Saskia is asking.

I open my eyes and see her concerned face swimming in front of me.

'Yes, sorry, I just feel a bit dizzy.' I struggle to my feet and force a smile. I'm worried that if I don't get out of here soon, I'm going to have a full-blown panic attack right here in front of her.

'Excuse me,' I blurt and lunge out of the room, down the stairs until I reach the hallway where I sit on the bottom step, hugging my knees.

'Would you like a glass of water?' Saskia asks. She's followed me down and she's standing over me, giving me a weird look. She's probably thinking she's made a mistake letting a strange woman into her house.

'Yes, thank you,' I say, heading into the kitchen and accepting a glass of water, cool liquid sliding down my throat as my heart rate slowly settles. 'Sorry about that. I'm not sure what came over me.'

'It's the heat, I expect,' says Saskia.

'Yes, that must be it.'

But it wasn't just the heat, I think. There was something else – something connected with that cupboard. It's puzzling and disturbing. And I can only think that I must have got myself trapped in there as a little girl. But trying to remember feels like pulling back layers of dressing on a festering wound and I recoil from examining the memory too closely.

'Well, thank you so much for letting me look around,' I say, draining the glass. 'My dad will be thrilled to see these pictures.'

'No worries,' says Saskia. 'Are you sure you're OK? Is there anything else you want to know?'

'Actually, there is one more thing,' I venture as I head

to the door. 'I wonder if there's anyone still living around here who would remember my family.'

Ryan and Saskia look at each other.

'You want to ask Moira two doors down at number thirty-eight,' says Ryan. 'She's lived here since God knows when. If anyone remembers your family, it'll be her.'

'Thanks,' I say. 'I'll do that.'

Outside, I lean against the wall, feeling shaky and sapped of energy. My next move is obvious – to call at number thirty-eight and see if this Moira person remembers my mother at all. But everything seems to be weighing down on me – from the sky which has clouded over to an ominous grey, to the air, heavy with moisture, which feels like it is wrapping itself around me.

I'm afraid, I realise. But I don't know what it is that I'm afraid of. All I know is that every instinct is telling me to get back in the car and drive as far away from this place as possible. And in my ears, there's a low threatening hum, a vibration that's getting louder, like the rumble of a train coming closer and closer.

Chapter Thirty-One

Number thirty-eight is the same as number forty-two, except it has a green door and the garden is a riot of colour; Japanese lilies, roses and love-in-a-mist all jostle for space in the small garden, and purple buddleia crawls up the walls.

A plump, middle-aged woman is outside, stooping to pull out weeds. She's so absorbed in the task that I have to call out a couple of times before she hears me.

'Hi,' I say brightly, when I finally attract her attention. 'Are you Moira?'

She straightens up and squints at me, shielding her eyes from the sun. 'No, I'm Fran. Moira's my mother. Can I help you?'

'Maybe.' I take a deep breath. 'It's just I spoke to Saskia and Jack at number forty-two and they seemed to think that your mother might be able to help me. I'm looking for someone who remembers my family. We used to live here about thirty years ago?'

'Oh yes? What's your name?'

'My name's Jessica Delaney. You don't know me, but my family lived here at number forty-two a long time ago when—'

I don't get to finish my spiel because Fran claps her hand to her face and laughs. 'Oh my goodness, Jessica Delaney. Little Jessica Delaney! Well, haven't you grown up?'

I stare at her, bemused.

'Of course, you won't remember me, but I used to babysit for you all the time,' she continues, taking off her gardening gloves and beaming at me. 'Why don't you come in? I'm sure my mother would love to see you.'

I follow her into a cool hallway and then out to a conservatory filled with plants where an old lady is sitting in a chair dozing, clutching a book of crosswords in her hands.

'Mum, wake up!' Fran shakes her gently awake. 'Look who I found outside.'

The old lady starts, snorts a little and opens a pair of rheumy blue eyes. 'Oh, hello,' she smiles politely at me.

'Mum, you remember the Delaneys who used to live two doors down, Eve and Brian?'

I breathe in sharply, unprepared for the casual way Moira mentions Eve. Eve and Brian, like they're a couple. Eve and Brian. Not Jean and Brian. *Eve* and Brian.

Moira rubs her eyes, blinking at me in confusion. 'Yes, of course I remember, why?'

'You remember they had a little girl called Jessica?'

'Yes,' she nods.

Fran grins. 'Well, guess what? This is her. This is baby Jessica.'

Moira's eyes widen. Then she claps her hand to her chest and laughs delightedly. 'Baby Jessica! Little Jessica Delaney. Well I never! You were such a sweet little thing. Frannie, move a chair here, please, so I can see her properly.'

Fran obligingly pulls up a chair and I perch on the edge, feeling slightly awkward and embarrassed by their obvious excitement. Moira leans forward and grips my hands in her bony hands. 'Let me take a look at you, Jessica. Well, you've grown into a lovely young woman, haven't you? You look just like your mother. Frannie, why don't you make Jessica a drink? What would you like, my dear? Tea coffee, whisky?'

I laugh nervously. 'It's a bit early for whisky for me. Some tea would be nice.'

Fran ambles off to the kitchen and I'm left with Moira, who won't let go of my hand.

'You know, I was such good friends with your mother,' she says. 'We always wondered what happened to you all. You disappeared so suddenly. One day Eve was round here drinking coffee – not a word about moving – and then literally the next day you were all gone,' she says. 'So, how are Eve and Brian and young Howard? I suppose he's not so young anymore. Are they here with you?'

'No . . . er . . .' I pick at an imaginary bit of fluff on the arm of the chair. 'Actually, I was trying to find out some way to get in contact with my mother, Eve. You see, I haven't seen or heard from her since she left.'

'She left?' Moira exclaims. She stares at me.

'You didn't know?' I say, my surprise mirroring the astonishment on her face. 'She went to Australia when I was three years old. I haven't seen her since.'

Moira shakes her head firmly. 'I had no idea, my dear. It must have been shortly after you moved.'

I think about this. I'm sure Dad told me that we moved after she left because he couldn't stand living in a place where they'd been so happy. But perhaps Moira is mistaken. After all, it was a long time ago and Moira must be nearly eighty.

Fran returns with a tray of tea and biscuits and places them on the coffee table.

'Can you believe this, Fran?' Moira says to her. 'Jessica here hasn't seen Eve for thirty years. Eve went to live in Australia.'

Fran stands there open-mouthed. She turns to me. 'Really? But why?'

I take a biscuit and start chewing. 'It's a bit complicated and I don't know all the details, but apparently she met a man called Michael and ran off with him.' I swallow back the tears that are suddenly and embarrassingly rising in my throat, and I try not to choke on the biscuit. It's ridiculous to be so upset by something that happened so long ago – a betrayal by a woman that I don't even remember. 'I was hoping that maybe you knew him. I'm thinking that maybe she married him and changed her name, and if I knew his surname, it might help me find her.'

'I don't remember anyone called Michael.' Fran frowns. 'Do you, Mum?'

Moira sucks her finger. 'Well, she did have a friend called Michael. Michael Westlake. I think your father disapproved of the friendship, but as far as I know they weren't lovers and he's certainly not in Australia. He still lives nearby, in Cheltenham.'

I lean forward, excited. 'Do you have his address?'

'Um . . . no, but I may have a telephone number for you.'

She stands up stiffly, hobbles into the other room and brings back a box of contact cards. 'Ah, yes, here we are,' she says, flicking through them. 'Michael Westlake.'

She hands the card to me and I take it and tap the number into my phone. I can't see how it could be the same Michael that Dad told me about, but anyone who knew my mother could be useful.

There's a short silence while Moira picks up a cup of tea in a shaky hand and takes a sip. 'I just can't believe it,' she says. You mean that Eve left you children? And she never got in touch?'

'I've got no memory of her,' I say. I didn't even know she existed until a few days ago, but there doesn't seem to be any point in telling them that.

Moira shakes her head. 'It just doesn't sound like the Eve I knew. Eve was devoted to you and Howard. That was clear for anyone to see.'

Tears well up in my eyes and Fran puts her arm round me. 'Mum . . .' she starts but Moira continues, oblivious. 'She adored you both. She can't have been in her right mind to leave you.'

I think about what Howie said about postnatal depression. 'Was there any sign that there was something wrong with her? Did she seem depressed? My brother said she suffered from depression.'

'She wasn't always happy,' Moira says, frowning. 'And she seemed worried in those last few months, but I didn't realise she was depressed.' She stares into the distance. 'Actually, now I come to think of it, she was very upset just before you left. Her dog had gone missing the week before; do you remember Milo, Fran?'

'Yes, Milo. He was a gorgeous dog. A collie terrier cross, wasn't he?'

Moira nods. 'She loved that dog so much and she was devastated when he disappeared.'

246

'Did you try to contact her after she left?'

'I did. I tried to track her down for a while. But it was 1991. It was more difficult in those days. There was no Facebook. Most people didn't even have email or mobile phones back then.'

I nod. 'What kind of person was she?' I feel a hunger to know this piece of my life that has always been missing.

'She was . . .' Moira hesitates, trying to find the right word '. . . a passionate person. Honest to a fault. Always trying to do the right thing, stand up for what she believed in. What else, Fran? She loved animals. Um . . . she played the piano really well, too. Do you remember, Fran? She played at that street party we had.'

Fran nods.

'She was a good friend,' Moira continues, her eyes misting over.

She leans over and pats my hand. 'She looked very like you, my dear. I think we've got a photo of her somewhere. Would you like to see it?'

I stare at her, dumbstruck. I never expected or imagined she would have a picture of Eve. And I'm so overwhelmed all I can do is nod.

Moira stands up stiffly and rummages in a drawer. 'It's a shame that all the photos are this digital rubbish now,' she grumbles. 'We take lots of photos and never look at them again. It used to be so exciting going to get them developed and waiting for them to arrive.'

She places the album on her lap and turns the pages.

'Ah, here we are,' she says, tapping a picture. It's a photo of Eve and Dad at a garden party. They're sitting under the shade of a large tree at a table smiling and raising their wine glasses to the camera. It's a small, slightly blurry image, and all I can make out of Eve is her thick red hair and the fact that she's wearing a pale green jacket with shoulder pads. She looks a little bit like me and a little like Jean.

I turn the page and there's another photo of her sitting on a swing cradling a tiny baby. I stare at it, my heart in my mouth.

'Can you guess who that baby is?' asks Moira, smiling.

'Me?' I venture. 'Or Howie?'

She slides it out of the album and reads the writing on the back. 'It says Eve and baby Jessica 1987. Weren't you a sweet little thing?'

In the picture Eve is looking down at me, head bent, with an expression of complete adoration in her eyes. For a moment I can't breathe. Grief and loss rise in my throat, choking me. Then I look closer and notice the pendant around her neck. It's small but clearly a swallow in flight. It's the same pendant Mum gave me just before she died, I realise with a thrill of excitement. So that's why Mum said it didn't belong to her, I think. It was never hers. It was Eve's.

'Can I have a copy of this?' I ask. 'Do you have the negative?'

'You can keep it if you like,' says Moira.

'Really?' I hold the album in my hands, trembling. 'Are you sure?'

'Of course I am,' she says, taking out the photo and handing it to me. I hold it delicately as if it were a precious artefact, and then I slip it quickly into my handbag before she can change her mind.

Chapter Thirty-Two

In the car, I take out the photo of my mother and pore over it, absorbing every detail: the freckles across the bridge of her nose, the gap in her teeth, the strand of red hair clinging to her neck, the look in her eyes, the warmth of her expression. Whatever she did later, even though she abandoned me, I'm sure that in that moment she loved me.

Tears of grief and anger roll down my cheeks. I'm crying for what I've never had – all the years I've missed. Why didn't Dad tell me? If he had, I would have had the chance to try and find her. I would have at least had an image of her. By denying her existence he's robbed me of even her memory.

I brush the tears away angrily and place the photo carefully back in my bag. There's no point in wallowing in grief and anger. Not while there's still a chance I can find her. I glance in the rear-view mirror to check that my eyes aren't too red, then I take out my phone and call the number Moira gave me. There's no answer, so I leave a message on Michael's answerphone and a few minutes later he calls me back and gives me directions to his house.

Twenty-five minutes later I pull up outside a small, modern bungalow. The garden is overgrown with wildflowers and nettles and dominated by a large mountain ash, with bird feeders dangling from its branches. There's a beaten-up grey van on his driveway and horrific pictures of animals being tortured sellotaped to his door.

I ring the bell, trying to ignore the pictures. And a large black dog looms up behind the frosted glass, barking loudly.

'Be quiet, Daisy!' a man shouts and the door bursts open.

He's about seventy maybe, tanned and wiry with a weather-beaten face and straggly grey hair tied back in a ponytail. Two dogs – the large black one and a Jack Russell – flank him, barking and growling at me.

'Sorry about them,' he says, pressing the big dog's head away. 'Don't worry. Their bark is worse that their bite. I'm Michael, by the way. Come in, come in.'

I follow him into a cramped, untidy living room, dominated by two sofas that are covered in dog blankets.

Michael lifts up a tabby cat sleeping in the armchair.

The cat gives a loud, indignant miaow and stalks away, tail quivering.

'Please, take a seat,' Michael says. 'Don't worry about Sheba. She thinks she owns the place.'

I perch awkwardly on the edge of the armchair. 'Thank you,' I say. 'And thank you for agreeing to see me.'

He sits opposite me and scrutinises me with shrewd, friendly blue eyes.

'So, you're Eve Delaney's girl,' he says.

'Did you know her well?' I ask. He seems like an old hippy and I wonder how he fitted into the respectable, middle-class life I imagine my mother had. The woman I saw in the photo looked conventional and smart. Not at all anti-establishment.

Michael bites his thumbnail. 'You could say that,' he says. 'We were very good friends for a while.'

Very, I think. *What exactly does that mean?* 'How did you meet her?' I ask.

He rolls up a cigarette and frowns. 'I met your mother in 1988 when she joined the animal rights movement I belonged to.'

I stare at him nonplussed. But I'm not sure why I should be surprised. It fits with what Moira said about how much Eve loved animals. My image of my mother is constantly shifting and all the time she's becoming more real to me.

'We hit it off right away,' he continues. 'She was a gem, your mum – one of a kind.'

I think about what Moira told me about Dad disapproving of Eve's relationship with Michael. 'I know this is a bit of a personal question,' I venture awkwardly, 'but were you ever . . . more than friends?'

The idea seems to amuse him. He slaps his thigh and chuckles. 'No, no, nothing like that. We were just friends. That's all.'

I feel a strange and unexpected sense of relief. I'm rooting for Eve and I want to believe in her. I want to believe that she was a person of integrity and that she was loyal to my dad. But it doesn't quite add up.

'Moira, my mum's neighbour, said that my father didn't approve of your friendship. Do you have any idea why?'

He shrugs. 'I belonged to an underground branch of the movement. We did things that weren't always strictly legal, like breaking into labs and abattoirs. Nothing to hurt anyone, you understand. Eve never got involved in breaking the law, but even so, your father didn't like it. He thought I was a bad influence. In the end she stopped telling him when she was meeting me, just to keep the peace.'

'Are you still in contact with her?' I ask, my heart in my mouth.

But he shakes his head sadly. 'No, I'm afraid I've no idea

253

what happened to her. She just upped and left suddenly without a word. I missed her for quite a while.'

'When was the last time you saw her?' I ask.

He stubs out his roll-up and chews his finger thoughtfully.

'It must've been a couple of days before your family left. She was going through a bad patch. Her dog went missing and she was fighting with your father.'

I lean forward. I'm getting closer to the truth about her disappearance, I feel it instinctively. 'What did they argue about?'

He shrugs. 'She didn't really tell me.'

'Do you think she could have been having an affair? Was there someone else in her life? Another Michael? An Australian maybe?'

Michael taps his fingers on the armrest. 'I'm pretty sure she wasn't having an affair. As far as I know, she was completely faithful to your father. And loyal. Maybe more loyal than she should have been.'

He stands up before I can probe further. 'All this talk is making me thirsty,' he says abruptly. 'I fancy a cuppa. How about you?'

'That would be lovely,' I reply dubiously. The glimpse I had of the kitchen as I passed earlier doesn't inspire confidence, but the longer I stay, the more I'm likely to find out about Eve.

'Sorry, I've only got soya milk. I hope that's OK,' he says, as he returns with two steaming mugs of tea.

'No problem.'

The milk has curdled slightly, and I take a cautious sip. His last statement has been preying on my mind. 'You said just now that my mother was more loyal than she should have been. What did you mean exactly?' I ask.

'Well . . .' He hesitates. 'I don't know this for certain, but I don't think your father treated her well.'

I feel a chill. 'What do you mean?'

'Are you sure you want to know?'

'Yes. I want to know the truth. All of it.'

'I'm pretty sure he was violent. I questioned her about it a few times, even suggested she leave him, but she would never admit that he hurt her or even consider the idea of divorce.'

I gape at him. My first, instinctive reaction to what he's saying is anger and disbelief. How dare this man say such vile things about my father? 'You don't know my dad. He would never lay a finger on anyone,' I protest.

He slurps his tea. 'Well, I admit, I didn't know for sure. All I know is that she often had bruises on her legs and arms, like someone had kicked her.'

'People get bruises all the time. She could have just bumped into a table or something . . .'

He flicks his hand impatiently. 'Yes, I know, but I think it was the way she reacted when I asked her about the bruises. She obviously didn't want to talk about it, and she acted guilty, like she had something to hide.'

I feel rage bubbling up inside me. 'You're wrong,' I say. My first impressions of this man were wrong. He no longer looks benign. He's a malicious scandal monger. No wonder my father didn't approve of him.

'Well, I have to go now,' I say coldly, placing my tea down on the table and standing up.

'So soon? Oh, I'm sorry if I've offended you. It's just you said you wanted the truth.'

'Well. Thank you for your time. No, don't get up. I'll let myself out.' I say tartly

He's wrong, I think, fuming in the car outside. My hands are shaking, my chest is tight, and I feel another panic attack coming on. Rooting in the glove compartment, I take out a beta blocker and swallow it down without water. Then I take out my phone and scroll through the photos I took at number forty-two. The house takes on a new aspect in my current frame of mind. It seems almost sinister – the windows look black and menacing, and from the angle of the photo it seems to loom over me. I shiver and click on another picture, and another, trawling through until I come to one of the garden and the sundial. I examine it closely, that distinctive statue of the boy holding a fishing rod.

Suddenly, something clicks in my head. I picture Mum sitting in our kitchen – a cup of tea shaking in her hand. She was rambling – her mind wandering and confused. At least I thought it was random rambling at the time.

He killed her, you know. He said it was the fishing boy who killed her, but I know it wasn't.

Is it possible that what she said wasn't completely arbitrary? Could she have been talking about the fishing boy on the sundial? I think about the way Mum seemed to muddle up time and place in her last few weeks. Recent events and things that happened a long time ago, all jumbled in her mind – chronology shaken up like a pack of cards, thrown up in the air and left to land randomly.

He killed her.

What if she hadn't been talking about Kate Chandry at all? What if she'd been talking about something that happened much earlier – something that happened in the garden of number forty-two?

Chapter Thirty-Three

Dark clouds are gathering as I drive out of town. There's a low rumble of thunder and lightning cracks the sky. *Michael was way off the mark*, I think angrily, hunching over the steering wheel. He didn't even know my dad. Dad isn't violent. He's gentle and easy-going. He doesn't even like killing slugs in the garden.

The rain intensifies and I switch on the windscreen wipers, swerving around a cyclist struggling up the hill. Then I slow down as I approach the village of Bibury. As I drive over the bridge, my rage gradually subsides, and doubt starts to creep in.

I've only witnessed Dad losing his temper maybe twice in my life, but both times it was dramatic and scary. It was as if he kept all his anger compressed until there was nowhere for it to go and he would just explode.

I haven't thought about it for years, but once during an argument with Mum when I was about fourteen, I remember him slashing a picture with a kitchen knife. I've no idea what led up to it, all I remember is the shocking moment when he sliced through the canvas and the sound of Mum screaming at him. And I recall other incidents which seemed insignificant at the time, hissed arguments late at night, overheard from the bedroom. And the time he threw a plate at Mum during a fight – he missed, of course, and I don't think he was actually aiming at her. But now, in the light of Michael's statement, all these incidents seem like they could add up to something sinister, fitting into a new narrative – a narrative where my father was a violent bully.

By the time I reach Oxford the weather has turned into a full-blown storm. My windscreen is drenched in rain even with the wipers on full speed, and leaves are being whipped up into a frenzy. It feels as if the storm is inside my mind as well as outside. My thoughts are in turmoil, the conversations I had this morning with Moira and Michael whirling around my head. There are things that don't make sense. Dad told me that Eve had left before we relocated to Wendover. It was the reason he'd moved in the first place, he said. He'd wanted to get away from everything that reminded him of her. So why was Moira so adamant that my mother and father had still been together when they'd moved?

The traffic moves sluggishly and then stops. *Of course, Moira is an old woman*, I think. And it all happened a long time ago. She could be confused. And I'd probably believe that she was mistaken if it weren't for the other glaring inconsistency in Dad's story. He also told me that Mum ran away to Australia with her lover, while both Michael and Moira seemed convinced that she didn't have an affair. Dad must have misinterpreted Eve's friendship with Michael because if he didn't, then he lied. And if Dad lied, then why? I can't think of any reason he would invent a story like that, unless . . .

I jump as the car behind hoots loudly. The traffic has finally started moving and I hadn't noticed. I stall the engine and then start it up again, crawling along slowly. *No, that idea is ludicrous*, I tell myself firmly. I'm overwrought and I haven't had enough sleep, that's all. I shouldn't have stopped taking my medication. My mind is playing tricks on me, the way it did in Spain. All I need is to take my meds and get a proper night's sleep. Once I've rested, I'll feel better about everything and I'll be able to see more clearly.

When I finally arrive home to my empty flat it's already dark. The rain has stopped, and the wind has died down a little. I realise I haven't eaten all day except for the biscuit I had at Moira's, so I heat up a packet of noodles and eat them in front of the TV. I stare vacantly at the news, something about a high school shooting in America and politicians arguing over a new bill, but I can't concentrate. I keep thinking of Mum, hearing her voice – the seemingly random things she said. The words beating out a rhythm over and over, like a drumbeat.

He killed her. I know too much. He said it was the fishing boy.

I turn up the TV to try to drown out the sound.

Eventually, I crawl into bed at about two o'clock. I'm so tired, but I can't get to sleep. Adrenaline is coursing through my body and the wind is howling outside, the branches of the apple tree scraping against the window, as if they're trying to get in. A suspicion has bored its way into my head and, now it's there, it's become a conviction. The reason I can't trace my mum, the reason that she didn't contact Moira or Michael or me or Howie was because she couldn't. Because she was already dead.

Chapter Thirty-Four

All night thunder has been rolling and rumbling, the air crackling with static, and I wake with pain drilling into my head. I climb out of bed and open the window, trying to breathe. But the storm has done nothing to alleviate the heat; the air is still humid and oppressive, and it feels as if I'm breathing in something viscous like syrup. I take a couple of painkillers and have a shower, letting the cool water sluice over my body, trying to wash away the suspicion tormenting me.

He killed her. My father killed Eve. No matter which way I look at it, it's the only explanation that seems to fit with the facts. Why else would he lie about whether she left before or after the move to Wendover? Why else would he invent a lover? And why else would she disappear so suddenly without trace?

I curl up in the corner of the shower, hugging my knees. I want these thoughts to go away, but they won't. They just keep getting louder in my head until they're hammering against my skull. He killed her. He killed Eve.

Maybe they were arguing, and he pushed her. Maybe she hit her head on the sundial. An accident then. At least an accident I could forgive.

But there's another suspicion, even more insidious, snaking its way into my mind. Did he kill Jean too?

I picture her in the living room the day I moved out. She'd been about to tell me something, hadn't she? I think about the way she clammed up when Dad came in.

He wants me dead. I know too much, she said. Was she talking too much, her tongue loosened by the dementia? It would have been so easy for him to slip some ground-up pills into her food.

Cold water drums on my head and back, stinging my skin. I want to stay here forever and pretend none of this is happening. But I can't. I must do something. But I don't know what to do. Should I go to the police?

I force myself up and out of the shower. And after drying myself and dressing, I google the Thames Valley Police, find their number and tap it into my phone. But as soon as I hear the ringtone, my courage fails and I press end call, my heart thundering. I've got no proof. They wouldn't believe me. All Dad would have to do would be to mention what happened in Madrid. They would get in contact with Dr Lopez and then I'd be screwed. Who would they be more likely to trust, a woman with a history of mental illness or an eminent psychiatrist and a concerned father?

I put the phone on the kitchen counter and make myself a cup of black coffee, trying to stay alert. I'm so tired and light-headed. God knows how much I slept last night. It can't have been more than a couple of hours.

The coffee is hot and bitter, and it scalds my throat as I gulp it down, but I barely notice. I'm trying to work out what to do. Should I confront Dad or tell Howie? I'm just about to ring Howie, the phone in my hand, when it vibrates and bursts into song, making me jump. It must be the police ringing me back, I think. I put it down on the table, letting it ring. But it carries on, loud and insistent, hurting my ears. So, at last I pick it up and swipe upwards to answer.

It's not the police. It's Ajay. He sounds rattled and a little out of breath. 'Um, sorry to bother you so early in the morning,' he says. 'But it's your dad. I'm afraid he's collapsed.'

The words take a moment to sink in. But when they do, the shock pierces my skull like a knife. It's the last thing I was expecting and despite all my suspicions, despite the terrible things I think he might have done, he's still my dad.

'Is he OK?' I manage, trying to breathe.

'Yes, I think so. We're at the medical centre. They're seeing him now.'

'OK, I'll be right there,' I say.

I jump in the car and speed along the country roads to Wendover, a cocktail of complicated emotions swilling around inside me. When I get there Ajay and Dad are in the waiting room and Dad is sitting there, clutching an ice pack to his head. He looks fine and I feel a rush of relief, immediately followed by anger. Why should I be relieved? Why should I care what happens to him?

'Are you OK?' I say tersely, sitting down next to him. My hands are shaking, and I feel nauseous.

'I'm fine,' Dad snaps irritably. 'It was just a dizzy spell, that's all. I don't know what all the fuss is about.'

Ajay smiles at me. 'There's nothing to worry about,' he tells me. 'The doctor thinks it was just dehydration and stress. It was a bit shocking, though. He just keeled over in the close and hit his head on the kerb. But no real damage has been done. Luckily, I was on my way to work and saw it happen.'

'Thank you so much,' I say automatically. 'Don't you have to get to the practice? I don't want you to be late for work.'

'It's no problem.' He looks at his watch. 'I haven't got any appointments today until ten.' He stands up and picks up his jacket. 'You take care of yourself, Mr Delaney.' He pats Dad on the shoulder. Then he turns to me. 'Well, I'll pop in after work to check on him. Are you all right? You look . . . quite tired.'

'I'm fine. I haven't been sleeping well, that's all,' I say. 'Thanks again for looking after Dad.'

And he smiles more widely this time. 'Anytime. What are neighbours for?'

After the doctor has checked Dad one more time, I drive him home. Sitting close to him in the car, I catch a whiff of BO and I realise he hasn't washed in a while. And as I open the door, I'm met with a smell of stale air and rotten food. In the kitchen, dirty dishes and mugs are piled up on the draining board. It's obvious he hasn't done any washing-up since I left. The sight should make me feel pity. He's an old man who's lost his wife, but now the initial shock of his accident is over, my suspicion is still simmering away beneath the surface. Is this all an act, I wonder – the respectable father, the loving, grieving husband?

'Do you want a cup of tea, Dad?' I ask once we're inside the house.

I can't confront him. What would he do if he knew what I suspected? If I'm right that he killed Mum because she was talking too much, he could be capable of anything – even harming me. No, I need to be clever. Cool. I need to find proof before I make any accusations.

'Oh yes, that's a good idea.' He sits by the window in the

266

living room, staring blankly out at the close. and I wash up two of the cups and make us some tea.

'Howard told me you went to Cirencester to visit our old house,' he says, as I hand him his mug. His tone is neutral, careful. But his eyes as they look up at me are suddenly sharp and watchful. He's trying to find out what I know, I think.

'Yes,' I say, equally wary. I feel like we're playing a game of poker, both of us unwilling to reveal our hand. 'I wanted to find out about Eve – my mother. I thought someone might be able to tell me where she'd gone or would know how to contact her.'

He shifts in his chair, adjusting his trousers. 'And? Did you find anything useful?'

'No, not really. I took some pictures of our old house, though.'

I show him the photos on my phone, studying his reaction carefully. When we get to the image of the bird bath, there's a flicker of something in his eyes. It's slight and quickly veiled but I've seen it and I can't unsee it. I know it could seem like such a small thing to base a feeling of certainty on, but somehow in that moment I'm sure that I'm right. My mother died right there in the garden of number forty-two. And I'm pretty sure now that it can't have been an accident. If it was, then why would he try to hide it? Why tell everyone that she left?

A wave of cold revulsion washes over me and I feel ice to my fingertips.

'That was in the garden while we were there, wasn't it?' I say casually, trying to keep my voice from cracking.

'Yes,' he says, 'I believe so.' He takes the phone in his hands and peers at it thoughtfully. 'The rest of the garden has changed beyond recognition, though,' he sighs. 'Apart from the apple tree. That's still there. You helped me plant that. Do you remember?'

'No, I don't.' I'm having trouble focusing on what he's saying, trouble hiding the rage bubbling up inside me.

'We were happy there,' he says. 'Your mother – I mean Eve – was happy.' Tears well up in his eyes. Jean wasn't the only one who was good at acting, I reflect.

He wipes his eyes and stands up. 'Excuse me, Jessica, I think I need to lie down. I still feel a little dizzy.' He turns and smiles at me. 'I love you,' he says and shuffles away to the door.

I don't answer. My father has never been a demonstrative man. I could count on the fingers of one hand the number of times he's told me he loves me. A few days ago, a protestation of love would have been surprising and touching. But now I just think, *Why? What's he playing at?* Suspicion twists in my gut. If he killed my mother, he needs to pay for it. I will make him pay. But before I can do that, I need proof. I stand up and stare out of the window. At Ajay's house and Polly's house.

As I'm looking out, Polly emerges from her door and opens the boot to her car. How do you uncover evidence of a murder that happened nearly thirty years ago? It's not as if there's a body to collect DNA samples from. Eve must be buried somewhere, I think. She can't have just disappeared. Where, though? In the garden at number forty-two? But someone would have discovered her remains when they re-landscaped the garden. No. If Eve's body had been found, it would have led to my father. And Dad's smarter than that. He wouldn't have done anything so obvious. I remember playing chess with him when I was a kid. He never made the straightforward move. He always managed to surprise me.

I rest my head against the windowpane. I'm so tired I can barely keep my eyes open. *Jean might have known where Eve is buried*, I think. She was there, living with us at number forty-two – she must have helped to cover up the murder. If only she was still alive, I could ask her. I swallow the grief rising in my throat. I wish I could speak to her just one more time. I would tell her that I love her and that I forgive her despite everything. I know she must have been operating under duress. She must have been scared. Perhaps she was scared for her life too.

I watch as a post van drives into the close and the postman hops out and slips a letter through Ajay's post box.

I'm struck by a thought. I can't speak to Mum, but maybe she can still speak to me.

Seized by a sudden sense of purpose, I go to her desk and tug open the top drawer.

The diary is still there, on top of all her papers. Dad hasn't got around to sorting out her stuff yet, thank God. I snatch it up quickly and slip it in my bag, closing the drawer carefully and quietly. Then I slip out of the front door. I don't bother saying goodbye.

Chapter Thirty-Five

At home I lie in bed reading Mum's diary again. I read it carefully, poring over each word, searching for significance in even the simplest statements.

I went to the hairdresser's today. I spoke to Polly. Howie and Vicky came around. They are building a new extension. We went to the Crow's Nest.

Here and there Dad has added a comment – a reminder of something she ate or said. There's nothing that sheds any light on her or Eve's death.

I flick through feeling frustrated, trying to make sense of it all. There must be something here, I think, some kind of clue. But there's nothing that seems to relate to Eve. I turn to the end of the notebook – to the neatly torn-out page at the back – and stare at it thoughtfully. Who tore it out and when? Did Dad remove it because she'd written something that implicated him? Or was it Mum herself? Maybe she simply needed a piece of paper for a shopping list or some other innocent purpose. Either way, I'm probably never going to know.

I close my eyes, feeling suddenly incredibly tired, and before I know it, I've dropped off to sleep with the notebook still clutched in my hand.

About half an hour later I'm woken by the sound of my phone buzzing loudly next to my bed. It's a message from Sean. I open it unenthusiastically. *Hey, just wondering when you'll be up for that drink*, he's written. *How about this Saturday?*

Can't he take a hint? Can't he accept that not every woman in the entire universe is dying to sleep with him? I mark the message as read, prop myself up against my pillow and open my photo file. I swipe through the pictures I took in Cirencester, looking for anything that I might have missed.

Then I pick up my handbag from where I dropped it by the bed and take out the photo Moira gave me – the picture of Eve holding me in her arms. I was so tiny, my feet and hands scrunched up, my mouth pursed as if I was about to cry. It must have been taken shortly after I was born.

I've never seen a photo of me as such a small baby. In fact, there are hardly any baby photos of me. I suppose Eve must have been in most of them and Dad decided to destroy them – along with all evidence of her. *How dare he?*

I think with a flash of intense anger. *How dare he have taken this away from me?* I trace my fingers lightly over Eve's face. She looks so beautiful, her face lit up with love. I trace my fingers down to the swallow pendant around her neck.

I'm thinking about Mum – Jean – sitting on her bed in the middle of the night, holding her jewellery box, guilt plastered all over her face. And then later, in the living room, pressing it into my hands. *Keep it safe*, she said. *There are lots of memories stored in there.*

I climb out of bed and tug open the bottom drawer of the chest. The jewellery box is there, where I stowed it for safekeeping, under all my socks and tights. I take it out and place it on the bed. Then I kneel next to the bed, like a child praying. Teasing out the pendant, I hold it up to the light, the diamonds glowing. *Eve wore this*, I think. *It was next to her skin.* Slowly, I bring it to my lips and kiss it. Then I fasten it around my own neck.

One by one I take out and examine the other necklaces and bracelets and earrings. It's mostly costume jewellery, some silver bangles, a gold chain, but otherwise nothing of any monetary value. Did they all belong to Eve or is some of the jewellery mixed up with Mum's? I wonder.

When the box is finally empty and the jewellery is sprawled all over the covers, I sit on the bed and weigh the box in my hands. I lift the lid slowly and run my fingers along the padded silk lining. Halfway along, I feel something small poking out of the join. With a thrill of excitement, I pick at it and tease out a piece of ribbon. *Now, why is that there?* I wonder. I give it a sharp tug and to my surprise, the bottom of the box lifts out, revealing a secret compartment.

My mouth falls open and I draw in my breath sharply.

Inside the compartment, there's a thick, lined piece of paper, neatly folded. I take it out and flatten it, running my finger along the torn edge with a mixture of excitement and fear. I'm almost certain this must be the missing page from Mum's diary.

From the beginning, it's clear that this is no normal diary entry. There's no date at the top and it's written like a letter, though I can't make out who it's addressed to. The words have been scrawled down in a rush with lots of crossings out. It's as if Mum knew, I think with a twinge of pain – as if she knew she didn't have much time left.

I squint at the page, but Mum's handwriting is hard to decipher in the dim light of the bedroom, so I go downstairs, turn on the stark strip lighting in the kitchen and sit at the table, my heart racing. As the words become clearer, I realise with a shock that the letter is addressed to Eve.

Dear Eve, I read.

I want to write this all down while I still remember. I'm getting old and my memory is fading fast – this damn disease! One day I know that I'll forget you. And I don't want to. I don't want to forget the good or the bad and I don't want to forget the things I did, even though they're painful to remember.

I wish you could forgive me. I did them because I loved him so much and I was a fool. I know that's not much of an excuse but it's the truth and I'm so sorry. I realise now that my love for him was misplaced, that there's something wrong with him; there always has been – something rotten at the core. You recognised it too late . . .

He said he knew a place where he used to play as a boy. We could bury you there, he said. So, we took your body in the middle of the night and we tossed you down the well like a worthless penny. I helped him dispose of you like you were no one, nobody. I helped him erase your memory and I'm so sorry . . .

I break off, struggling to breathe. I feel like I've been stabbed in the heart. Here it is: definitive proof that Dad killed Eve. Even though it's what I suspected, it still comes as a massive shock to see it written down in black and white. Not only that, but Mum knew. *She knew and she said nothing . . . She helped him cover it up.* My hand is shaking and I'm choking on angry tears as I force myself to read on:

Eve, my darling sister, I want to make amends. The least I can do for you now is remember you the way you deserve to be remembered – to give you the memorial you were denied.

You were Eve Susannah Delaney née Leyton. You were born in 1951 and you died in 1990.

A loving mother and wife, a sister, and a fearless fighter for what you believed in.

There's more. More about the kind of person Eve was and the things that she did during her short life, but I can't read any longer . . . not right now. My eyes are burning with unshed tears.

I stagger to my feet. Suddenly overwhelmed by a feeling of intense weariness, I climb the stairs stiffly like an old woman. I know that anger will come, but at the moment I think I must be in shock because a heavy numbness washes over me as I brush my teeth and turn out the light.

It was a kind of eulogy, I think, lying in the darkness. The last part was almost like the inscription on a gravestone. But of course, Eve hasn't got a gravestone. She's been denied even that small dignity. She's been dumped in a well *like a worthless penny.*

In a well . . . Whether she knew it or not, Mum obviously wanted me to find that letter. She would have wished for me to find Eve's remains, wherever they are, and give her a proper burial – and that's what I'm determined to do. But where? Where is the well that she mentioned?

I close my eyes, trying to sleep, but my mind won't let

me rest. It keeps on worrying away at the question, until suddenly my eyes fly open.

A place where he used to play as a boy. Where else but the estate where Dad grew up – more than ten square miles of parkland? I'm guessing it would be a good place to hide a body if you knew where to go.

My heart hammering, I turn on the light, fumble for my glasses and pick up my phone. I type 'disused wells UK' into the search engine, and it comes up with the National Well Record Archive from the British Geological Survey. A couple more clicks and I find a map of all the old boreholes in the UK. I zoom in on Cirencester, swiping sideways to the large estate where Dad grew up. There's only one well marked in that area, a circle, coloured dark red to indicate that it is of unknown depth. *That's it*, I think triumphantly. *That's where she is.*

Chapter Thirty-Six

Vicky is at the door, eyes big and startled.

'Jess, how lovely.' She air-kisses me. She looks happier than the last time I saw her. I'm guessing it's because the au pair has returned and it's nearly time for Brandon to go back to school. 'Do you mind taking off your shoes? I've just hoovered and—'

'No problem.' I kick off my trainers and my feet sink into the ridiculously clean, ridiculously white carpet of the hallway as I follow her to the state of-the-art living area.

'Is Howard around?' I ask, hoisting myself up onto a bar stool at the island that divides the kitchen and dining room.

She nods. 'He's upstairs having a shower. He'll be down in a minute. Can I get you a drink?'

'Something cold, please.'

'It's Jessie!' Howard exclaims as he pads into the room

barefoot in shorts and crisp white T-shirt. 'How are you, little sister?' He takes a beer from the fridge, puts his arm around Vicky and grins at me. 'What do you think of our new table?'

I'm not in the mood to admire his furniture. 'We need to talk.' I glance at Vicky. 'Privately.'

Vicky flushes. 'I'll just go and check on Brandon.' And she slips tactfully out of the room.

Once she's gone, Howard sighs and flops into an armchair. 'What's up, Jess? How was your trip to Cirencester? Did you find any leads?'

Inside my pocket I finger the piece of paper I found in the jewellery box. I won't show him yet. I need to take him through this step by step – take him through the same journey I've been on – to convince him of what I know.

'I met a friend of Eve's,' I say.

Howie leans forward. 'Really?'

'Yes. Do you remember someone called Moira? She lives two doors down from our old house.'

He pinches the top of his nose and then rubs his eyes.

'They had a daughter called Francesca. She would have been about your age.'

He grins. 'Oh yeah, I remember Fran. She was quite a babe. She used to sunbathe in the garden in a really skimpy bikini.'

I roll my eyes. 'Well, apparently Fran's mother, Moira,

279

was very good friends with our mother but she completely lost contact with her after we moved. Don't you think that's weird?'

Howie frowns and shrugs. 'Not really. Mum didn't keep in contact with anyone, not even us.'

'Mmm,' I agree. 'But Moira said that Eve didn't mention anything about leaving Dad, or about moving. She said that she saw Eve the day before we moved. It doesn't fit with what Dad told me. He said that we moved here after she left. Which of them is right, Howie? When did she leave? Was it before or after we moved?'

Howard seems annoyed by the question. 'I don't know. I was at boarding school, remember? All I know is that when term started, we lived in Cirencester and when it finished, we'd moved to Wendover and our mother wasn't with us anymore. But I would've thought Dad would remember better than some random neighbour.' He stands up and fills the kettle.

'So, you didn't find out where she is now?' he says. 'Well, it's probably for the best. She clearly doesn't want to be contacted. We have to face it, she didn't want us, Jess. She wanted Michael.'

'That's just it, though. Michael wasn't her lover,' I say.

Howard tips his chair back, frowning. 'What do you mean?' he says. 'Dad told us. She ran off with Michael to Australia.'

'I met a friend of Eve's called Michael. He's still living in Cheltenham on his own. He was friends with Mum, nothing more.'

Howie sighs impatiently. 'There could be more than one person called Michael. Anyway, how do you know he's telling the truth?'

'Just instinct, I suppose.' I take a deep breath. 'There's something else. Michael said he thought Dad was abusive towards our mother.'

Howie was older than me; he would have been more likely to have been aware if there was any violence in our household at that time. But Howie reacts the same way I did initially, with denial. He gives a loud, dismissive snort. 'Dad? Seriously?'

My stomach churns with anxiety. I know it's going to be difficult to convince Howie. 'Did you ever see him hit Eve or did he lay his hands on you?'

Howie stares at me. 'Absolutely not.'

'Don't you think it's odd, though? Our mother disappears without a trace? And Dad lies about when she left, where she went, why she left?'

Howie narrows his eyes. 'What are you driving at?'

'There are things Mum – I mean Jean – said before she died. For example, she told me one day that she was afraid he wanted her dead, because she knew too much . . .'

He tips his head to one side, a faint trace of amusement

accompanying the obvious anger in his eyes. I think he's guessed where I'm going with this.

'Go on,' he says.

I take a deep breath. 'She didn't say who she was talking about. At first, I thought she meant Ajay because she said she'd seen him push his wife from the window . . .' Howie rolls his eyes and opens his mouth to speak but I plough on . . . 'But I think now that she was talking about something else, something that happened much longer ago.' My voice lowers to a whisper. 'I think she meant Dad . . .'

Howie gives a hostile laugh and then stops abruptly. 'Oh, you're serious?' he says. He speaks slowly as if I'm an idiot. 'Mum had Alzheimer's. She was losing her mind. She said all kinds of weird shit.'

I feel tears starting at the back of my eyes. I mustn't cry. I mustn't sound too emotional. I need to convince him with cold, hard logic. 'Yes, but you weren't there when she said it, Howard. She was so scared.'

Howie leans in close, lowering his voice. 'Let me get this straight. Are you trying to tell me that our father killed Eve?'

I hold my breath, my heart pumping. It's the first time I've expressed these thoughts out loud to another human being.

I nod slowly. 'Yes . . . I know he killed Eve. Maybe he was having an affair with Jean or he was jealous of Michael, I don't know, but whatever the reason, they had a fight and I think he pushed her, and she hit her head on the sundial.' I can imagine it all too clearly – the anger on Dad's face, the sickening crack as Eve's head hits the stone.

Howie stands up and walks away towards the window. Then he turns abruptly. 'You realise how crazy you sound, Jess? I mean, this is Dad we're talking about.'

'I have proof.' I tug out the paper in my pocket and hand it over.

He reads it, a look of incredulity spreading across his face. 'Is this a joke? What is this? Where did you find it?'

I explain about Mum's jewellery box and the diary with the page torn out. 'I think she wanted me to find this. She wanted me to find Eve.'

He scrunches up the paper and throws it in the bin. Then sits opposite me. 'This is nonsense, Jess. You must see that. Mum wasn't in her right mind when she wrote this. She had all kinds of delusions. She probably felt guilty about marrying her sister's husband and her guilt morphed into this crazy story.'

'No, I'm sure I'm right. That's not all.' I can see the disbelief hardening in his eyes, but I plough on regardless. 'I think he killed Mum too.'

He rocks back in his chair and sighs. 'What?'

'The pills she took. I think he gave her them to keep her quiet – because she was starting to talk.'

Howie doesn't answer right away. He stands up and comes to sit next to me, looking thoughtful. Then he puts his arm round me. 'Look, Jess,' he says gently. 'You're upset, grieving – we all are. You've not been in your right mind lately. You feel guilty because they were your pills that she took. And you're trying to find someone else to blame. But this story – this crazy concoction – you've got to see that it's just insane.' He takes a deep breath. 'Listen, Dad told me all about Madrid, Jess. I'm worried about you.'

His words hit me like a battering ram. Is it true? Is that what all this is about – a way for me to find someone else to blame, a distraction from my own sickening culpability? I sink back into the sofa. My eyes fill with tears and guilt rises in my throat, choking me.

Steam pours out of the spout of the kettle and Howie stands up and gets out two mugs. 'How about a cup of tea, Jessie? There's nothing like a nice cup of tea to help clear your head.'

I feel suddenly so tired of the whole thing. Tired and confused. I accept the cup he offers meekly and take a gulp. The liquid is hot and burns my throat. Is he right? Is it my fault?

I walk to the rain-smeared window and look out at the garden. I can't stop hearing Mum's voice, remembering the terror on her face when she said *he killed her*. Another memory surfaces – Mum in the living room, gripping my arm. *I've done something really terrible.* The way she broke off so suddenly when Dad walked in the room. I hadn't thought of it before, but it was almost as if she was scared of him. Listen to your gut, isn't that what they always tell you? My gut is telling me that Howie is wrong about Dad and that I'm right.

I turn to Howie, who is checking his phone, frowning.

'Mum wanted to confess something to me, right before she died. I think she wanted to tell me that she helped him cover up the crime.'

Howard bites his lip. 'Mum? Seriously, Jess. I don't think she ever even had so much as a parking ticket. Can't you see you're not thinking straight? I mean, if he killed her, where's the body? Somebody would have found it by now.'

'I thought about that.' I go to the bin and retrieve the paper, smoothing out the creases. 'It's here. Look, it says, "we tossed you in a well, like a worthless penny."'

'Jess . . .'

I take out my phone and show him the map of all the boreholes in Cirencester and I point to the single red dot on the Langley estate.

Howie opens his mouth to speak. Then his phone beeps and he checks it with an irritated tut.

'There's a problem at work,' he says, shoving his phone back in his pocket. 'Look, Jess, I haven't got time to deal with this – with you. Can't you see this isn't normal? All this crazy fucking stuff about boreholes.' His voice rises. 'You need to get help.'

I sit down on the sofa. My head's spinning.

'Anyway, I've got to go now,' he adds more gently. 'You look exhausted, Jess. Why don't you go home and go to sleep? I'll call you this evening.'

He doesn't believe me, I think, as I drive out through the electric gates. And if my own brother doesn't believe me, then what chance do I have of convincing anyone else? I brush away a tear with my fist as I head back towards Aylesbury. I can't afford self-pity. I need to be strong. I'm on my own.

At home I wash the dishes that have accumulated on the draining board and empty the bin, which is starting to stink. The living room is still half painted, the splatter of white paint staining the carpet. I sit in the middle of the room on the floor, trying to work out my next move.

My phone beeps and I see there's a missed call from Dad and one from Claire Matteson, as well as a couple of messages from Sean and one from Alice. *I'll read them later*, I think. I feel tired and emotionally drained. I rip the sheet off the sofa and lie down, exhausted. My eyes close and I'm just drifting off to sleep when the phone rings loudly.

It's Howie. I answer reluctantly, prepared for another

286

tirade. But he sounds calm, contrite even. 'I'm sorry about earlier, Jess. I lost my temper,' he says. 'Are you OK?'

'I'm OK,' I say. I sit up, holding the phone to my ear.

'I shouldn't have been so harsh,' he continues. 'I want to help.'

'Help me how?' I say warily. If by 'help' he means taking me to another psychiatrist, then I'm not interested.

'How about we take a trip to Cirencester ourselves and check out this well?'

For a moment I'm stunned. He's actually taking me seriously.

'Really? You believe me then?' I say incredulously.

'I don't know,' he admits. 'But I'm willing to keep an open mind and I figure if we go there and you see for yourself that there's nothing there, then maybe you'll realise that the whole thing is in your head.'

'When shall we go?' I ask.

'How about tomorrow evening? I could pick you up after work at about eight thirty.'

Chapter Thirty-Seven

It's a perfect summer evening and the sun is still shining brightly when Howie, good as his word, pulls up outside my house in his shiny silver Porsche. He hoots the horn and I snatch up my bag and rush out of the door.

Howie revs the engine and we purr through the village, accelerating as soon as we get out onto the open road, roaring along the motorway towards Oxford.

'Thank you for this,' I say, gripping the seat as he swerves around a lorry and nips just ahead of it. 'I appreciate you coming along with me. I know you think it's a wild goose chase.'

'No problem,' he says. 'To be honest, it's just good to get out of the house. Vicky's been moping around all week and as for Lara, I don't know what's wrong with the girl. She's been like the Wicked Witch of the East lately.'

'She's seventeen. It's a difficult age.'

'Mmm, yes, I suppose so.'

He keeps glancing over at me, a worried frown on his face. 'Anyway, how are you, Jess?'

'I really am fine now,' I say. 'I realise what I said must seem a bit crazy . . .'

'Just a little . . .' he smiles at me. 'With what happened in Madrid, I just wanted to check you're OK?'

My heart sinks. It's the second time he's mentioned Madrid in the past couple of days. Has he been talking to Dad again? Has he told him what I said yesterday? And if he has, how will Dad react? Fear coils in my belly. He's not going to just sit back and wait for us to find Eve.

'You didn't tell Dad what I said yesterday, did you?' I blurt.

'Of course not,' Howie reassures me. 'I haven't spoken to him all week. But when I last spoke to him, he just mentioned that you'd had a bit of a hard time in Spain.'

If I tell Howie the truth, it will just confirm his suspicions that I'm crazy and he'll never believe me about Eve.

'I was just very stressed, that's all, and the stress turned into depression,' I say. 'But I'm fine now.'

'Dad said that there was an incident at the school where you worked?'

'It was just a misunderstanding.'

'Are you sure?' he asks.

'Yes.'

'OK.'

Howie seems to have lost interest in the conversation. He switches on the radio and the *Desert Island Discs* theme tune wafts over us, but I'm not listening.

I'm trying hard to keep the memories at bay, but it seems I can't stop them flooding back. And in my mind, I'm back there – in Madrid, locked in that classroom, with little Anna Maria crying inconsolably and begging to be let out as a dark stain spreads down her tights and Rachel, the school principal, hammers on the door.

I'm not quite sure how long we were there. Long enough for it to get dark outside and for Anna Maria to stop crying and curl up in a ball on the floor, whimpering away in Spanish.

'Don't worry,' I kept saying. 'He can't hurt you now.'

But even in my delusional state, I realised from the way Anna Maria flinched as I tried to comfort her that at that moment, she was more scared of me than of her father. Even so, I was sure that I was doing the right thing; that she would thank me one day. And when they finally broke down the door, I launched myself at her dad, scratching and kicking like a wild cat while Anna Maria screamed at me to stop and Rachel tried to restrain me.

'What the hell were you thinking?' Rachel said in her office after Anna Maria and her father had left. 'You'll be lucky if they don't want to press charges.'

'Yes, Jessica, what were you thinking?' echoed Matteo, who had come to pick me up because Rachel didn't think I was in a fit state to go home alone.

'I couldn't let her father take her,' I said. 'He's been abusing her.'

Rachel frowned. She interlaced her fingers, resting her elbows on the desk. 'That's a very serious allegation, Jessica. How do you know? Did Anna Maria tell you that?'

'No,' I admit.

She exchanged a look with Matteo. 'Are there any marks on her, any injuries?'

'No, not that I know of.'

She sighed. 'So, what makes you think he's abusing her?'

I was confused by the question. Everything was fuzzy in my head. I was trying to remember why this all started, why Anna Maria and I ended up locked in that classroom. All I knew was that I'd had an overwhelming feeling that she was in danger. 'He ... he locked her up,' I stammered weakly, unconvincingly. But even as the words came out of my mouth, I realised it wasn't true.

'No, you're the one who locked her up,' Matteo snapped impatiently. 'My God, Jessica. That poor little girl was so scared she wet herself.'

I dropped my head into my hands, feeling suddenly drained. Lucidity was returning and with it doubts were creeping in. I was beginning to realise that I must have made a terrible mistake.

The next few days and weeks come back to me in flashbacks, like fragments of a nightmare – that awful journey home on the Metro, the consultation with Dr Lopez, the moment I realised I would have to leave Madrid because I knew Matteo would do everything he could to get me sectioned.

I grip the car seat, trying to hold on as Howie pulls sharply into a layby. I'm trying not to let the memories – all those feelings of guilt and shame – overwhelm me. It must have been a terrifying experience for Anna Maria, and I was lucky her parents didn't press charges.

Is it possible I'm making the same mistake now? Once again, I'm making wild accusations. Is this all just my illness – the delusions returning? *But, no, this is different*, I tell myself firmly. *This time I have evidence.*

'Hey, Jessica. Are you all right? I asked you a question. Didn't you hear me?' Howie is asking loudly, tapping my shoulder, bringing me back to the here and now.

'Sorry,' I say shakily. 'I was just thinking about Madrid.'

'You seemed lost in your own world there for a moment,' he says, starting up the engine again. 'Are you sure you're OK?'

'Yes, I'm sure,' I say, trying to pull myself together. 'What was your question?'

'What?'

'The question you asked me.'

Howie shrugs. 'Oh, it wasn't important. I just asked what you would have as your *Desert Island Discs*?'

It's such a light-hearted topic, compared to my dark, spiralling thoughts, that I'm momentarily floored. But I guess that Howie is trying to distract me and I'm grateful for that. I need to be distracted right now, so I give the question some consideration.

'That's tricky,' I say at last. 'I'd definitely have the *Moonlight Sonata* by Beethoven as one of my choices.'

He jerks his chin upwards and looks at me sideways. 'Why *Moonlight Sonata*?'

'I don't know,' I say. I struggle to express how it makes me feel. 'It just always gives me this feeling of deep peace. I can't really explain it.'

Howie raps his fingers on the steering wheel. 'I can.'

'You can?' I stare across at him surprised.

'Yes, our mother, Eve, she used to play it at night. Almost every evening she would sit at the piano and play it after we'd gone to bed, don't you remember?'

I shake my head. I don't recall it consciously, but there's a part of me buried deep inside that must have remembered somehow. That has to be the reason why I love it so much: I associate it with my mother. In a way, through music, my mother has always been with me and the thought fills me with a deep, bittersweet sadness.

We drive the rest of the way in silence, each of us lost in our own thoughts. By the time we reach Cirencester, the sun has disappeared behind layers of smoky grey cloud and we park just outside the park gates, which are closed so we head up the hill to the side entrance. The light is fading. There's a chill in the air as the evening draws in and I wish I hadn't left my jacket in the car.

'King's Park Comprehensive is at the top of this hill,' Howie says conversationally, as we walk along the dual carriageway. 'I used to go this way every morning.' On one side a few cars and a lorry whizz past and on the other there's a high stone wall. 'I used to cycle up and down every day. It was great coming home. You didn't have to pedal at all.'

'What?' I say, puffing to keep up with him. 'But you went to secondary school at St Bartholomew's?'

Howie stoops to do up a shoelace. 'No, they sent me there when I was fourteen – the year before we moved to Wendover.' He sounds resentful and I'm surprised on two counts. I'd just assumed he'd gone to private school from the age of eleven. And I'd always assumed he enjoyed himself at school. I always slightly resented the fact that he had gone to such an expensive school, while I was left to go to the comprehensive in Aylesbury, and I'd wondered why my parents sent him there when we weren't exactly rolling in money.

At the time I thought it was plain sexism – the fact that

he was a boy and I was a girl. But now I think I know the reason. Dad and Jean wanted to get him out of the way. He knew too much. They didn't want to risk him letting something slip to me. No wonder they always kept us apart.

Howard stops by an imposing wrought-iron gate and tries the handle.

'Fuck. It's locked already,' he says. 'I thought the side entrance would be open. Never mind, I know another way in.'

We walk a bit further up the dual carriageway and come to a lower wall. We clamber over into the field with two horses in it. The horses snort and gaze at us warily as we cross the paddock and squeeze through a gap in the fence on the far side.

On the other side of the fence, Howie brushes leaves and dirt off his shorts and grins at me, his teeth garishly white in the fading light. 'I feel like Sherlock Homes and Dr Watson,' he says, like we're going on a fun jaunt. How can he be so cheerful, knowing why we're here, what we might find? *Unless it's because he doesn't believe me*, I reflect. To him, this is all an exercise in proving me wrong.

We scramble up a ditch and onto the gravel path.

'Which way?' asks Howie and I check the map and point up the hill towards another path bisecting this one, and a large, old stone folly.

Howie sets off purposefully, and I almost have to jog to keep up with his long stride. The park is completely empty and silent, not a soul about. There's nothing but the hiss of the wind in the trees and the rustle of small creatures in the hedgerows.

'Where now?' he asks as we reach the folly. I sit on the metal bench inside and look at the map on my phone. 'This way,' I say, pointing into the woods.

Howie checks the map over my shoulder, nodding, and we set off again. As we veer off the path, it gets much darker and the trees seem to be stooping over us, their branches reaching out to us like long arms. I'm glad that Howie is here with me. I would be even more scared if I was out here alone. As it is, I start when I hear the snap of a twig behind me and something like the bark of a small dog makes my heart thump out of my chest.

'Did you hear that?' I ask Howie, peering through the gloom, but I can't see anything.

Howie shrugs. 'Maybe it was a deer. There are a few in the park.'

'It sounded more like a dog,' I say. Not that I know what deer sound like. Howie is probably right, but I can't shake the feeling of being followed – that someone is watching us.

We walk for a long time, venturing deeper and deeper into the wood. I'm beginning to think we're lost when my phone beeps in my pocket, making us both jump.

'Jesus, Jess!' Howie laughs nervously. 'Are you trying to give me a heart attack?'

I glance at the screen and am surprised to see that it's a message from Holly. After all these years of silence! At any other time, I would be excited. Finally, she's got back to me. But I'll have to read it later.

The trees are getting denser, closing in on us, and the ground is soft and muddy in places. We walk on in silence. There's only the sound of our own footsteps until we finally reach a small clearing. I glance at my phone again. According to the map, it should be here. But as I look around, there's no sign of a well.

'It's supposed to be here,' I say, disappointed, sitting on a large tree root and taking a stone out of my shoe. Perhaps this is a wild goose chase after all.

'Hang on a moment,' says Howie. 'You wait here. I'll just have a scout around, see what I can see. These old maps aren't always all that reliable.' And he disappears into a thicket.

Once Howie is gone, I put my shoe back on and look around. It's very quiet. Too quiet. The wind in the trees sounds like someone breathing and the sensation of being watched that I had before is even stronger now. Fear crawls in my belly. Every rustle and snapping twig makes my heart race. Could Dad have found out about our plans? Could he have followed us here? 'It's nothing,' I mutter to myself. 'Just my imagination.'

I take out my phone again to distract myself, tap it and

the screen lights up. There's a bubble with a picture of Holly in it and a message:

> *Dear Jess,*
>
> *I'm sorry that it has taken me so long to get in contact with you and I was so sorry to hear of your mother's death – she was a lovely lady and I remember her with a lot of affection. I'm sorry that I didn't come to the funeral, but the truth is that I was scared . . .*

Scared? I think, confused, feeling a twinge of unease. But I don't get to read anymore because just then Howie returns, panting slightly. There's a gleam of excitement in his eyes. 'I've found it,' he announces. 'It's just over here.'

My heart skips a beat and I struggle to my feet, Holly's message temporarily forgotten. This is the moment of truth.

'Did you see anything?' I ask in a whisper.

He smiles grimly. 'No, it's covered with a grille. It's quite heavy. I'll need your help to shift it.'

I follow him through some dense overgrowth, brambles scratching at my legs and deceptively soft stinging nettles brushing against my skin. I'm deeply afraid of what we will find.

We step over a fallen branch into another small clearing.

In the centre Howie has pulled back some vegetation to reveal a rusty metal grille. I'm surprised that he found it so easily. It looks like it was completely hidden by brambles. We tug at the rest, ignoring the scratches on our hands, until it's completely free. Then we try to wrench up the grille. But it won't shift.

'We need something to lever it,' Howie says at last, red-faced with exertion. 'I might have something in the car we can use. You wait here.'

While I'm waiting, I creep to the edge of the well and peer through the small squares in the grating, my heart hammering. There's a smell of damp. Stale, cold air creeps up and touches my face, but it's too dark to see anything. *Are you down there, Eve?* I wonder with a shiver. *Are you down there waiting for us?*

I wish Howie would hurry up, I think, shivering. I step back away from the well and take out my phone again, reading the rest of Holly's message.

I was afraid that you wouldn't believe me. But I owe it to myself and to you to tell you the truth. It's not something we can really discuss in a message but I'm down in London next week for work and I thought we could arrange to meet up somewhere. But please don't tell anyone you're meeting me – especially not your family.

The message leaves a bad taste in my mouth. Why doesn't she want me to tell them? I stare down at my feet, thinking hard . . .

There's a noise in the thicket and Howie pushes his way through. He's holding a crowbar in one hand.

'This should do the trick,' he says.

I look at the well thoughtfully. It's flat to the ground. There's no wall around it, nothing to indicate where it was. And from the vegetation that's been torn away, it looks as if it was completely overgrown when Howie found it. My mind moves slowly, sluggishly, as if through thick murky water.

'How did you know where the well was?' I ask.

'Just luck, I guess,' he shrugs. 'Come and help me, Jess. Don't just stand there.'

He squats by the well, digs the crowbar into the edge of the grille and heaves. With a grunt, he manages to prise it up.

'Hold this,' he says. I take the edge of the grille so that Howie can jemmy up the rest. I watch as he shines the light from his phone into the well, illuminating damp green moss and lichen at the top. And the beam of light sweeps downwards, shining on black water down below.

'There's nothing there,' Howie says, turning off the light. 'Are you happy now, Jess?'

'We don't know how deep it is,' I say. 'There could be anything down there.' There's an old metal ladder, its rungs embedded in the wall, but it only goes a short way down and it looks rusty. It looks like it would snap under our weight. There's something else bothering me.

'Why did you have a crowbar?' I ask. 'That's not a normal thing to keep in your car, is it?'

'What?' Howie stares at me, his face strained with the effort.

'The crowbar, why was it in your car?'

He wipes his face with his hand. 'I lent it to a friend a few weeks ago and forgot to take it out.'

He's lying. Howie's car is spotless. He must have it cleaned at least once a week. There's no way he would leave a rusty old crowbar in his boot.

I can't avoid the obvious conclusion anymore.

The reason Howie has a crowbar is because he knew he was going to need it, and the reason he found the well so easily is because he's been here before.

Chapter Thirty-Eight

He knew the well was here. He knew exactly where to come and what he would need. And that can mean only one thing. He knew Eve was dead. He knew Dad killed her. He must have come here with our parents and helped to dispose of her body.

I look up at him and he grins at me. He's actually enjoying this, I realise. He's enjoying himself, not because he doesn't believe me, but because he knows that I'm right.

We stand staring at each other, on opposite sides of the well.

'I know she's down there,' I say.

Howie gives a short, derisive laugh, suddenly reminding me of Matteo. 'You can go down there and check for yourself if you want, Jess. Be my guest.'

I can't help myself; the anger spills out of me.

'You know she's there. You've known all along that she's been there. You knew Dad killed her. How could you, Howard? You let me believe she was alive. You let me think I was going crazy.'

He doesn't deny it. He squats on the ground with his back to a tree, clutching the crowbar.

'You're nearly there,' he smirks. 'Come on, Jess. You can work it out. I thought you were supposed to be intelligent.'

I gawp at him. Something clicks inside my brain. *I did it because I loved him*, Mum said. *Him*. She never actually mentioned Dad by name.

That one thought is like a domino that sets off a cascade of other thoughts. It's as if I've lived underground all my life, and now I've stepped outside into the light. Everything viewed from this new perspective makes a kind of terrible sense, and I experience an awful, blinding clarity.

Howie.

Howie has always been ruthless and lacking in empathy. He will do anything, trample over anybody to get what he wants – from wives and children to business rivals. He never feels guilty about anything. Why have I never seen it before? All the time Howard has been the cancer at the heart of our family, not Dad. *I did it because I loved him.*

Mum was talking about Howie all along.

303

Chapter Thirty-Nine

Howie weighs the crowbar in his hand. Then he looks up at me. The expression on his face is dispassionate and thoughtful, as if I'm a puzzle to be solved; an obstacle to be removed. It sends a chill to my heart.

Why bring me here if he knew I was right? He must know we'll find our mother's body. So why bring me here? Unless . . .

'It's getting dark,' I say, and my voice comes out as a frightened squeak. It would be comical if I wasn't so terrified. 'We should get going.'

'I don't think so, Jess,' he says.

He couldn't risk me going to the police, I realise. They might have taken me seriously. That's why we're here, the two of us, all alone late at night. This was never about finding our mother's body. This was about silencing me the way he silenced Jean. And I am gripped by a sudden terrifying certainty:

He's planning to kill me too.

'It was you,' I blurt. 'You killed Eve. Mum and Dad lied to protect you.'

He doesn't seem phased by the accusation. He doesn't even try to deny it. He just shrugs as if we're talking about a minor misdemeanour rather than murder. 'I told them it was an accident. I was only fifteen. They didn't want to ruin my life.'

'And was it?' I whisper. 'An accident?'

I'm still willing to give him the chance to excuse himself. If I pretend to believe him and agree to keep his secret, then maybe he will be able to let me go.

'Not really.' He frowns thoughtfully, staring at the ground. 'I mean, I was really angry. I'd heard her talking to Dad the night before. She was trying to persuade him to send me away to boarding school. She said that she couldn't handle me anymore.' He digs angrily into the ground with his toe. 'She didn't want me, so I decided to kill her. I thought if she was out of the way then I could stay at home.'

I'm edging away towards the trees. Maybe I can make a run for it while he's still talking, absorbed in his thoughts. But just as I think I'm going to make it, he looks up, gives a short bark of laughter and stands up, striding over to me with one swift, easy motion.

'I'm sorry, but I don't think I can let you go now, Jess,' he says, grabbing me tightly by the wrist.

'Let go of me,' I yell, trying to wrest my arm away, but his grip is too strong. And he just smiles tauntingly and holds on to me as if it's the easiest thing in the world.

'You killed Mum too. It was you who gave her the overdose.' The words spew out of my mouth, choking me. At this second my anger is stronger than my fear. And tears of rage roll down my face as I think about Mum, who always loved us both and would have done anything for me or for Howie. *Had* done everything for him. She lied for him, turned her life upside down for him. She even committed a crime for him, hiding her own sister's death. But as soon as her mind started going and she became a liability, he didn't think twice about killing her.

'I saved her from a long, degrading illness,' he says. 'Anyway, it was you who made me realise she was getting dangerous, when you told me the things she'd been saying.'

That's right. It was me who told him. The realisation almost breaks me.

'At least tell me she didn't suffer.'

He shrugs. 'I don't think so. She just fell asleep. If you think about it, it was a good way to go. I did her a kindness.' As he speaks, he's dragging me towards the well, and I'm scared that he's going to push me in. But instead he picks up the crowbar and raises it high above his head.

Terror sears through me. *I'm going to die here in these woods. He's going to kill me.*

'Please don't!' I beg desperately. 'I won't go to the police, I promise. You're my brother. Please. We can just cover this up again and pretend it never happened.'

For a split second he pauses, and I can see that he's considering what I'm saying. Then he smiles – his slow, charming smile. 'I wasn't born yesterday, Jess. What kind of an idiot do you think I am?'

'I know you're not an idiot,' I say, thinking rapidly. 'And that's exactly why you won't hurt me. I mean, think about it, Howard. How would you explain my disappearance?'

'Good point,' he says thoughtfully. He looks at me, his head tilted. 'Give me your phone,' he says. And without waiting, he rummages in my pockets and fishes out my phone.

Shit. I've lost any chance I had of calling for help.

'Maybe a message to Dad from your phone will do the trick,' he says thoughtfully. 'Let me see, what can I say? You've decided to go away and you don't want him to contact you.' He taps away at the phone, thumbs flying. 'It wouldn't surprise him given the argument you had recently. No one knows we came here together, so there's nothing to link me to your disappearance. And if Dad is satisfied, who else is going to bother searching for you? Let's face it, Jess, who would miss you really?'

It's true, I think with a heavy despair as he lifts the crowbar and I cower, bracing for impact. But as I step back, my foot slips and I pitch over the edge of the well.

Chapter Forty

Everything seems to happen in slow motion. I'm falling like Alice in Wonderland down the rabbit hole. Although in reality it's probably no more than a split second, my mind works at lightning speed and I have time to think about Dad, about how I wish I'd told him I loved him, and to wonder what it was that Holly had wanted to tell me.

Howie's face silhouetted against the moonlight is the last thing I see before I smack into a pool of water and hit my head against hard stone.

For a second, everything is blank. Then I come to, floundering and gasping for breath, gulping in mouthfuls of cold, foul-tasting water. I struggle to my feet, trying to orientate myself. I'm waist-deep in water, standing on something hard and lumpy. Rain is pattering above me. I am panicked and confused and my head is throbbing with pain. I touch it tentatively with my hand and my elbow grazes against rough, wet stone. Where am I? With an effort of will, I drag my scattered senses together. I'm in the well. I fell in here. Howie was trying to kill me. He killed Eve and he killed Mum and now he's left me here to die.

I can't see anything. It's pitch-black down here, almost complete and total darkness. There's not even a chink of light. He must have replaced the grille and covered it over with something, I realise with a jolt of fear. I fumble about in the darkness, trying not to panic, running my palm over the rough stone wall encircling me. As I move, my foot nudges something on the ground beneath me. Stooping down, I plunge my hand into the water, pick it up and trace my fingers around it. It's smooth and slimy, bulbous at the tip. A distinctive shape, familiar somehow.

I drop it in horror as I realise suddenly what it is.

A bone.

I flail about in disgust and panic and kick against another under my feet, then another and another. There must be hundreds of them down here. There are two hundred and six bones in the human body, I remember from my biology lessons at school. And I'm standing here amongst them – the bones of a human being. The bones of my mother.

Chapter Forty-One

In a frenzy of horror, I call out, 'Help!' It comes out as a croak at first and then rises to a scream until I'm shouting at the top of my lungs. 'Help me, please! Help!'

There's no answer, of course, just the sound of the rain and the steady drip of water. Far above I can hear the coo of a wood pigeon. The darkness feels heavy, as if it's pressing down on me, and I reach upwards trying to push it off, fighting a wave of nausea and panic. I can't afford to panic. I must stay calm. I need to try to work out a way out of here. My survival depends on it.

There must be a way. There's always a way. I think about Mum and the way she always used to say 'where there's a will there's a way' when I was struggling with something. More often than not, she was right. I pat and stretch my arms and legs experimentally. At least nothing seems to be

310

broken. Maybe the well is not that deep after all and the water must have broken my fall, or I wouldn't have survived unscathed. Perhaps I can climb out. I run my fingers along the wall and find a handhold in the stone. Digging in with my nails, I try to hoist myself up. For a moment I hang on through sheer determination but then, when I try to claw my way higher, my arms give out and I slide back down, scraping against the stone. Then I try again and get a little further. God knows how many times I attempt this, but each time I only get so far and then drop back down, defeated.

At last I give up, exhausted, crying with rage, frustration and fear. It's useless. Even if I could climb up to the top, how would I move the grille when I got there?

Hopelessness washes over me. I am going to die down here alone. No one will ever find me. I will be buried here forever with my mother. How long will it take for my body to turn to bones too? My throat constricts and I feel waves of panic wash over me. The walls of the well seem to be closing in on me. This is my worst nightmare come true – I'm stuck in a tiny space with no means of escape. Tears roll down my cheek at the thought of how much of my life I've wasted feeling sad and scared. Now I'm about to lose it, life seems incredibly precious and beautiful. Tears turn into sobs of despair and I cry inconsolably, clutching Eve's bones.

*

The sound of scrabbling brings me to my senses. Moonlight appears above me and I stare at it, fascinated and bemused. Am I hallucinating? How long have I been down here? I have no idea. It could be minutes; it could be hours. There's more scraping above me and I realise that there's someone up there. My first thought is that Howie's had a change of heart. *He's come back to get me out*, I think with a rush of incredulous hope – but then fear grips me as I realise that it's more likely that he's come back to finish the job he started . . .

A black shape appears in the circle of light.

'Jessica!' A small, scared voice hisses. 'Are you OK down there?'

'Jessica!' she calls again more loudly, and I realise with a jolt of astonishment that it's Vicky. Relief and joy flood through me. I'm not going to die. Somehow, miraculously, I'm saved. Vicky has found me.

'Yes,' I call back. It comes out as a weak, inaudible croak. So I try again more loudly. 'Yes, I'm down here.'

'Oh my God! Are you hurt?'

'I think I'm OK,' I say. I feel fine. In fact, I'm so giddy with happiness and relief, I want to jump and dance. 'I'm so glad you're here. How did you find me?'

'Shh,' she whispers. 'I'm not sure he's gone. I'm going to go and get some help.'

'Can't you just call the police?'

'I tried,' she says. 'I can't get signal. I would need to go back to the road.'

'Don't leave me here . . .' I beg. The thought of being left alone again fills me with terror. I'm terrified that Howie will come back again.

There's a short silence 'All right. I'll do what I can.'

I listen impatiently to Vicky straining to move the grille, wishing I could help her. But she's obviously stronger than I gave her credit for because it doesn't take her very long to heave it out of the way.

'Bella's lead is in my pocket. I'm going to lower it down,' she calls down to me breathlessly. 'Do you think you can climb up it?'

I think about this. I remember trying to climb a rope at school, never getting much further than halfway.

'I'll try,' I say.

'Good.' Vicky's face disappears for a moment and then appears again. 'Be careful, the end is metal,' she says. 'I don't want to hit you with it.' And then she flings something down to me. It bounces in the air, swinging next to me like a pendulum. I grab it and rub the thin extendable lead dubiously between my fingers. I'm not sure that it's strong or thick enough to take my weight.

'I'm going to try to help you from this end,' Vicky says. 'But I think you'll have to do most of the work yourself.'

What other choice do I have? It's worth a try. I take a

deep breath and attach the metal clip to my belt loop. If I lose my grip, there's an outside chance it might hold me. Then I grasp the rope, fumble to find a foothold and I heave myself up. My hands burn on the rope, but I grit my teeth and tighten my grip, sliding one hand up higher, shifting my feet incrementally upwards. This way I slowly and painfully make my way up. Every muscle is burning, strained to full capacity, and my arms feel as if they're being tugged out of their sockets. But I try not to think about the pain and focus on the circle of light above me and Vicky's whispered encouragement.

'Keep going, Jess,' she says every now and then. 'You can do it.'

Then, somehow, I reach the metal rungs at the top of the well. I grasp them and, as I clamber up them and reach the rim of the well, Vicky grabs hold of my wrists and pulls. I give one last push with my legs and I flop, exhausted, onto the ground, panting for breath and shivering in the cool, damp night air.

And Vicky kneels next to me and smiles.

'You made it,' she whispers, patting me on the shoulder. I look up at her. There's a full moon shining brightly above us, which is a relief after the total darkness in the well.

'I'm alive,' I say, dazed.

I can hardly believe it. I'm alive. I'm going to live. I start laughing and crying, and Vicky is laughing and crying too and hugging me. She puts her hand to my head and brings her finger away covered in blood.

'Jesus, Jess,' she says in an appalled whisper. 'You've got a bad head wound. We need to get you to the hospital.'

Vicky's helping me to my feet when she starts and looks over her shoulder warily.

'Come on,' she says. 'We need to get out of here.'

I don't want to move. Every part of my body is screaming to stay where I am, but there's an urgency in her voice. And reluctantly, I scramble to my feet. I feel dizzy so I lean on Vicky. I'm standing there swaying when I feel her stiffen.

'Shh,' she hisses. And then I hear it too. The crunch of feet on dry leaves, the snap of a twig as someone makes their way through the undergrowth towards us.

'What the fuck . . . ?' says an amused voice and Howie steps out into the clearing. He's lugging a large rock, which he sets down on the ground when he sees us.

Why's he got that? I wonder vaguely. But the answer comes to me before I've even finished asking the question. And I shudder. He couldn't afford to leave me down there alive and he's brought the rock to finish the job. If he'd dropped that on me, it would've crushed my skull like a watermelon.

'What the fuck do you think you're doing, Victoria?' he says, glancing from me to Vicky, with a look of almost comical bemusement. There's no fear in his eyes, just mild, amused annoyance, as if we're gnats or flies that are bothering him.

'Howie . . .' Vicky lets go of me. She stretches out a hand in front of her, palm forward like a stop sign, as if she has superpowers and can keep him at bay with the force of her mind. 'Please . . .'

He glances down at the crowbar still lying amongst the nettles. Vicky follows the direction of his gaze and at the same time, without a word, they both lunge for it. Vicky gets there first and snatches it up, dodging Howie's hand as he tries to grab it. I move towards Howie. Maybe together we can overpower him. But as I stumble forwards, my legs buckle under me and I sink to the ground. I feel very dizzy; everything is swaying and blurring and I'm trying hard not to faint.

I'm dimly aware that Vicky is waving the crowbar over her head.

'Don't come any closer,' she warns.

Howie laughs mockingly. 'What exactly do you think you're going to do with that?' he says.

It does look comical: Vicky trying to look fierce, determination etched on her delicate features.

'I've phoned the police,' she lies. 'They're coming soon. You'll only make things worse for yourself if you hurt us.'

For a second there's a flash of indecision in his eyes. Then it's displaced by anger.

'You stupid bitch,' he grunts, lunging at her and grabbing the crowbar. Vicky valiantly does her best to hold on to it and for a moment I watch them tussling. The scene swims in front of me. Darkness is creeping at the edge of my consciousness. I close my eyes, sinking into blackness.

'Help me, Jess!' Vicky screams. The sound pierces my dull brain and with a huge effort of will I wrench open my eyes.

It's not good. Howie has prised the crowbar from Vicky's hands and is about to swing at her. They're both standing dangerously close to the edge of the well. I need to act now, or Vicky is going to die.

Adrenaline surges through my body and I stagger to my feet. A roar of rage seems to come from deep inside me and I charge recklessly at Howie. Using my shoulder as a battering ram, I hit him square in the belly. He's caught off balance.

'Oh shit,' he says. His eyes are mildly startled, his mouth open in a wide 'o'. He makes one last attempt to regain his footing as he teeters on the edge, his arms flailing wildly. Then he tumbles over. And I watch in shock as he disappears, sucked backwards into the darkness.

Vicky and I sit dazed on the grass at the lip of the well, ignoring his angry yells from down below.

'What do we do now?' I ask weakly. My head is starting to throb.

'We need to phone the police and get you to a hospital,' Vicky says decisively.

I look back at the well dubiously; Howie has already started attempting to climb out. I can hear him scrabbling around down there. He's way stronger than me.

'What if he gets out?'

'Help me with this,' Vicky says, tugging grimly at the cover.

Together we drag it towards the well and slot it back into place while Howie shouts at us from below. Finally worn out by exertion and stress, I sway backwards. Lights flash in front of my eyes. I try to hold on to Vicky. Then everything goes black.

Chapter Forty-Two

I wake up in the hospital lying between crisp, white sheets, listening to the old woman in the bed next to me snoring.

There's no serious damage done, the doctors tell me, and after they've given me a few stiches and kept me a couple of nights for observation, they allow me to go home.

Vicky comes to pick me up in Howie's car so that I don't have to drive.

'They've arrested Howie,' she tells me as we speed along the motorway towards Aylesbury. 'He's going to be charged with murder.'

I stare out at the flat fields whizzing past – at a few sheep grazing on yellowing grass. *It must be a huge shock to her*, I think, closing my eyes and letting the world drift past. I'm still very tired and the medication they've given me at the hospital is making me sleepy.

'How did you know where to find us?' I ask when Vicky breaks suddenly near Oxford, jolting me awake. 'How did you know what he was going to do?'

'I didn't,' she admits. She looks a little embarrassed. 'I thought he was having an affair with his secretary, so I installed a GPS tracker on his phone.'

I can't help laughing. 'Really?'

She nods. 'I know it sounds crazy, but I wanted to see him for myself because I knew, if I confronted him, he would just lie.'

'It's what he does,' I agree.

'After you left our house on Monday night, he told me he was going to meet a client in London the next evening and that he'd be late home. I knew he was lying. I've learned to read the signs. So, I switched on the tracker yesterday evening, I saw that he was heading towards Oxford and I just followed the signal.'

Vicky breaks as we join the back of a queue of traffic around Oxford. 'When I arrived in Cirencester,' she continues, 'and found the park gates closed, I thought that I must have made a mistake, that the software must be faulty or something. But when I saw his car parked nearby, I knew I was on the right track.

'I climbed over the gate. Then I just followed the signal, keeping hidden in the trees, until I heard you and Howard up ahead of me talking. You were by the folly.'

I think about the conviction that I'd had that we were being followed. 'I think we heard you,' I say.

Vicky nods and revs the engine. We crawl along for a few metres and then stop again. 'I realised you'd heard me, so I kept very still and waited until you were out of earshot before I moved. By then I'd heard your voice and knew that it was you that Howie was with, not Zoe, so I decided to give up and go back.'

'Weren't you curious about what we were doing in the woods so late in the evening?'

'I was, but I was more scared that Howie would find out I was there. I knew he'd be furious if he thought I'd been spying on him. Anyway, I was just heading back down the path when I heard you scream.'

The traffic has ground to a complete standstill. Vicky sighs and turns off the engine.

'I couldn't leave without checking you were OK,' she continues, 'even if it meant Howie found out I'd been following him. So I ran in the direction of the sound.' She shudders. 'And when I reached the clearing, I saw him there. He looked so calm that for a moment, I thought everything must be all right. It took me a while to make sense of what I was seeing. He was just coolly scooping up earth and leaves and dropping them in the centre of the clearing. Then I noticed the crowbar and I heard the muffled sound of shouting coming from inside the earth. I couldn't believe it at first. How could your voice be coming from underground?'

She shudders as we start moving again and I stare up at shredded clouds in a blue sky. I'm trying to forget the memory of being trapped inside the well, of the darkness pressing down on me.

'It took me a while to work out what was going on, but when I did, I was so scared, Jess. I literally couldn't move. I just crouched there frozen to the spot as he covered over the well. Then he sat on top of the mound of dirt and leaves he'd created. I didn't know what to do. If I had tried to phone the police or to move, he would have heard me. So I just stayed there for what seemed like forever and waited for him to go.'

'Thank God you did.'

I smile at this woman and realise I've underestimated her massively. There's a strength in her that I never appreciated.

'How are the kids coping?' I ask. 'It must be hard for them. I know they idolise their father.'

Vicky shrugs. 'I'm not sure. Brandon doesn't know anything. He's too young. I've just told him his father is away on a business trip. Luke seems to have taken it all in his stride. He's gone back to stay with Louise. It's Lara I'm worried about. She's refusing to leave her room; she's refusing to eat or do anything. Do you think you could come and talk to her when you feel well enough? She likes you. I know she'll listen to what you say.'

Chapter Forty-Three

'What's going on?' I ask.

It's a few days later and I'm at Howie's house. Howie isn't there, of course, thank God. He's currently in jail awaiting trial. Vicky is sitting amongst boxes. Half the furniture is gone. She's not wearing any make-up and her hair is tied back in a simple ponytail. It makes her look young, fresh-faced and innocent.

'I'm divorcing him and we're selling the house,' she explains, chipping away at her nail varnish. 'Apparently Howie owes lots of money, so none of this really belongs to us anyway.'

'Oh Vicky, I'm so sorry,' I say, flinging myself down on one of the few chairs left. Vicky has always had expensive taste. It's hard to imagine her having to rein in her spending.

'Don't be,' she replies. 'We've got a flat in town. It's perfectly fine for the four of us. Luke will be at his mum's most of the time and Lara will be away at college soon.' She looks around at the state-of-the-art kitchen. 'I was never really happy here. I'm glad to see the back of all this stuff.' She gestures around the room and, as she does, she winces suddenly and clutches her shoulder.

'Are you OK?' I ask. 'Did Howie hurt you at the well?'

She nods and bites her lip. 'I think I pulled something when we were fighting over that crowbar. Mind you, it wouldn't be the first time he's hurt me,' she adds, raising her eyes to mine.

I stare at her, appalled, as this sinks in.

'You mean . . . ?'

'He slammed my head against that kitchen counter once.' She points at the beautiful marble countertop. 'And he smashed my hand in that door.'

How come none of us saw it? How could I have been so blind?

'I never—'

'Knew? No, well, usually he didn't leave marks and, if he did, I covered it up well.'

I wonder about his first wife, Louise. Did he abuse her too?

'I know what you're thinking,' Vicky says ruefully. 'I should have said something or left him but . . . I don't know ... I kept telling myself he would change, that he would go back to the way he was in the beginning ... And he could be really sweet at times.'

I think about the irony of describing someone who killed their own mother as sweet. But I know all about self-delusion. I kept telling myself Matteo would change and now I realise that, perhaps in some warped way, when I got together with Matteo, I was subconsciously seeking out someone with a personality like my brother's. We gravitate towards the familiar, even if it's not good for us, that's what Claire has told me. I remember the secret cupboard at number forty-two and the dread I felt when I saw it – the feeling of being shut in. It wasn't my imagination, I've decided. It was a memory – a deeply buried memory. Someone locked me in there. And I'm pretty sure I know who now.

'I should have left him, but I was a coward,' Vicky says, shaking her head.

'You're not a coward,' I say firmly. 'You're an amazingly strong woman. You fought off a man twice your size. You should have seen yourself.'

'Thanks,' she grins shakily. 'We made a kickass team, didn't we?'

I smile at the way she says 'kickass.' So prim and proper.

'Is Lara upstairs?' I ask.

Lara doesn't answer my knock, so I push the door open tentatively and peer in.

'Lara?'

She's curled up in bed, clutching a pillow. As I walk in, she jerks her head up and scrapes a hand through her greasy hair.

'Go away, please,' she mumbles.

'Vicky's worried about you,' I say, hovering awkwardly by the bed. 'And so am I.'

She gives a little snort and rolls over, turning her back to me, so I perch on the edge of the chair by her bed, trying to decide what to say. I know that there's nothing I can tell her that will make things any better for her. Her father has been charged with murder. It's impossible to put a positive spin on that fact. I go over to the window, peer out at the garden and fiddle with the curtain. Then give a deep sigh and turn to face Lara again. On the bedside table there's a lamp, a phone and a hardback book, face down. I sit back down and pick up the book, turning it over, staring at the cover. On the front there's a picture of a bunch of red tulips and *Love Poems* is written in large gold letters. I flick through the pages thinking of Sean standing in Wendover high street, a book tucked under his arm. I read the first line of the first poem. It's by Robert Burns. *Oh, my love is like a red, red rose . . .* Then I flip back to the cover page.

Someone has scrawled in large, messy handwriting:

To Lara, I'm sorry. Can we start over? All my love, S.

I snap the book shut, feeling sick.

'Where did you get this, Lara?' I ask.

She rolls over and snatches the book from me. 'A friend gave it to me, if it's any of your business, which it isn't.'

'That friend wouldn't happen to be called Sean White, would he?'

That gets her attention. She sits up, fully alert, crosses her legs and looks at me through narrowed lids.

'How long have you been seeing him?' I ask.

She lifts her shoulders listlessly. 'About a year, I guess.'

It's worse than I thought. 'You should stay away from him, Lara. He's bad news.'

Her eyes darken. 'Yeah, well, maybe we're suited then. I'm bad news too. I'm just like my father. I've done things . . . bad things.'

I stare at her. 'What kind of bad things, Lara?'

She glares back at me defiantly.

I think about the text Ajay told me about at Mum's funeral: *Back off bitch, Sean is mine.* 'It was you,' I say slowly. 'You sent the message to Kate Chandry.'

For a moment I think she's going to try to deny it. But then she slumps back against her pillow, not meeting my eyes. 'Yes,' she whispers hoarsely. 'When I found out he was having an affair with her, I was so angry. I wanted her to know that she wasn't the only one.' Her face twists. 'So, you see I'm bad to the core, just like Dad.'

I sit next to her on the bed and sigh.

'You're not the same as him, Lara. Her death was an accident; it was nothing to do with your message.'

She gives a loud groan and punches the pillow viciously. 'No, it wasn't. You don't understand. She killed herself.'

She says it with such certainty that my stomach coils with fear. 'How can you possibly know that, Lara? You weren't there.'

She stares at me defiantly. 'Yes, I was. I went there that day – the day she died.'

I catch my breath. 'No, you can't have been. You were at the clinic with Ajay . . .'

Lara shakes her head. 'I lied,' she says simply. 'I didn't go to work. I called in sick and I went to Sean's; I knew he had the morning off. But he wasn't at home, so I drove to *her* house. I wanted to see with my own eyes if it was true that they were having an affair. And sure enough, there he was, his car parked outside. I waited in my car fuming, trying to build up the courage to go in and confront them both. But just as I was about to get out of the car, Sean came storming out. I could tell they'd been fighting. He was so angry he didn't even notice me.'

So, it *was* Sean that Polly heard arguing in the garden, I think in surprise.

'I was just trying to decide what to do next when I saw her at the window,' Lara continues. 'I saw her climb up on

328

the ledge.' Her eyes blaze with pain and her voice drops to a whisper. 'I saw her jump.'

I blink, shocked. 'You saw her jump?' I repeat.

Her face twists and she nods. 'I was so scared. I couldn't think straight. I just drove away as fast as I could.'

'You didn't stop to check if she was still alive?'

She wrings her hands. 'No. I saw someone come out of the house opposite, so I knew they had seen, and I didn't want to have to answer any questions about why I was there.'

She gazes at me, her eyes bright with tears. 'Do you hate me now, Jess?'

I take her hand as silent tears roll down her cheeks. 'I could never hate you, Lara. And you can't blame yourself. You couldn't have known she would do that. It's not your fault.'

Chapter Forty-Four

About a week after my conversation with Lara, I meet Holly
in London. She hasn't changed much. Not really. And it feels
like all the years drop away as I hug her thin shoulders and
she says, 'Watcha, Jess.'

We sit by the Princess Diana Memorial Fountain,
watching the kids splash in the water. And we talk about
our lives – the things that have happened to us in the seventeen years we've been apart – cramming as much as we
can into a short space of time. I don't mention Howie. I'm
not sure Holly is ready for that, and I know I'm not.

But finally, Holly sighs and says, 'I suppose you've
guessed what my message was about – what I was going to
tell you?' she says.

'I'm not sure,' I say with a heavy heart. 'But it had something to do with Howie?'

She nods. 'I didn't use the word "rape", not at first, not even in my own head. I didn't realise what he'd done was rape until years later . . .' She looks down at her hands, twisting in her lap. 'I thought because I'd let him kiss me and take off my top that I'd led him on.'

'Oh, Holly,' I say inadequately and my heart plummets. It's worse than I'd even suspected.

Her small, sharp face pinches with pain. 'It was the summer of 2002. You'd gone off on holiday with Jean and Brian, and Howie was left in the house on his own. I guess he was bored because he started taking an interest in me, making flirty little comments, which, of course, I loved. I couldn't believe my luck – you know how I idolised him. Then one day he came around to my house while my parents were out, and we went to my room . . . When things got serious, I asked him to stop but he didn't.' She breaks off, wincing.

'It's OK, you don't have to tell me the details,' I say.

'Afterwards, he laughed at me when I cried.'

'He *laughed* at you?' I repeat, appalled.

'Yeah, he said I was a baby and that I shouldn't start things I wasn't able to finish.' Tears well up in her eyes and my heart aches for her – for her now, and for who she was, my innocent little fifteen-year-old friend.

'I was so ashamed,' she says, brushing her eyes. 'I know it sounds crazy, but I blamed myself.'

We all blame ourselves, I think. Anger twists in my belly. How many people's lives has he tarnished or ruined?

'I'm so, so sorry,' I say, holding Holly's hand.

'It's OK, I'm over it now,' she laughs through her tears. 'I know it might not seem like it right now, but I hardly ever think about him these days. It's just that there's a part of me that would like him to know how much he hurt me.'

'There's no point,' I say heavily. 'He doesn't care.'

I tell her all about Eve and Mum and how Howard is now in prison awaiting trial and she listens, round-eyed.

'At least he can't hurt anyone else now,' she says when I've finished.

'It's been good to see you, Jess,' she says, smiling as we part at the Tube station in the fuggy air and fumes. 'Let's not leave it seventeen years next time.'

I watch her walk away, her distinctive, light, springy step. When she reaches the top of the escalators she turns and raises her hand in a kind of salute. And she disappears, sucked into the crowd.

Chapter Forty-Five

A few days later Ajay appears on my doorstep. He's holding a plastic bag with a box inside. He looks sheepish, shuffling from foot to foot as if the ground is too hot. He smiles and clears his throat. 'This is for you,' he says.

'Come in,' I say. And he follows me into the kitchen, where I switch on the kettle and pop teabags into mugs. Then I look inside the plastic bag and gasp. It's a Nikon D850.

'Is that all right?' he asks. 'I don't know much about cameras.'

'It's too much,' I say, shaking my head. 'It must have cost a fortune.'

He lifts the box out of the bag and runs his hand over the cardboard lid. 'It's not brand new,' he says. 'It was Kate's. She only used it a couple of times. It might as well get used.'

'Thank you.'

I take it out of its box and experiment with the shutter and the focus. Then I take a couple of snaps of Ajay. He smiles at me, his hands resting on the kitchen counter. I wonder if the camera has caught the complexity of his expression. All the sadness, compassion and something else, which I can't quite read but I think might be hope.

'Brian told me what happened,' he says, looking at the floor. 'But I don't know all the details.'

I smile and pat the bandage on my head. 'No, well, it's a long story.'

'Tell me,' he says. 'I like long stories.'

And somehow it all spills out. Everything – all the things that Howie did and all the lives he's ruined. I even tell him about Madrid, about Matteo and my breakdown.

'But you're OK now?' he asks anxiously. He raises his eyes to mine. And something new in them makes me catch my breath.

'Yes, I'm OK. My head is on the mend.'

'What about . . . mentally, though, I mean?' he says. 'That's some fucked-up shit you've been through.'

'Oh, I'm a complete nutcase,' I laugh. 'But then, that's nothing new.'

He smiles back. 'You know I've missed you since you moved from the close. Is that weird?' he says.

I laugh. 'Kind of. You hardly know me.'

'Izzy misses you too. She keeps talking about you.'

'She does?'

'Yes.' There's an awkward pause. 'When you feel ready,' he blurts, 'I was wondering if you'd like to go out somewhere, or maybe come around for dinner?'

My smile broadens. 'Are you sure you want to get involved with someone as fucked up as me?'

'I'll take my chances.'

Chapter Forty-Six

Dad is out on bail. He's been charged and is pleading guilty to perverting the course of justice. He faces a jail sentence of several years if he's found guilty. I've tried talking to him about his case, but I honestly don't think he cares what happens to him. I think losing Mum and then reliving the loss of Eve has just about broken him.

Maybe I should be angry with him, but I don't feel like I have any more room for anger. All I feel is pity for this sad, old man. He did what he did out of love for his child and, however misguided he was, I can't blame him for that.

Together we climb up Coombe Hill. The chalky path is wet and slippery from the recent rain, but the sun is out, warming our backs, and the air is fresh.

'I know you're wondering why we did what we did,' he

says as we reach a shady bridleway and pause by the gate to catch our breath.

'You were trying to protect him. I understand,' I say.

'I believed it was an accident . . .' He breaks off, unable to finish.

'It's OK, Dad, I understand.'

'No, no, let me finish.' He gives a deep shuddering sigh and continues. 'At first, Howie told us she tripped and fell, but it was obvious, even to me, that that wasn't what had happened. There were bruises and cuts all over her face and arms.' He shakes his head. 'Still, I told myself it was just a terrible accident. Sure, he'd lost his temper, but he hadn't meant to kill her.'

'But he did mean to kill her,' I say. 'He told me that he planned it when he found out she was going to send him away to boarding school.'

Dad gapes at me and then shakes his head. 'He's worse than I thought. I should've listened to Jean. When Eve died, she wanted to go to the police, but Howie seemed so upset. He begged us not to. He even threatened to kill himself if we did. It was just after there had been a scandal about a spate of suicides in young offenders' institutions and I really thought his life would be in danger if we turned him over. We argued long into the night and eventually Jean relented.'

'But why hide the body? Couldn't you have just told them it was an accident?'

337

'We knew that if the police saw the injuries on her body, we wouldn't be able to pass it off as an accident.'

I think about the bruises Michael mentioned. Of course, it wasn't Dad who gave her them. How could I have ever believed it was?

'It wasn't the first time Howie was violent towards her, was it?' I say.

Dad sighs. 'No, you're right. He'd hit and kicked Eve a few times before. She'd showed me the bruises, but God forgive me, I told myself she was exaggerating the extent of his violence. I told myself it was normal for a teenage boy to lash out at his mother every now and then.'

'And when Milo disappeared, I thought Eve was crazy to blame it on Howard. Now I think she was probably right.' He sighs deeply. 'I was so blind, wilfully blind. It was only later on, after Eve died, I began to notice things – small, nasty things he would do when he thought no one was watching. Jean insisted on sending him away to boarding school – to keep him away from you, to protect you from him. But we should have done more . . . we should've gone to the police.'

They should have, I think. A lot of people would have been better off: Holly, Vicky, me. And Mum would still be alive. But there's no point in regretting what's done, that's what Claire says. You can't undo the past. You have to look it square in the eye, acknowledge the effect it's had and then move on.

338

We carry on up the hill until we reach the monument. Then we sit on the stone plinth. Some children are taking it in turns to jump off the monument steps and there's a young couple with a border collie huddled together against the wind. I look out over the fields and houses, tiny dots on the landscape from this vantage point. The day is clear, and I can see a long way. I can see Chequers and on the horizon a couple of wind turbines revolving slowly in the distance.

'I'm sorry that I lied to you,' Dad says, staring straight ahead, 'about your mother.'

I don't answer. That one lie led to so many others. All the stories they told me about their past. *Was anything the truth?* I wonder. *Does he even remember what the truth is anymore?*

'Did you really meet Mum when her car broke down?' I ask.

He smiles sadly. 'Yes, but Eve was in the car too. It was Eve I fell in love with.'

'Mum said you climbed up the trellis to her bedroom window?'

'That was Eve too.'

'What was she like, my mother . . . I mean, Eve?' I ask.

He stares out at the fields and houses spread below us.

'She was brave, unfiltered, very loving. She adored you. She always felt guilty about that, you know – the fact that she loved you more than your brother.'

I think about the photo of me in her arms – the look in

her eyes. I've framed it now and it's got pride of place in my newly decorated living room.

'I'm so, so sorry,' Dad says simply as I watch the tears roll down his cheeks. It's the second time I've seen him cry in the space of a few weeks and I pat him awkwardly on the back.

'It's OK, Dad, I forgive you,' I say, hoping that saying it out loud will make it true. Life is short – too short to hold on to anger and bitterness. After all, Dad's the only family I have left now, and we need to stick together. That's what Claire says, anyway.

It's funny, but lately I've grown to like and respect Claire a lot. I'm beginning to trust her too. The other day, I even felt comfortable enough to open up for the first time about my breakdown in Madrid – about Anna Maria and the child I thought I heard under the floorboards.

Claire didn't say anything at first, just sat staring pensively at her hands, twisting them in her lap. Then she gazed up at me in that frank, compassionate way she has.

'Do you think it could have had anything to do with what your brother did to you? Locking you in the cupboard when you were little? The child you thought you heard was trapped too.'

'I suppose it could,' I said slowly. It hadn't occurred to me before. 'I think you could be right.' Everything seemed suddenly so simple and my mind felt light and clear for the first time in as long as I can remember.

Perhaps all the time, while I was so desperately trying to rescue Anna Maria and that imaginary child in Madrid, the person I was really trying to save, after all, was myself.

Epilogue

1990

Jessica is trying not to cry. But sitting in her pushchair, the tears keep on coming anyway, big, round, fat tears that roll down her cheeks and stuff up her nose. She scraped her knee in the park. It still hurts and beads of blood are oozing out from the dirt-covered graze. But she mustn't cry. Howie gets cross when she cries. Thinking of Howie makes her belly hurt and she cries even more, big sobs that come from her chest.

'Never mind, darling,' Auntie Jean says, whisking her up in her arms as they reach the front door. Auntie Jean's arms are soft and smell like marzipan and Jessica feels a little comforted. 'We'll give it a wash and get a plaster and it'll soon be right as rain.'

Jess shakes her head. 'I want my mummy,' she whimpers.

Auntie Jean is nice, but she's not Mummy. Mummy always makes everything all right.

Auntie Jean smiles at her and kisses her on the cheek. 'OK, sweetie, I think she's out in the garden. Let's go and see, shall we?'

Jessica wipes her nose and stops crying. She's comforted by Auntie Jean's cheerful, no-nonsense manner and as Auntie Jean carries her through the house, she's distracted by the pearl necklace at her throat. She twists the small white globes, gazing in fascination as they catch the light.

'Oh!' says Jean as they reach the big glass door. Her face is suddenly all white like her necklace, and her mouth is wide open, a capital 'O'. She's staring at Mummy and Howie, who are in the garden playing musical statues. Mummy is lying on the ground and Howie is standing over her, trying to trick her into moving. *Silly Mummy*, thinks Jessica, *she'll get all dirty lying in the leaves and mud like that.*

'Oh my God, no!' Jean wails and her voice sounds strangled. She sets Jessica down on the ground and rushes up the garden, giving a cry that reminds Jessica of Milo when Howie pulls his tail. Then Auntie Jean flings herself to the ground next to Mummy and presses her head against her chest.

Jessica follows her up the path, trying not to tread on the grass between the paving slabs.

Auntie Jean is breathing heavily like she's been swimming underwater.

343

'Quick, get your father!' she says to Howie. She sounds cross and Auntie Jean is never cross.

'It was an accident, I swear. She tripped and fell on the fishing boy,' says Howie.

'Just go and get your dad!' Jean is shouting now. 'Tell him to call an ambulance!'

Howie doesn't move. 'It's too late anyway,' he says blankly.

Why is Mummy still lying there? Why doesn't she move?

'I want Mummy,' Jess says to the stone sundial as her father arrives and talks in a hushed, urgent voice with Auntie Jean.

'I want Mummy,' she says, sitting on the damp grass while the adults argue above her and the breeze stirs the wind chime in the apple tree.

ACKNOWLEDGEMENTS

First and foremost, I would like to thank my wonderful editor Rachel Neely. Thank you for believing in me and for always giving invaluable advice. I'm grateful also to the whole fantastic team at Quercus, especially my eagle-eyed copy editor, Lorraine Green, and the brilliant cover designer, Henry Steadman.

Although *Deny Me* is not intended to be a serious portrayal of dementia, it was inspired by my father who suffers from dementia and my mother who looks after him.

I would like to take this opportunity to draw attention to the plight of the many people who suffer from this debilitating illness. I'd also like to thank the vast unseen and unpaid army of carers, often elderly themselves, who look after people with dementia, often without any help, 24 hours a day. They are true heroes!

While writing *Deny Me*, I read Nicci Gerrard's excellent book, *What Dementia Teaches us about Love* and I would like to thank her for insights. I have always been a fan!

Lastly, I would like to thank my two boys, Max and Toby for bringing joy and laughter into my life and my husband, Jim for everything.